The Canal Murders

ALSO BY J. R. ELLIS

The Canal Murders

A YORKSHIRE MURDER MYSTERY

J.R.ELLIS

THOMAS & MERCER

This is a work of fiction. Names, characters, organizations, places, events, and incidents are either products of the author's imagination or are used fictitiously. Any resemblance to actual persons, living or dead, or actual events is purely coincidental.

Text copyright © 2024 by J. R. Ellis
All rights reserved.

No part of this book may be reproduced, or stored in a retrieval system, or transmitted in any form or by any means, electronic, mechanical, photocopying, recording, or otherwise, without express written permission of the publisher.

Published by Thomas & Mercer, Seattle

www.apub.com

Amazon, the Amazon logo, and Thomas & Mercer are trademarks of Amazon.com, Inc., or its affiliates.

ISBN-13: 9781662515897
eISBN: 9781662515880

Cover design by @blacksheep-uk.com
Cover image: © Ghost Bear / Shutterstock; © D P Mitchell / Alamy Stock Photo

Printed in the United States of America

The Canal Murders

From the *Airedale Mail*

15th January 1984

Hugely Enjoyable Evening with Folk Group Rowan

The weather outside may have been cold and snowy, but inside The Farmers Arms at Baildon, we were all warmly entertained by the up-and-coming folk group, Rowan.

Rowan consists of Ben Shipton and Roger Aspinall on guitars, Bridget Foster on flute and Bob Anderson on drums. Vocals are provided by Liz Aspinall and Annie Shipton. They perform their often poignant songs about the lives of ordinary people in old northern landscapes with great tenderness and skill, singing about hardship, love and loss. They are a hugely creative group who write all their own material.

It was fascinating to see how young and energetic folk musicians like this can recreate the past so vividly through their modern take on the old traditions of folk music. They deserve greater prominence in the folk music scene, and they will surely achieve it. They have a great future ahead of them.

Last night's performance was all the more impressive in the light of the fact that their youngest member – Simon Anderson, 19 – was recently killed in a tragic accident on the A1 late at night after a concert in the north-east, when the group's van, driven by Annie Shipton, veered off the road and crashed.

Prologue

At 127 miles, the Leeds and Liverpool Canal is the longest canal in Britain built as a single waterway. It was constructed between 1770 and 1816 at a cost of £1,200,000. It has 91 locks, including the Bingley Five Rise and a mile-long tunnel at Foulridge. Originally built to link Yorkshire's industrial towns with the port of Liverpool, it is now used mainly for leisure and residential purposes.

'Come on, Andy, hurry up!' Stephanie Johnson called out to her boyfriend. Their brightly painted narrowboat had just entered a lock on the Leeds and Liverpool Canal below Saltaire on the outskirts of Bradford in West Yorkshire. Andy was operating the gates, while Steph was preparing to steer the boat through.

Andy Carter stood at the edge of the lock looking confused. He held up an L-shaped iron contrivance with a handle at one end and a socket at the other.

'What's this thing called again?'

'A windlass!' called Steph from deep in the lock.

'Oh, yes. So which gates am I doing first?'

Steph looked up, and shook her head in mock despair. 'We're going up this lock, so close the bottom gates behind us and shut the sluices. Then go to the top gates and open the sluices there.' She waited for a moment before deciding to give him a quick test. 'And what will happen then?'

'The water will fill the lock and raise the boat to the higher level. Then you'll take it through the top gates.'

Steph laughed and clapped ironically. 'Hurray! He's got it at last.'

Andy laughed too, gave her the finger, then pushed the big balance beams that closed the gates at the bottom of the lock. He fitted the windlass on to the spindle and turned the cogged wheels at either side to close the sluices. He then went to the top gates and opened the sluices there. The water churned as it poured in and began to fill the lock. Andy, relieved that he'd got it right, stood and watched as the narrowboat rose.

Suddenly Steph called out, 'Andy, get hold of the centre rope and steady the boat! It's going to smash into the sides!'

Andy had forgotten that when a lock fills, the rush of the incoming water can move the boat around quite roughly. He grasped the rope and pulled the boat towards him, stabilising it against the damp, dark side of the lock.

As the boat rose, Steph appeared, frowning at him, and he grinned sheepishly in return. The truth was that when Steph had suggested this holiday, he hadn't appreciated what was involved. Andy had been brought up in Croydon, coming north several years ago to join the West Riding Police in Harrogate. He and Steph were both detective sergeants working for DCI Jim Oldroyd, though they lived outside of Harrogate in an apartment in Leeds that overlooked the River Aire.

Andy knew nothing about canal boats. He had imagined when they booked this break that he and Steph would be cruising down a wide waterway with locks operated electronically by waterways staff. They could sunbathe on the boat, and he would look after a crate of beer. He'd had a rude awakening when he had to learn how to start the engine, steer, and operate the locks without help from any officials. Luckily Steph had been on a narrowboat before and revelled cheekily in her superior knowledge by appointing herself captain.

'OK, crew,' she said, laughing as the boat reached the level of the water above the lock. 'Open the top gates now.'

Andy saluted ironically and leaned into the balance beams on the top gates. Steph switched on the throttle and the boat moved slowly through the gates. She guided it to the bank so that Andy could get on board.

'Good, well, that wasn't so bad, was it?' she said, her blue eyes sparkling at Andy.

'No, I actually quite enjoyed it. I think I'm getting the hang of things. Where next?'

It was nearly six o'clock on a calm and pleasant afternoon in early September. They hadn't set off from Leeds until late in the afternoon due to the loading up of the boat and their briefings about how to handle it. There wasn't time to go much further.

'Just on to Saltaire. We'll moor up for the night. There's a lot to see there: great art gallery in the old mill with Hockney paintings, and there's a World Heritage Site village nearby too.'

'Sounds great!'

The longboat moved slowly and serenely along the canal, its engine puttering as Steph operated the tiller. Andy sat on a little bench at the front of the boat and surveyed the peaceful scene. Despite his initial difficulties with operating the boat, he was having a good time. Steph was right: there was something very calming about canals and being on the water. Maybe it was because the pace was slow, or simply due to the presence of birds and other wildlife along the banks and in the water. He watched as a group of mallards moved out of the way of the boat, and noticed two moorhens hidden among the reeds, their red beaks just visible. It was wonderful. Ever since he'd moved to Yorkshire, he'd been learning to admire and enjoy the countryside, and this was another aspect he could get very used to.

A little further along the waterway, they reached the massive Salts Mill, and navigated between huge stone walls linked by a covered walkway high above the water. There were large windows along the four storeys of the two mill buildings, but they couldn't see anything inside.

'Wow – it's amazing to think all this used to be full of machinery and people making cloth,' observed Andy.

'It was,' Steph said. 'And the canal was used to transport it all the way to Liverpool. Then it would go abroad. It would have been a noisy world in there with the clattering looms compared to the peace out here, though there would have been a lot more activity with boats being loaded up and stuff like that.'

The boat went under a road bridge. On the other side, the canal suddenly got busier. There was a canal basin, including a small marina where one or two boats were advertised for sale. Several boats were stationed on wooden jetties parallel to each other.

On the canal side there was a general shop incorporating a chandlery. People walked around talking in little groups. More boats were moored a little further down the water next to a canalside pub called The Navigation. Many of the boats looked as if they were permanently moored – part of a community of people who lived on the canal. Some had numerous pots of flowers lined up on the outside of the boat and there were little gardens near the water's edge, complete with chairs for sitting out. Most of the vessels had colourful and elaborately painted castles and flowers on their hulls, part of a long tradition.

Steph and Andy found a space just past the basin. Andy pulled the boat in and tied it to the small capstans at the front and stern.

He saw with approval the pretty pub building which looked as if it must have been there since the canal was constructed in the late-eighteenth century. The beers would be good. Steph saw him gazing and knew what was on his mind.

'Not yet,' she said, smiling. 'Let's have some tea first, shall we? Once you get in there that will be it for the evening.'

'Sounds good to me,' replied Andy with a laugh.

They both went down into the neatly appointed boat, which was kitted out with every modern convenience: well-equipped kitchen, sitting area, shower room, toilets, comfortable bedrooms. It was more luxurious than Andy had expected when Steph had first suggested they went on a canal boat holiday. He had no idea that so much could be fitted into a narrowboat.

In the kitchen – Is that the galley? he thought, trying to use his nautical terms correctly – he made a garlicky tuna and tomato sauce while Steph boiled some pasta. One of the advantages of narrowboating was freedom from car driving, and while it was also illegal to operate a boat under the influence of alcohol, now they were moored for the night they opened a bottle of red wine.

By the time they'd eaten, the early September dusk was beginning to fall. They sat on the boat finishing their wine. The canal was illuminated orange in the setting sun. Two coots swam across the water.

Steph sighed. 'Beautiful, isn't it? And so peaceful. Who would have thought there was a busy urban area over there.' She pointed towards the nearby town of Shipley and the city of Bradford beyond. There was the vague sound of traffic in the distance.

'Absolutely,' replied Andy, who was rather distracted by the noise of music and singing coming from the pub.

Steph smiled. 'OK, I can see you're desperate for a pint. Let's tidy up and go over there. It sounds lively!'

◇

The Navigation was indeed lively. A local folk band were playing in the spacious bar, which was packed with a range of people mostly middle-aged and beyond. In their style of hair and clothing, many looked as if they had been part of an alternative cultural scene for many years – men with greying ponytails, and women dressed in dungarees embroidered with flowers.

As the band finished a song to enthusiastic applause, a dark-haired woman in jeans came into the bar and looked around. Her brow furrowed as she saw the person she was looking for, and she went across to where they were sitting with a group of friends. 'Shipton!' she called out sharply.

A woman immediately looked towards her. She had medium-length grey hair with a fringe, and wore a necklace with multicoloured beads. Her attractive face was rather lined and her blue eyes were cold. She smiled sarcastically.

'What's the matter with you?' she said.

'I've read that bloody blog you write.'

The grey-haired woman laughed. 'And?'

The other woman produced her phone and read from it. '"There are problem people in all boating communities – refugees from the town who don't know how to behave. People who play rock music late at night and let their dog crap on the towpath. Perhaps we need a separate basin on the canal where these people can moor up, throw their litter into the grass, have fights, and piss into the water when they're drunk."'

Some of the people sitting with the grey-haired woman tried to stifle giggles at this, which inflamed the reader still further. She raised her voice.

'Don't think I don't know you're talking about me and Darren.' She looked around the table with contempt. 'You and all your bloody hippy friends, you're just a bunch of snobs who think you own the canal. Most of you've never done a hard day's work in your bloody life. Darren and I worked in factories in Bradford and saved up to come and live here and—'

'Calm down,' said a man wearing a colourful waistcoat and rimless glasses, whose name was Bob Anderson. 'You're making a spectacle of yourself.'

She completely ignored him and continued to stare at Shipton. 'Just because we like a drink and play some of our music. It's better than the crap you get in here.' She waved a hand towards the small performance area where the group were about to start their song. There was such a buzz of conversation that no one seemed to have registered the confrontation except the people at the table.

However, the landlord – a burly man called Phil Cunliffe – had noticed. He came across from the bar and stood behind the dark-haired woman.

'OK, Laura, that's enough. We don't want any bother in here, do we?'

She turned her angry face towards him and was met by an implacable stare. She didn't want any trouble with Phil, fearing that he might ban her from the pub. She turned away, gave Shipton a final filthy look, and flounced out of the bar, brushing roughly past a surprised Andy and Steph at the door. They had arrived just in time to witness the end of this encounter.

'Bloody hell, what's got into her?' observed Andy.

Steph shrugged her shoulders in response to his question, and looked after the retreating woman.

'Oooh! Narrow escape there, Annie!' This was said rather sarcastically to Shipton by a woman with permed greyish-blonde hair, a flowery dress and long, black, laced-up boots. She was called Bridget Foster, and was Bob Anderson's partner.

Shipton laughed. 'Curious how her behaviour confirmed what I implied in the blog. She must be drunk again.'

9

Phil was still there and answered. 'Well, she's not been drinking in here.' He frowned as he looked at Shipton. 'I've seen that blog, Annie. It's a bit strong don't you think? Surely we want to welcome everyone into the canal community.'

'You might, because you want them to spend their money in here,' Shipton said sharply. 'But some of us want people who can behave as if they are part of a community, and not like they're yobs who don't care about anyone but themselves.'

Phil didn't want to pursue the argument but was clearly not convinced. He shook his head as he went back over to the bar, followed by Andy and Steph. Andy ordered their drinks as the group began another song.

'What was going on there?' he asked the barman, his professional interest in averting trouble having been alerted.

'Oh, just a little disagreement,' he replied as he pulled Andy's pint, which was a local bitter brewed by the Saltaire Brewery, and handed Steph a glass of white wine. 'Are you passing through here?'

'Yes,' replied Andy. 'We're on our way up to Skipton and then a place called Gargrave, I think.' He turned to Steph who nodded. 'Just moored up here for the night.'

'Good, well, you're here on our folk night, if you like that kind of thing. They're just about to start.'

'Oh, we do,' replied Steph, and they both turned towards the band in the corner of the bar as the song began.

Back at the table, Bob listened to the song rather wistfully.

'Takes you back, this one, doesn't it? Early nineties. It was that group from the Eden Valley – Misty Fells, weren't they called? We played this a few times ourselves, if I remember rightly.'

'We did, Bob,' replied Annie. 'They were good vocals.' She started to hum along with the tune.

10

'Roger liked the guitar part as well, didn't he, Liz?' Bob looked at the woman sitting next to him. She had long, frizzy, auburn hair and wore green dungarees. Her face looked troubled.

'Yes, he did,' she murmured, remembering her dead husband.

The conversation flagged a little after this until Bridget asked, 'How's Brittany doing, Annie?'

'Oh fine, Bridget. She's still teaching at the same school in Oldham. Seems to enjoy it. Her and Harry have got a nice semi nearby. She lives a more conventional life than her mother ever did.'

'That wouldn't be difficult,' replied Bridget, laughing.

Annie smiled. 'No, I don't suppose it would.' She finished her wine as she listened to the next song. Then she stood up. 'Anyway, I'm off. It's an early start for me tomorrow – I'm taking the boat up to Skipton for some repairs.'

'Are you going to Benson's?'

'Where else? I'm going to get there for when they open – should get back in good time, then.'

She wished them all goodnight and walked to the door where she ran into someone who was just coming in – a tall, strong-looking man with a moustache. He frowned at her.

'Bloody hell! Off back to the boat already, are we? Must have already spent up. You shouldn't be here at all. You should be saving up to pay your debts. Do you get drinks on t' tick from Phil?'

Annie calmly returned his gaze. 'Shut up, Gary. You know you'll get paid.'

He didn't move out of her way. 'Oh, that could well be true. The question is when, isn't it?'

Annie shrugged. 'You won't get anywhere trying to intimidate me, Gary Wilkinson. Now can you please move?' She pushed past him and walked off into the dark.

'Just don't come anywhere near the shop until you bring some money with you!' he called after her, before swearing at her lack of response and continuing into the bar.

~

The lights from the Saltaire streets above the canal reflected on the water in the basin as Annie walked carefully along the unlit towpath back to her narrowboat where she lived alone. She switched on the lights, climbed down the steps into the boat's interior, and made hasty preparations for going to bed.

Hearing that song back in the pub had reminded her of the past. She spent some time looking at old photos of the folk band called Rowan. Formed by a group of friends, there had been a number of years where they had toured and performed together, with Shipton on vocals.

She took the photos and spread them on her quilt in the small bedroom, which had a window looking out on to the water. She lay in bed, staring at them for a while, and then fell asleep.

Sometime later there was laughter and conversation outside as the folk group completed their performance and people began to leave the pub, but it didn't wake her up. Then all the lights turned off apart from the those on the main road; the waterfowl roosted near the bank, and everything went quiet except for some tawny owls hooting in the nearby woods.

~

The next morning Steph woke early in the small bedroom of the barge with Andy still asleep next to her.

She glanced at her watch – it was half past six. She looked out of the window and saw a gorgeous scene as the sun was just rising on another clear day and the light was filtering through the trees. The canal was still and reflected the sun. There appeared to be no one about. She decided to get up and go for a walk.

She smiled at the sleeping figure of Andy, who would probably not wake for a while. He had consumed several pints of real ale the previous night. He never used to be big on beers and ales until DCI Oldroyd had introduced him to a number of local breweries. She had to admit, their enthusiasm had even rubbed off on her, but she could pace herself better than the two men.

Carefully, she eased herself out of bed, got dressed and unlocked the door at the back of the narrowboat. It was a beautiful morning and she sat for a while looking at the colourful boats, the pub, the canal, the waterfowl and the huge mill that they'd passed yesterday. There was the rattle of a train passing nearby and a cyclist pedalled by on the towpath, but otherwise it was very quiet. She was about to go back down to the kitchen to make some tea before her walk when something caught her attention.

It was a blue narrowboat, coming downstream at a strange angle across the water. The name *Moorhen* was painted on the side, along with some of the little birds with their red bills. The engine seemed to be ticking over in neutral. It was moving almost silently – like a ghost ship – and that made Steph feel uneasy. A couple of coots swam away from the barge, and she watched as it came towards her slowly and then drifted past.

Then she saw the body of a woman slumped at the back of the boat, against the tiller. There was a lot of blood around her neck and chest and on the wooden boards. She recognised the body as the woman who had been involved in the argument the night before in The Navigation.

She rushed back down into the boat. 'Andy!' she shouted. 'Get out here quickly. I think there's been a murder!'

13

One

Old Adam was a shepherd
On the moorlands of the north,
He walked o'er twenty mile a day
Was never paid his worth.

Upon the moors,
Upon the moors,
The moorlands of the north.
Upon the moors,
Upon the moors,
Was never paid his worth.

He dug his sheep out of the snow,
As ewes gave birth in frost,
He walked in ice and sun and rain,
And counted not the cost.

Upon the moors,
Upon the moors,
As ewes gave birth in frost.
Upon the moors,
Upon the moors,
And counted not the cost.

From 'The Shepherd' performed by Rowan © 1993
lyrics by Bob Anderson, music by Bridget Foster

The canal basin was cordoned off with blue and white incident tape. A crackle of police radios disturbed the tranquillity that Steph and Andy had been enjoying. A number of police cars and an ambulance were lined up on the road that led over the bridge and up into the town.

Andy and Steph stood by their boat watching the police officers and the forensic team at work. It seemed strange to be merely observing and not involved in the action. They'd done what they could, ringing 999 and rousing some of the other boaters who had been moored up nearby. Luckily the drifting boat had gone into the side of the canal quite near to the basin entrance. Working together, a group of them had been able to grasp the ropes, pull the boat into a space in the basin and secure it.

Andy had produced his warrant card and advised everyone to keep off the boat, while Steph went on board to check that the victim was dead. Two other people looked briefly at the body and confirmed that it was Annie Shipton, the owner of the boat.

When the local police arrived, Steph and Andy handed everything over. This was not their patch, and they weren't officially on duty.

'Bloody typical,' Andy said, as they waited for the local officers to take their account and statement. 'This would have to happen when we're here on holiday. You can't seem to escape this job, can you? It follows you round.'

Steph shook her head. 'It does seem like that. But we don't have to get more involved. Our boat's not stuck in the basin. We'll just get on our way to Skipton soon and—' She seemed distracted by something happening near the barge, but then her face lit up. 'Hey, wait a minute – look who it is!'

She pointed to a plain-clothes officer who was talking to some others in uniform by Shipton's boat.

Andy stood up. 'It's Jav!' He called out, 'Hey, Jav, what the hell are you doing here?'

The officer looked over, puzzled, before his face burst into a broad smile of recognition. He came over quickly, and they shook hands.

'Andy and Steph! I don't believe it! It's been too long!'

Javed Iqbal had served as a detective sergeant at the Harrogate station for several years before returning to his native Bradford for promotion to detective inspector. He was tall, trim and – as always – smartly dressed.

'It has, Jav. Oh, sorry, I suppose it should be "sir" now.'

'Oh, nonsense . . . We don't worry about rank and titles and forms of address – call me Jav, at least when we're by ourselves.' He laughed. 'You know I still miss you guys. We used to have so much fun in Harrogate. And the boss! DCI Oldroyd – what a man, eh? I've never met anyone like him!'

'Me neither, Jav,' said Steph. 'I don't think there is anyone like him.'

Jav nodded. 'He was the man who gave me the confidence to believe in myself as a detective and to apply for this job as an inspector at Bradford.'

'Good for you,' said Andy. 'Steph and I keep thinking about applying for promotion and moving on, but it's never felt right so far.'

'It will one day. All in good time,' said Jav. 'Anyway, never mind what I am doing here, what are you two doing here? You must be on holiday, right?'

'Well, we were,' said Steph. 'We've hired one of these boats for a few days, and we were on our way to Skipton.'

'And now this has happened,' mused Jav. 'But don't worry, once you give a statement about finding the body, I'm sure you can get on your way.' He glanced over to Shipton's boat. 'Look, I think the pathologist has finished, and I need to go and talk with her. Why don't you come with me? Just listen to what she's found out?'

Andy looked at Steph who nodded. They were not officially on duty, so couldn't get involved in the crime scene, but the truth was their professional interest was piqued by what had happened, even though their holiday had been interrupted. They followed Jav over to the boat where a woman in her fifties, wearing protective clothing, was packing up her things.

'Ah . . . Inspector Iqbal.' She smiled at the detective who introduced Andy and Steph.

'This is Dr Miriam Coates,' he said.

Dr Coates looked very sympathetic when she realised they were also detectives. 'Oh dear,' she said. 'Finding a body while you're having a break from police work. I think that's what used to be called a busman's holiday.'

The three detectives looked puzzled; none of them had heard the saying before.

She continued to pack up as she talked. 'My initial opinion is she's not been dead long, not more than two hours. The cause of death was likely a stab wound to the neck, which pierced the throat and severed veins and arteries, hence all the blood. I'll have to do more work in the lab, but I'm pretty sure that she was stabbed from behind. One curious thing: there was no sign of a struggle. It seems as if she was taken by surprise while she was steering the boat and then fell by the tiller. I'm not sure how. It's a very confined area for a murder to take place, and unless the killer was invisible, I find it hard to believe our victim didn't notice someone was there.' She picked up her case. 'Anyway, I'll leave you to it and send my report as soon as I can.'

Jav thanked her and turned to Andy and Steph. They were quiet for a moment as they thought about what the pathologist had said.

'It sounds like it's going to be a tricky one, Jav. If Miriam is right, how did the murderer get behind her? When you're steering, you're at the back and looking down the length of boat in front of you. And there's not much space to sneak up behind someone. How was she attacked?' asked Andy.

Jav frowned. 'Right, I need to talk to the forensic people and see what evidence they've found. There must have been someone on the boat who somehow managed to get behind her. It's the only way to explain that wound.'

Jav went over to *Moorhen*, and Steph and Andy went back to their boat to get a bit of late breakfast. It wasn't too long before Jav, looking very perplexed, came over to talk to them and drink a cup of tea.

'Well, it's getting more mysterious by the minute. According to the forensic team there's no evidence of anyone else having been on board, apart from the victim. In particular, there are no footprints in the blood, which they said would be very difficult for the killer to avoid. It's only provisional information at this stage, but it's turning into a puzzler.'

'It doesn't surprise me,' said Steph. 'As soon as I saw that boat drifting down the canal, I sensed that something weird was going on.'

Jav didn't reply for a moment and then he gave Andy and Steph a mischievous look. 'Do you know, I'm thinking that this is just the kind of case that would appeal to DCI Oldroyd.'

'What? You're not serious,' said Steph.

Jav's mouth cracked into a wide smile. 'It will be like old times. Look, I work for DCI Haigh at Bradford HQ and we're short of staff. He'd be delighted if you and DCI Oldroyd were here to assist me.'

'Hey! Who said anything about us? We're on holiday!' said Andy.

'But you can't resist it. Go on, admit it! Oldroyd himself would say a true detective can never pass up a mystery like this. And afterwards you can just carry on to Skipton.'

Steph shook her head. 'But, Jav, we don't know that the boss is free, and it would be highly irregular for a DCI to conduct an investigation in another district.'

'He's not conducting it – I am. He will officially be a consultant providing me with assistance. Of course *we* know that he will really be in charge.'

Steph looked at Jav with her head on one side. 'You've got this all worked out, haven't you? Did you know that this was going to happen?'

Jav's good-humoured face continued to smile. 'Not exactly . . . but now it has happened, it seems too good an opportunity to miss. And we'll all learn something. You always do, working with him. I would like to have been on more cases with him when I was in Harrogate. I think I missed out compared to you two, so it would be great to have him here.'

It was impossible not to get caught up in his enthusiasm. Andy exchanged glances with Steph and then laughed. 'It would be amazing for us all to work together again. Do you really think you could swing it with the Bradford people?'

'Yes, I'm sure I can.'

'OK, I'll contact the boss, but I wouldn't hold out too much hope. He might very well be involved with a case now. We've been out of the loop for a few days.'

'It's worth a try,' said Jav.

❧

DCI Jim Oldroyd was finishing a late breakfast with his partner, Deborah, in their house in the pretty village of New Bridge, just outside of Harrogate. He finally had a day off, after several long sessions at work. They had only been in the property for a month, and were still enjoying the novelty of living in a house with a garden, albeit currently a somewhat overgrown one, having previously shared a flat in Harrogate overlooking The Stray. So far, they were happy with how things were going: Oldroyd didn't have a long commute into Harrogate, and Deborah, who was a psychotherapist, was able to see her clients from home.

'Well, Jim, it looks like we could have some good weather this weekend. Maybe it's time we tackled the garden.' She glanced at him and immediately saw that this was not welcome news. 'Remember, you promised me that you would help to get everything in order. It's too much for me to do by myself.'

Oldroyd smiled as he crunched through a piece of toast and marmalade. 'Of course. I'm not going back on what I said, but do you think we could get a walk in too?'

'Yes, I don't want to garden all weekend. I . . .' She stopped as Oldroyd's phone began to ring.

'Oh, it's Andy Carter,' he said, looking at the screen. He answered the phone. 'Hello, Andy. What can I do for you? Aren't you and Steph away on holiday somewhere?'

'Good morning, sir,' Andy said on the other end of the line. 'Yes, Steph and I are on the Leeds and Liverpool Canal on a narrowboat. We set off from Leeds and got as far as Saltaire yesterday. We moored up outside this pub by the water, near a canal basin.'

'Yes, that'll be The Navigation. I know it. They serve some good local beers there.'

'You're right, sir . . . I tried one or two last night.'

Oldroyd took a great deal of pride in the fact that he had converted Andy from a generic lager drinker into someone who appreciated real ale, but he sensed that Andy wasn't calling simply to discuss local brews.

'Anyway,' continued Andy, 'this morning everything kicked off here big time.' He told Oldroyd about Steph's early encounter with the blue narrowboat and Shipton's body. And, also, how Jav had turned up to investigate.

'Good Lord, Javed Iqbal! It's been a few years since he was with us, hasn't it? I'm glad he's doing well over there. Very bright lad, very dapper and always such good fun, wasn't he?'

'He was, sir, and he hasn't changed.' Andy paused. 'In fact, he's made a suggestion. I don't know what you'll think of it.' He explained how they wanted him to come over and unofficially lead the investigation.

'Well . . .' said Oldroyd, caught off guard and momentarily at a loss for words. 'I'm very flattered, but I can't see how it would work. I can't just desert Harrogate and muscle in on someone else's patch. I mean, the chief inspector over that way is David Haigh. I know him.'

'Don't worry about that, sir. Jav says they're short-staffed in Bradford and DCI Haigh will jump at the chance of extra help. The main question is whether you are busy at the moment.'

'Well, as it happens, no, but . . .' He looked at Deborah, thinking about his promise to do some gardening.

'Then why not come over, sir? It's a case that will fascinate you.' Andy outlined the strange circumstances of the murder. 'The body of a woman has been found stabbed to death in a narrowboat, but there's no forensic evidence that anyone else has been on the boat. We've no idea how it was done, sir. Me and Steph are going to delay our holiday and come back to work to help Jav. It would be great if you were here too.'

Oldroyd took a deep breath. A mysterious case like this always intrigued him. Why not go over and take part? His own boss, Superintendent Walker, was always easy about lending him out if things were quiet in Harrogate; he felt it brought prestige to his district. Oldroyd was sure that Deborah would understand.

'OK,' he said decisively. 'You're on. I'll have to have a word with Superintendent Walker, and I'll need to speak to David Haigh as well to make absolutely sure he doesn't mind.'

'Fantastic, sir! Let me know when you're on your way.'

Oldroyd ended the call with a broad grin on his face and a spring in his step. They were behaving like a bunch of teenagers on an exciting jaunt. But why not? Working with enthusiastic people on a challenging case like this was the real joy of policing for Oldroyd.

'Wow, what a smile! Has Matthew Watkins resigned?' asked Deborah. Matthew Watkins was the trendy, managerial and deeply unpopular chief constable of West Riding Police, particularly hated by Superintendent Tom Walker, although it was true that Oldroyd didn't have much time for the man either.

'No, something much more interesting,' he said, and explained what had happened in an animated fashion.

'I see,' replied Deborah, pleased to see her partner so positive and looking forward to a new challenge, but suspecting that any joint effort during the coming weekend might now be in jeopardy. 'So it looks like gardening is going to be put on hold, then?'

'No, not completely. I'm not going to work flat out every single day and over the weekend.'

'OK, but don't forget that Louise is coming up soon. We need to sort out a few things in the house before then.'

Louise was Oldroyd's daughter. These days she lived in London and ran a women's refuge centre. She'd also recently been invited to take a leading role in a government inquiry into provision for women who were at risk or had suffered from domestic violence. Oldroyd had always been proud of her, but she really was doing something special with her life, he thought.

23

'Louise won't mind,' he said. After all, she had inherited his passion for work, and would understand why this case would be irresistible to him.

'Maybe not, Jim, but the spare room is full of boxes we haven't unpacked yet. It's not a very welcoming space. All I'm saying is don't get so immersed that you can't do anything else but investigate the crime.'

'I won't, I promise. Come here.' He gave her a kiss. She had always been very understanding about the difficulties of his work and how it could encroach on his private life. In return Oldroyd tried his best to support Deborah when her work took an emotional toll. His former wife, Julia, Louise's mother, had found it much more difficult to deal with Oldroyd when he became wrapped up in a case, and this was what had caused their marriage to fail. With Deborah, however, they seemed to complement each other very well indeed. 'Right! I'll get off and I promise you I'll help at the weekend.'

'OK,' replied Deborah, although she sounded sceptical.

The people who lived in the narrowboats moored in the basin were waking up to the grim news that a murder had occurred on the water.

Bridget Foster stood on the small deck by the tiller on her boat. It was brightly coloured in pinks and greens with scenes from folk group gigs painted along the side, and the name *Rowan* in a flowing script at the front of the hull. She'd spoken to the police, who had told her what had happened. The body had been identified as that of Annie Shipton before it was removed. All around the basin groups of people were talking in huddles.

Bridget was waiting anxiously for her partner, Bob, to appear. He'd probably gone for a walk and called in at the village to do some early shopping. Then she saw him walking down the road and across the bridge on to the towpath. He had a rucksack on his back, and he looked curiously at the police tape around Shipton's boat, and at the presence of police officers.

'What's going on?' he said as he arrived and saw his partner.

Bridget was relieved to see him. She spoke unsteadily, resting her arm on the tiller. 'It's Annie – she was found dead on her boat. She was murdered, stabbed in the neck, so people are saying. I saw blood all over the deck by the tiller. It was awful.'

'What? Murdered? When?'

She looked at him. 'Where have you been all this time?'

'I woke up early. It was a lovely morning, so I went for a walk downstream. Then I looped back and went up into the village and did some shopping.' He held up the bag.

'You didn't see anything when you left the basin?'

'No. What's this all about? You sound like the police doing an interrogation.'

Bridget looked round to see if anyone was listening. 'I was worried when they discovered her dead, and then I realised you were missing.' She looked at him. 'You know why.'

'Don't be ridiculous. That was all a long time ago.'

'Yes, but I know you're still really angry about what happened.'

Anderson picked up the bag of groceries. 'Let's go inside. I don't want to talk about it here.' He went down the steps into the boat carrying the bag. Bridget followed him, still anxious.

∼

Liz Aspinall, who had lived alone on her barge, *Meg*, since her husband Roger died, appeared on the deck in her dressing gown.

She yawned. She had stayed late at the pub the previous night. She looked around the basin and saw the unusual activity. The tall man who had confronted Annie Shipton in the entrance to The Navigation the previous night was walking past.

'Hey, Gary!' Liz shouted. 'What's going on? Why are the police here, and all that blue and white tape?'

'Have you just got up?'

'Yes.'

Gary Wilkinson came close to her and whispered. 'It's Annie – she was found dead on her boat this morning.'

'What? Who by?'

'Believe it or not, the police found her. Did you notice a couple in the bar last night – visitors? Apparently they are police officers on a narrowboat holiday.'

'Bloody hell! But what happened to her?'

'Stabbed. You can see lots of blood on the deck, though they've taped the boat off.'

'So, somebody went on board and killed her?'

'I don't know. Somebody said the boat was drifting down the water when they saw the body and the blood, and so they pulled it into the basin.'

Liz put her hands to her face. 'God! Poor Annie.'

'Go back in and sit down,' said Gary. 'It's a shock. Sorry, I can't stay. I have to get over and open up the shop.'

Liz nodded and, without another word, went down the steps into her boat.

Gary continued round the basin back to a long building that was his shop: a chandlery that sold everything required for narrowboating as well as some basic provisions. He lived in the flat above the shop.

Next door to Gary's place was a smaller building that housed the office of the Canal and River Trust, which was responsible for the running of inland waterways. A woman in her early thirties called Ros Collins was just arriving, dressed practically in black jeans, trainers and an oversized grey hoodie. She worked for the trust and was about to unlock the door of the office when she also noticed the presence of the police, and turned to Gary, who was just about to unlock his own place.

'What's going on then, Gary?'

'You're the second person to ask me that this morning.' He explained about the murder of Annie Shipton.

Ros put her hand to her mouth. 'Oh my God! That's terrible!'

'I know. I still can't believe it. I was speaking to her last night at The Navigation.' He paused. 'Actually, I was having an argument with her. She owed me quite a bit of money. She was always popping in for bits and pieces and saying, "Put it on the tab." Then she never paid. It was my fault for letting her do it, I suppose, but I tend to trust people in the boating community.'

'Don't worry, you weren't the only one. Between us, she was well behind with her mooring fees. She gave me the impression of being the kind of person who drifts through life and ignores the rules, especially those to do with paying bills.'

'I think you're right. I doubt if we'll get our money now. Anyway, I'd better open up. I've got some customers.' Two people were waiting nearby, browsing the shop window, and Gary bid them good morning as he opened the door.

Ros stood for a moment looking around the basin and at Shipton's boat cordoned off by police tape. Then she went into the trust's office.

~

A mile downstream from Saltaire there was a row of terraced houses between the canal and the railway. Sam Wallace, who had cycled past Steph and Andy's boat shortly before Steph saw *Moorhen*, lived in one of these. His bike leaned against the wall by his front door.

Sam was in his early twenties and still lived with his mother Janice. She had brought him up as a single parent after his father had died in an accident at a textile mill when his son was ten. The compensation from his employer was insufficient and it had been a struggle financially. Janice worked in the kitchens at a local high school and her wages were not high, but they managed. She'd always instilled ideas about thrift and not wasting money into her son, who had been well behaved when he was a small boy. It was when he reached his teenage years that the problems had begun.

He had never been a high achiever at school and left at sixteen not really knowing what he wanted to do. And then he fell in with the wrong crowd. He began to stay out late in the evenings, knocking about the streets with his gang and getting into trouble. He developed a short temper, and got into several fights.

Janice had moved quickly. She had lived in the area all her life and knew a lot of people, so she persuaded a roofing contractor to take her son on as an apprentice. Sam had been resistant to the idea initially, but she made him go to work each day. He was a strong young man, and he took to the work after a while.

Janice – knowing it wasn't enough to use a stick and that you needed a carrot as well – bought him a bike in an attempt to provide him with a hobby that would take him away from the undesirable gang. There was a cycling club in Saltaire, and some other men his age were members. This plan was also successful. He became so keen on cycling that he went out for rides in the early morning before going to work. She hoped his wilder days were well and truly behind him.

Mother and son were now eating breakfast in the small kitchen, Janice already in her work clothes. Sam was quiet and seemed distracted.

'Better hurry up, Sam,' she said, looking at the wall clock. 'Mr Ferguson won't want you to be late.'

'It's fine, the job we're on is just up the road from here.'

'Right.' She looked at him, overcome suddenly by a mother's sense that all was not well. 'Are you OK?'

'Yeah.' He wasn't looking at her.

'Have you been out on your bike this morning?'

He stopped chewing his toast. 'Yeah, just up the towpath.'

'Everything all right along there?'

'Yeah, Mum, stop fussing, will yer?'

'You didn't see that woman again, did you?'

'Which woman?'

'The one you had the big row with – the one who told you off for cycling too fast up the towpath.'

He looked away from her. 'That bitch!'

'Sam! Don't use that word about a woman. I don't care how much you dislike her. It's disrespectful and nasty.'

'She thinks she owns the canal – her and those other old weirdoes in the basin. That towpath is a bridleway. I checked it with Martin at the club. We have a right to cycle on there.'

Janice had a drink of her tea. She noticed that he hadn't answered her question, but there wasn't time to talk about it.

'Yes, as long as you don't go too fast. Anyway, we can't go through all that again right now – you'd better get off to work.'

'OK. See you tonight.'

Sam got up from the table, picked up a small rucksack, which contained sandwiches Janice had made for him, and left the house on his bike.

Once he was gone, Janice got to thinking. What was that woman's name? Yes, she remembered – Annie Shipton. She'd met Shipton a few times around the village. Stuck up, full of her own importance. Someone said she'd once been in a folk group, but she seemed too stern and unfriendly to be an entertainer. Sam had had a big row with her and had apparently shouted some unpleasant things. It was near the basin and people had needed to restrain him. She couldn't justify him abusing anyone but she could understand how Shipton had got under his skin. Sam hated being told off, especially about anything to do with cycling. He had become fiercely defensive about the rights of cyclists.

Janice cleared the breakfast things away and left the house to catch the bus to the school. She thought about her son on the journey. Sam had had some run-ins with the police concerning his fights and she was concerned that he might encounter them again. She felt that was the slippery slope to getting a criminal record, losing your job and dropping out of mainstream society. She frowned. It wasn't going to happen if she had anything to do with it. What had he been up to on the bike ride this morning? If she couldn't get it out of him, there were plenty of people whom she could ask.

~

It was later in the morning and the three detectives had been loaned a back room at The Navigation from a shocked Phil Cunliffe to use as their base of operations. They were drawing up an action plan as they awaited Oldroyd's arrival.

'We obviously need to talk to everybody on these boats to find out all we can about the victim – who she was, who might have wished her harm, and so on,' said Jav.

'Yes, and whether anyone saw anything. I mean, how come the boat was just drifting downstream like that? Was she on her way somewhere?' said Steph.

At that moment, a detective constable entered the room. 'Detective Chief Inspector Oldroyd has arrived, sir,' she said.

Jav, Andy and Steph went outside, where they could see Oldroyd's battered old Saab parked near the canal basin. Oldroyd himself was already looking at Shipton's boat.

'Sir,' called Steph.

Oldroyd turned to see them, a big smile on his face. 'So good to see you again,' he said as he shook Jav's hand. 'And thank you for inviting me to help you with this case. I want to make it clear you're in charge. I'm here as a kind of consultant.'

'Thank you, sir, but feel free to direct operations. I think this case needs someone with your experience.'

'OK. You'll also have to tell me about life at Bradford HQ. I want to know all the gossip!'

Jav laughed. 'Well, sir, I have to say life is good at Bradford, but I've missed Harrogate a great deal. How long has it been? Two years?'

'Three, I think,' said Oldroyd. He turned to Andy and Steph. 'So, you come for a quiet holiday on the canal, and you haven't even got as far as Skipton before you find a body!'

'It was Steph you have to thank, sir,' said Andy. 'I was fast asleep after drinking those ales last night. It would have drifted past us to goodness knows where if it had been down to me. Then it might have been someone else's problem.'

'But it didn't, and now we're all here,' said Oldroyd, rubbing his hands together and smiling. 'I've spoken to Superintendent Walker and he's happy for me to work with Jav on this. I also called DCI Haigh . . . He's relieved to have some help because he's so short-staffed. So everything's OK.' He turned to Andy and Steph. 'It's very good of you two to come back to work to help.'

'Thanks, sir,' said Steph. 'The thing is, once I'd seen the body and the odd circumstances in which it was found, I had to know what had happened. Andy felt the same. I think it's the detective in us. We've been working with you for so long, sir, we can't resist the challenge.'

'Well, I'm glad I've inspired you with my enthusiasm and unique abilities,' replied Oldroyd with his customary mock self-satisfaction. 'As well as bringing people to justice, we share the deep desire to solve mysteries such as this.'

'It's true,' said Jav, nodding. 'And what better way to do it than with a group of colleagues who work so well together!'

Oldroyd laughed. 'Yes, you're making it sound exciting. Like a *Boys' Own* adventure from the old comics.'

Jav briefed Oldroyd on the circumstances of the boat and on what they planned to do.

'So it seems as if she was stabbed from behind while she was at the tiller?' said Oldroyd, sprawling back in a chair and thinking with his eyes closed. 'And there was no sign of a struggle?'

'Not according to the forensic team and Dr Coates,' said Jav.

Oldroyd opened his eyes and looked as if he were relishing the challenge. 'Very intriguing. Let's get to work.'

Laura and Darren Ward were having breakfast on their boat. They were both taking the morning off having worked through the previous weekend – Darren as a window fitter and Laura waitressing at a branch of Nando's. After Laura's encounter with Annie Shipton the previous evening, they had gone on to a club in Shipley and stayed late.

Darren had a stocky figure with heavily tattooed arms and a virtually bald head. He peered out of the window of their narrowboat at the police tape and the officers in uniform.

'What's going on out there?' he asked.

'Where?'

'In the basin. I'm going to go and have a look. There are police all over the place. I hope nobody's broken into Gary's shop.'

He climbed up the steps and out of the boat.

He was back within a few minutes shaking his head. 'Bloody hell! I went round to see Gary. There was no break in – it's much worse than that.'

'What's happened?' asked Laura through a mouthful of toast.

'There's been a murder. And you'll never guess who's been killed.'

'Go on then.'

'That Shipton woman. She was found on her boat. Stabbed. There was blood all over the boat by the tiller.'

Laura turned to him sharply and knocked a cup of tea over. 'What the hell?'

'Hey, steady on!' Darren picked the cup off the floor. 'I thought you didn't like her, anyway.'

'I didn't, she was a snobby bitch, but that doesn't mean I'm happy that she's dead.'

Darren looked at her mischievously. 'Hey . . . You could have done her in, couldn't you? You could have got up early, crept out of here, gone over there and stabbed her. And I would never have known.'

'Shut up!' Laura looked distressed.

'It's a joke!' said Darren in a sing-song voice.

'Maybe. But think about it. The police will find out that I had that big row with her last night and that will make me a suspect. I had a motive for bumping her off.'

'Get away! Just because you didn't like what she wrote in that stupid blog?'

'The police won't see it like that; they'll be on to it like a terrier with a stick.'

'You won't be the only suspect, and certainly not at the top of the list. I've heard she had a few enemies and owed money all over the place, so don't worry.'

Laura shrugged her shoulders but said nothing. She didn't seem to be convinced.

∾

The detectives decided to split into two groups as they began their investigation: Oldroyd with Steph, and Andy with Jav, who went over to the trust's office to see what they could find out. After that they would speak to the owner of the chandlery. Oldroyd was keen to talk to Phil Cunliffe – pub landlords were always a good source of information. He and Steph sat at the bar with Phil standing behind an array of colourful beer pumps offering a range of local beers. Oldroyd couldn't resist asking about them.

'You've got a nice selection here, Mr Cunliffe.'

'Thank you. All brewed locally.'

'I like a nice traditional amber bitter, something similar to the famous Taylor's Landlord, you know.'

'Well, if that's your type of beer you can't do better than this Original Bitter. Try it.'

Phil pulled Oldroyd a taster which he eyed keenly. 'Oh, that's good. Lovely depth of colour, and that scent of—'

'Sir,' said Steph firmly, with a certain look on her face.

'Oh, yes.' Oldroyd grinned sheepishly. 'Mustn't get distracted on duty. Another time.' Instead, he asked Phil what he knew about the victim.

'She lived alone. I don't know what she did before she came here but I think her and few others who live in narrowboats in the basin were in a folk group together back in the day. I've heard them talking about it. They were in here last night,' began Phil. 'They always come to the folk night. And they always sit over there.' He pointed to a table in a corner.

'So there's a group of friends who have permanent moorings here in the basin?' asked Oldroyd.

'Yes, they've been living here for years. They're all over sixty now.'

'I don't suppose you know much about their past lives either?' said Oldroyd.

'No, you'll have to ask them.'

'Can you give us some names?' asked Steph, who was ready with a notebook.

'OK, the people who were in the folk group – there's Liz Aspinall, she lives on *Meg*. That's the cream and red boat. She's by herself. I think her husband died a few years ago. Then there's Bob Anderson and Bridget Foster. They live on *Rowan* – that's the really fancy one with all the paintings on the side. There are some other people who have permanent moorings too. There's a boat just out of the basin called *Gypsy*. It looks a bit rundown. Laura and Darren Ward live in that one. They're a lot younger and they don't get on with the others. It's a bit of a class thing. I only mention them because last night there was a big row between Annie Shipton and Laura.' He looked at Steph. 'I think you were here.'

'Yes, we saw a bit of that as we came in,' said Steph, writing everything down. 'What was it about?'

Phil shook his head. 'Something to do with a blog Annie wrote. She must have said something unpleasant, and Laura thought it was about her and Darren. She was quite shouty and aggressive.'

'Did she threaten Ms Shipton with violence?' asked Oldroyd.

'No, I went over and broke it up before it could get any nastier.'

'OK. Thanks for all that. Were you aware of anybody else who might have had a motive for killing Annie Shipton?'

Phil thought for a moment. 'No, but there were rumours that she owed money to a number of people. I don't know who.'

'Thank you.'

Oldroyd and Steph left Phil to make hasty preparations for opening time. He'd been badly distracted by the events of the morning.

～

Jav and Andy walked across towards the Canal and River Trust office. They passed the marina section of the basin where there were some narrowboats and canoes for sale, which piqued Andy's interest. There was a small office, but it was shut.

'Are you interested in buying?' said a voice behind them. It was Ros Collins from the trust. 'Peter Swales is only here at the weekends, but I can take your details if you like.'

Jav explained who they were, and Ros led them into the trust's office. It was an interesting place full of colourful displays of photographs of canal life in the past and present, and lots of leaflets and books. She took them into a small back room where she had a desk with a computer and some filing cabinets containing copies of the publicity material and forms.

'What does your job involve?' asked Andy.

'We're the agency that looks after the waterways. We maintain them and enhance them with the help of volunteers. We also issue permits for various things such as mooring. I run this office, which also acts as an information point for visitors.'

'I assume you know why we're here?' asked Jav.

'Yes. I've heard about Annie Shipton. It's terrible.'

'How well did you know her?' asked Jav, noting that Collins looked a little anxious when he mentioned Shipton's name.

'Only as a client. There is a charge for permanent mooring here at the Saltaire basin, payable to the Canal and River Trust, and it's my job to collect it.'

'And did she pay the charge regularly?'

Ros hesitated and then said, 'As a matter of fact, no. She was badly in arrears. I sent her a letter recently giving her notice that she was facing eviction if she refused to pay. You'll probably find the letter in the boat unless she destroyed it.'

'Did you get any response to the letter?' asked Andy.

'No,' Ros said, but a slight hesitation and the fact that she looked down suggested to Andy that this was not entirely true.

'Do you have any idea why she didn't pay?' asked Jav.

'No, but I'm aware she owed money elsewhere. I was talking about it this morning to Gary Wilkinson who owns the chandlery next door. She owed him money too.'

'I see. Do you live near here?' continued Jav.

'Just up in Shipley. It's close enough to walk most days, which I did this morning. I got here at about half past eight. I open the office at nine. When I got here, I saw the police tape, and knew something was wrong. Then Gary came past and told me what had happened.'

'Do you know the people in the boating community here?'

'Not that well. But they seem good people who follow the rules, don't pollute the canal or cause any trouble. They pay their mooring fees, which gives them access to facilities like the water hose to top up their tank and the bilge pump to get rid of their waste. The community seems to function well, although I am aware of some friction between the long-established residents and a couple who arrived recently.'

'Who are this newer couple?' asked Andy.

'Laura and Darren Ward. They came here from Bradford. They're a lot younger than the others. I suppose you could say they have a different attitude.'

'In what way?'

'They're not quite so sedate, if you like. They have a more . . . lively and noisy lifestyle.'

'And does that annoy people?' asked Jav.

'I think so. There was certainly no love lost between them and Annie Shipton.'

'Did they threaten her?'

'Not to my knowledge.'

'And do you know of anyone else who might have had a motive to harm her?'

'No. I really don't know people here that well on a personal level. I don't think there's anything else useful I could tell you.' She thought for a second before adding, 'But before you go, another of my jobs is recruiting members to the trust.' She produced two membership application forms with leaflets and gave the detectives a cheeky smile. 'So how about joining us? You'll be helping support the maintenance of our wonderful network of waterways and all the wildlife that flourishes in them. And you get lots of benefits, like a booklet about walks and a regular magazine.'

Andy and Jav glanced at each other and smiled. They'd not expected this; she was certainly serious about her job. 'Thank you, we'll take the forms and have a look,' said Jav. 'An officer will call round to take a statement from you.' The detectives pocketed the leaflets as they left.

Ros sat behind her desk, looking into space and thinking. Hopefully that interview might be the end of her involvement in the case. Unless . . .

The unusual goings-on down on the canal had not gone unnoticed in the surrounding area. Part of the huge former textile mill had been converted into an arts centre and gallery.

Nicholas Spenser, the manager of this complex, was an energetic, lean and physically fit man in his forties. He was always smartly dressed, and had serious plans for the Mill Centre involving an ambitious expansion with a new building.

He'd called at the office of one of their suppliers on the way to work, so arrived at the centre a bit later than normal. As he got out of his Audi, he noticed the presence of the police cars and the blue and white tape down on the canal. Inside the centre, he spoke to the young receptionist who was sitting behind a counter in the modern atrium, which had been constructed within the old mill.

'Morning, Julie. Have you seen what's going on out there over by the canal basin?'

'Morning, Mr Spenser. Yes, I was here earlier when the police started to arrive. Bert went over and found out what it was all about.' She leaned forward rather conspiratorially. 'Apparently there's been a murder!'

'What?'

'Yes, someone's been killed on one of the boats. Isn't it awful?'

Nicholas shook his head. 'Do we know who it is?'

'No. Bert said the police wouldn't tell him anything else. He came straight back to tell us, but I expect he'll be going over again soon and will talk to any witnesses. He'll find out.'

Bert Marshall was one of the caretakers at the centre. He was a very nosy individual who spent more time gossiping and prying into people's affairs than doing his work.

'Well, let me know if you find out anything else, will you?' Nicholas said.

'I will, Mr Spenser.'

Nicholas went quickly up the stairs and into his office. He stood at the window overlooking the canal, the mill, the river and the park that lay beyond. He enjoyed this view, and thought of the achievements of Sir Titus Salt, the philanthropic industrialist who had created all of this back during the Industrial Revolution, including the sturdy homes designed for his workers. Nicholas liked to think that Titus Salt would have approved of the work he was now doing in developing the mill as an arts centre, giving it a new purpose that still enriched the lives of working people.

He sat down, switched on his computer and tried to start work, but he was still thinking about what he had seen at the basin. He hoped that the trouble down there would not impinge on the smooth running of the Mill Centre. Those boat dwellers were always bad news.

He frowned. There had been conflict between him and that group, and one of them in particular had made his life very difficult. And there were other things too about his plans for the centre that he hoped would remain a secret. But what if the police investigation were to unearth them? That could ruin everything.

About half an hour later, Julie knocked on the door of his office.

'Mr Spenser,' she said as she came in. 'We've just had some news through. A friend of mine was talking to the people on the canal. She says it was that woman who's against the plans who's been killed. You know . . . Annie Shipton, was it?'

Nicholas frowned. 'Annie Shipton? What happened?'

'She was stabbed to death on her boat. Melanie said there was a lot of blood. She could see where she thought the body had been. It must have been awful. And Annie was in the pub the night before apparently. It's terrible, isn't it?'

'Yes,' replied Nicholas. This was really bad news – of the type he'd been dreading. It could make things awkward and bring in unwanted publicity for the area, further endangering his plans for the mill. 'Thanks for telling me, Julie.'

When the receptionist left, Nicholas swore, and then picked up his phone. He'd better call his wife to tell her about the murder on the canal and that the police were likely to come and interview him. He didn't want her finding out about it from anyone else.

~

Oldroyd and Steph approached the narrowboat called *Meg*. It was adorned with pots of flowers and herbs.

They showed their warrant cards to Liz Aspinall, the narrow-boat's owner, who invited them on board. The interior of the boat was decorated in an ornate manner with a variety of colourful cushions and rugs. A battered guitar sat in the corner. There were crocheted blankets draped over the sofa. One wall was covered in rather faded photographs and press cuttings.

The detectives sat on the bench seat at the dining table while Aspinall took a chair opposite. She was wearing blue denim dungarees and Birkenstocks, and her long auburn hair was swept back into a ponytail, showing off her large, silver hoop earrings. Oldroyd looked around the neat interior of the boat and its facilities, and then glanced out of the window on to the water where two beautiful swans were gliding along. Narrowboats were cosy, and being on the canal had clear attractions. Maybe he and Deborah could come on a boating holiday too. He'd once been on one himself on the Stratford-upon-Avon Canal and had a great time.

'We've been told that you were a friend of Annie Shipton,' began Oldroyd.

'Yes. I've known her a long time. It's devastating.' She spoke in a quiet voice with a Yorkshire accent and then looked away and paused as she recollected the past. 'I met Annie through my late husband Roger, when we were all at music school in Manchester in the nineteen-eighties. It's a long time ago now. Annie and I were singers. Roger played the guitar. That's one of his.' She pointed to the guitar propped in the corner. 'It was his favourite.'

'What happened to him?' asked Steph.

'He died of cancer two years ago.'

'I'm sorry.'

Liz gave a wan smile. 'Thanks. We would have had a good life together, except we lost our daughter Meg. Also from cancer. She was ten years old. We named this boat after her. Her death cast a shadow over everything. We couldn't have any more children. I've lost both of them now.' She picked up a framed photograph from a small table. 'This is the three of us.'

Steph and Oldroyd looked at the image of a younger Liz with a red-haired man who they assumed must have been Roger, and a girl of about nine. They were all smiling into the camera. It was a heart-breaking image, knowing what would eventually happen.

'I'm sorry, again. That's awful,' said Steph, handing the frame back.

Liz nodded and for a moment seemed beyond words. After taking a few seconds to recover, she continued. 'Anyway, when we left college, we decided to form a folk group. Annie's husband Ben also joined us. He's a bass guitarist. They're separated now and he lives over in Oakworth. We also recruited Bob Anderson and Bridget Foster – Bob's a drummer and Bridget plays the flute. They live over on *Rowan*. The boat's named after our group – Rowan. Ever heard of us?'

Steph and Oldroyd looked at each other. 'I'm afraid I don't listen to folk music very much. How about you, Steph?'

Steph shook her head.

'Well, we were very popular in the north in the nineties. We played in clubs and halls all over Yorkshire, Lancashire, Cumbria and Northumberland. We even got a recording contract. Our songs were all about northern life and ordinary people from the past and the present. You know? Shepherds, mill workers, sea farers . . . Bob even wrote one about the men who worked on the canal. Bob would often do the lyrics, and Roger wrote the music.'

'Are those photographs and cuttings from your time in the group?' asked Oldroyd, looking at the wall.

'Yes. It was a hectic life, but great fun. We never had a lot of money – it's not the kind of music that gets super-popular and makes you rich. We lived in caravans for a while because we were constantly on the move. It's OK when you're young, but eventually Roger and I got tired. We wanted to settle down and start a family.'

'So how did the group come to an end?'

'It got a bit acrimonious because Annie wanted us all to carry on. She insisted we could improve our performances and become more famous. She accused us of letting everybody down. But Roger and I just didn't have that ambition, so we left. Some fresh people joined after that. It was never the same, though, and it wasn't long before Bob and Bridget fell out with the Shiptons over copyright issues, and they also left.'

'What did you do after that?'

'We settled in Bradford. Roger worked giving guitar lessons and I trained as a music teacher. We missed the excitement of performing, but the settled life was good. We rented a terraced house in Heaton. Bob and Bridget went to Leeds – we still saw them quite a lot.'

'But Rowan continued?'

'Yes, but not with the same success. Roger and I made guest appearances at times, as did Bob and Bridget. I think they were the most popular gigs, but Annie would never have admitted it.'

'So was there still animosity between you?'

'A bit. It took a long time for Annie to forgive us for breaking up the group, but she seemed glad to see us when we went back. Rowan didn't last too long after that, however. That was when Annie got pregnant with Brittany. She's a primary school teacher in Oldham now.' Liz put her hand to her mouth. 'Oh! She won't know what's happened.'

'She will have been visited by the local police. It's always our priority to contact the next of kin of the deceased.'

'I see. Poor Brittany. We'll look after her.' Liz looked very upset at the prospect of Annie's daughter suffering.

'So how did you all end up here on the canal?'

'It was Annie's idea. She and Ben went on a boating holiday and really enjoyed it. The group had dissolved by this time. She contacted us and asked, how did we fancy living near each other on the canal at Saltaire? She said it would be fun, and we could all grow old together. It was also much cheaper than living in a house. Roger and I weren't sure at first, but when we came down here and saw the boats, we were instantly drawn to the idea. And it made sense financially. We were paying out large amounts for rent at the time, but we could afford to buy a narrowboat. It's a bit restricted in terms of space, but that never bothered us. Bob and Bridget felt the same, so we all acquired boats and moored them here. There were no young people to think about. We lost our daughter, Bob and Bridget don't have kids, and Annie's daughter Brittany had left home. We've been here for five years now.'

'And do you all get on with each other?' asked Oldroyd.

Liz momentarily hesitated, something that the sharp-eyed Oldroyd immediately noticed and made a mental note of. 'Yes. We don't argue about the group any more and we're not reliant on each other. We lead quite separate lives but it's nice to have everyone nearby and meet socially. We've known each other for so long and we have such a history despite any past disagreements. The only falling-out was when Annie and Ben split up a couple of years ago.'

'What caused that?'

Liz shrugged. 'It was always a bit of a stormy relationship. They used to have rows about the group's music. They had different ideas about what we should be playing. Annie always regarded herself as the unofficial leader of the group who should have the final say on things. To be fair, she always did most of the organisation and finance of the group, so she had a right to think that way. But I don't know what caused them to split up. Annie just announced one day that Ben had left, and that was that. He did come back, occasionally, however. I was up late one night, and I heard shouting coming from *Moorhen*. I'm sure it was Annie and Ben arguing. Then a bit later a car drove off.'

Steph noted this down. 'So what do you all do here?' she asked.

'Roger continued with his guitar lessons until he was too ill. The kids used to like coming here to the boat. I took up sewing and rug-making, and I make cushions too.'

'Yes, I can see,' said Steph, looking round. 'They look great.'

'Thanks. I share a workspace in the Mill Centre. There's a section that's been converted into workshops for craft workers. I sell my stuff at local markets. As far as the others go . . . Bob became a sort of consultant for budding folk groups – gave them advice and mentored them. Bridget teaches the flute. She's managed to get quite a few local pupils and she conducts a little amateur orchestra. None of us have ever been any good at making money, but we survive. The poorest of us was Annie, who never had any kind of job, to my knowledge, from the time Rowan finally split up. I don't know how she survived, especially after Ben left. We all helped her a bit when she came round asking for bits and pieces, like a few eggs or something. We were always buying her drinks in The Navigation. I think she owed money to a number of people.'

'Did Annie have any enemies that you know of? People who might have wanted to kill her?' asked Oldroyd.

Liz looked at him and then out of the window at the water. A narrowboat was chugging past the basin. 'Annie could be a difficult character. She was very outspoken and stubborn if she thought she was in the right. She fell out with Bob once over some copyright issues, but that was a while ago. Recently she got involved in a big row with Nicholas Spenser, the manager of the Mill Centre.'

'What was the row about?'

'There's a scheme to build an extension to the galleries. The design is very modern, and Annie was very opposed to it. She said it didn't harmonise with the old mill buildings, and felt it would bring in too many tourists, which would spoil the feel of the area. She organised a petition against the development and took it into Spenser. I think she was quite aggressive towards him.'

'OK,' said Oldroyd as Steph wrote down the details.

'Then there was that business with the cyclist.'

'Go on,' Oldroyd said, sensing she was unsure if this was relevant.

'Annie was a fierce defender of the canal being mainly for the narrowboaters, even though people have a right to walk and cycle on the towpath. She told anyone off if she thought they were misbehaving, and she got into a big argument one day with a local man – I don't know his name – about him cycling too fast on the path. I wasn't there, but apparently it got nasty . . . And then there's that business with the blog and the couple who live on *Gypsy*.'

'Yes,' Oldroyd said. 'We heard about that from the landlord at The Navigation, including the row in the bar.'

Liz took a deep breath and looked out of the window again. 'I don't think I can tell you any more. Annie was a person who made enemies. You're going to have a difficult job narrowing down who might have taken an argument further.'

'How did you find out about things this morning?' asked Oldroyd.

'We had a fairly late night at The Navigation. I was woken up by the commotion outside. When I came out on to the deck, Gary Wilkinson – who runs the chandlery – told me what had happened. I've been on the boat ever since. I'm just too shocked to do anything.'

'Do you know why Shipton might have taken her boat on to the canal at such an early hour?'

'She told us last night that she was setting off early to go up to Skipton boatyard for some repairs.'

'Did she say whether anyone was going with her?'

'No, and I can't think who would have gone. Annie had become a loner since Ben left.'

Oldroyd brought the interview to an end, but as Liz was showing them out, she spoke again.

'Look, there is something else. I wasn't going to mention it because it didn't seem to be my place to tell you.'

'Go on,' said Oldroyd.

'Early on, when the group formed, there was another member: Simon Anderson. He was Bob's younger brother, who played the violin. He was very talented.' She paused and looked down. 'He was killed in a road accident and some people blamed Annie. I'd much rather you asked Bob himself about it before I say anything else, if you understand.'

'OK, we will,' said Oldroyd, thinking that it was an avenue worth pursuing. You never knew how far back the roots of some crimes could run.

When the detectives left, Liz stood by the tiller looking over towards Shipton's boat, *Moorhen*. Annie was gone. Life on the canal would never be the same again.

∾

Bridget Foster watched the police leave *Meg*. When they were out of sight, she went across to talk to Liz on her boat.

'What did they ask you about?' she said as they sat drinking tea.

'They're obviously looking for suspects. They wanted to know all about Annie's history, all the details about Rowan and our involvement, and what we've done since . . . And did I know anyone who would want to kill her? I told them about the blog, the business with the Mill Centre, and the confrontation with the cyclist.' She looked at Bridget. 'I also mentioned our arguments with her . . . that copyright business with Bob, and Simon's death.'

Bridget looked shocked. 'Why did you tell them about all that? It draws suspicion on to Bob.'

'Look, you have to be straight with the police and tell them everything you know. If you try to conceal anything or lie to them, they'll find out later and then you'll be in real trouble, bringing suspicion on yourself. But if you tell the truth, you've got nothing to be afraid of.'

'No . . . no, I suppose you're right,' replied Bridget, but she didn't sound very convinced.

'What's the matter? You surely don't think Bob had anything to do with it?'

'No, but he was out on a walk early, and didn't come back until after the body was found. I know it's silly, but I just wish he'd been with me all the time. I can't give him an alibi. I know the police will be coming to us soon.'

'They will, but as I say, don't make anything up to the police. And I've saved you a lot of time and effort – they won't need to ask you as much about our group and stuff like that. Where did Bob go?' asked Liz.

'Just for a cycle ride and then to do a bit of shopping.'

'There you are, then.'

Bridget shook her head. 'I just remember how unpleasant that whole business about the songs was. And the things Bob said about her, not to mention Simon.'

'But that was a long time ago. We've all been friends again for years now.'

'I know. I'm just being daft. But it's such an awful thing. What do you think happened?'

'She was stabbed on the boat, according to what I've heard.'

'But where did it happen?'

'Somewhere upstream, I suppose? She told us she was going to Skipton, didn't she?'

'Did somebody get on the boat with her, then? Who, for God's sake?' Bridget was getting quite upset as they contemplated what had happened, and started to cry.

Liz put her hand on her friend's arm. 'I don't know, Bridget. But I wonder if she met that cyclist again. We know he's capable of violence.'

'Yes. I wouldn't be surprised if it was him.'

'The other worry I have is Ben.'

'Ben?!'

'You know how they used to argue when they were together. I always thought Ben had a violent streak in him. He used to frighten me at times with his bad temper. And you know what Annie was like – always up for a fight.'

'But he hasn't been around for a long time.'

'I know, but maybe they've been in contact recently and fallen out about something. You know how Ben used to come back now and again. I told the police I heard them arguing late one night. I think something was going on between them.'

'Oh, Liz, that just makes it worse if it was one of us!' Bridget was on the verge of tears again. 'Surely Ben wouldn't do that.'

'I hope you're right, Bridget. I just don't know.'

Jav and Andy went straight from the Canal and River Trust office to the chandlery next door. Inside, the shop floor was absolutely packed with a cornucopia of boating paraphernalia. Neither of them had ever seen anything like it.

There were rolls of different kinds of lines and ropes in different colours and thicknesses, door locks, windlasses, tools, batteries, Calor gas cylinders, bilge pumps, and plastic containers of toilet fluid. Against one wall there was a tidy display of boat paints and another of ornamental boards and decorated metal chimneys. There was even a specially designed keyring with a ball of cork that would float in the water to prevent your keys from disappearing into the depths if you dropped them into the canal.

The detectives presented their warrant cards to Gary Wilkinson.

'I presume this is to do with Annie Shipton's murder?' he said.

'Yes.'

There was no one else in the shop and Gary locked the door. 'OK, come through here.' He beckoned for them to go behind the counter and led them into a back room similar to the one at the Canal and River Trust office, but this one was piled high with boxes and containers. Near the door there was a battered old desk with a computer and some chairs. They all sat down.

'I don't know anything about what happened,' Gary said. 'I was early as normal, but the police cars and the incident tape were already here. As the cordoned boat was *Moorhen*, I thought something must have happened to Annie. I managed to get a closer look and, sure enough, saw her lying near the tiller.'

'What did you do then?' asked Jav.

'It was a shock, but I was curious to find out more. I talked to some other people who were standing around chatting and one of them told me he'd seen the boat being brought into the basin and the body was by the tiller.'

'How well did you know Annie Shipton?' asked Jav.

Gary looked away and Jav thought he seemed suddenly nervous and uncomfortable.

'She's been here for several years, and she came regularly into the shop. But we didn't have a very good relationship, to be honest.'

'Why?'

'She asked if she could open an account . . . you know, pay at the end of the month? As she was a regular customer I agreed, but it was a mistake. She was always late paying, and then she stopped altogether.

She owed me over two hundred pounds when she died. I suppose it's my fault for being so lenient but she always had a sob story – she'd not been well or she'd had to send some money to her daughter or she'd had to pay for repairs to the boat. In the end I realised I was being manipulated. I bumped into her last night as she was coming out of The Navigation, and we had a bit of a row. I told her not to come into the shop any more. I should have banned her a while ago.'

Jav exchanged a glance with Andy. 'OK, it was sensible of you to share that with us. You said you arrived early this morning – how early? Was it early enough to have another confrontation with Shipton?'

Gary shook his head vigorously. 'No. When I got here, she was already dead, and the police were all over the place.'

'OK. Someone will be in touch to write down your statement later, so please stick around.'

Gary got up, went into the shop and opened the door. A small queue had formed outside. He came back to see the detectives out. 'I shan't be going anywhere. I've got a business to run.'

~

All four detectives met back in the room at The Navigation, where they gathered round a table to share what they had learned. Phil had kindly provided some coffee. Oldroyd sipped his, thinking, before he finally spoke.

'Right,' he said. 'First of all, Jav, can you confirm the Shiptons' daughter and Annie Shipton's estranged husband have been informed of her death?'

'Yes, sir. Officers visited them early this morning.'

'Did we manage to retrieve Shipton's phone?'

Jav shook his head. 'No, sir. The boat has been searched. I think it's very likely she had her phone by her when she was attacked and it went into the water.'

'Blast!' exclaimed Oldroyd. 'You're probably right. But it would have been useful to have it. Anyway, let's go through what we know and what we don't. It seems that Annie Shipton left the basin in her narrowboat very early this morning and went upstream towards Skipton. The night before, she had said to her friends that was her intention. We don't know for certain whether anyone went with her.'

'Or hid in the boat, sir,' ventured Steph.

'Yes.' Oldroyd nodded before continuing. 'It seems to me that she can't have got very far. I know this canal. There's a lock just upstream, so she wouldn't have gone beyond that else the boat could not have drifted back down to here. The lock would have blocked it.'

'Unless the murderer turned the boat round after they killed her? Then they went through the lock and abandoned the boat to drift down by itself.'

'That's possible, but why do it? It would have been time consuming and very risky, increasing the likelihood that they would be seen by someone on the towpath or in another boat. I think they did whatever it was quickly, seizing the opportunity when there was no one else around.'

'Any thoughts on how the murder was committed, sir?' asked Jav.

Oldroyd shook his head. 'No sign of a struggle according to the pathologist and Forensics, who are saying there was no evidence of anyone on board. If she'd been shot it would be different – you can be shot from a distance, but you can only be stabbed at close quarters . . . unless there's an expert knife thrower involved. But if that was the case, we would presumably have found the knife still in her body. But perhaps we can learn more about what really happened if we can determine who was responsible. What about the suspects?'

'There appear to be a fair number of people with a motive, sir,' said Andy, consulting his notes. He always made a detailed written record during a case. 'Though whether any of the motives is strong enough for a murder, I'm not sure. So we've got the couple who were insulted by the blog – Laura Ward had a big row with Shipton about it in the pub last night. Then there's this mysterious cyclist, who seems to be an aggressive character.'

'One of my detective constables has been asking people about this and he's come up with a name: Sam Wallace. It seems he also had a row with Shipton. He lives further down the canal somewhere. We'll find out exactly where,' said Jav.

'Good work,' said Oldroyd.

'A cyclist passed me coming down the towpath just before I saw the boat, sir,' said Steph. 'I didn't get a good look at them, but that could have been this man, Wallace.'

'There's the husband, Ben Shipton,' said Andy. 'We need to interview him and find out more about his relationship with his estranged wife. That's usually a fruitful area. Liz Aspinall, another member of the former folk group, reported that she recently heard the sound of an argument coming from Shipton's boat when her husband was paying a visit.'

'Yes, most people who are murdered are killed by a family member or friend,' added Steph.

'Also, sir, you mentioned that there had been some arguments between the members of this folk group, including over copyright?'

'Yes. We also need to interview the couple – Bridget Foster and Bob Anderson who live on *Rowan*. They are the other remaining members of that folk group. Aspinall also told us that Anderson's brother was killed in a road accident. And that Shipton was somehow involved in that.'

Andy continued, 'There are at least two people to whom Shipton owed money – Gary Wilkinson at the shop, and Ros Collins at the Canal and River Trust. Although we're not talking about huge sums.'

'No,' observed Oldroyd. 'But sometimes people get into rows, lose their temper and do something violent even when the stakes are low. It's the provocation experienced rather than the amount of money at stake.'

'Finally, sir,' said Andy, 'there's this business of Shipton's opposition to the extension at the Mill Centre. She appears to have made an enemy of the manager there.'

'Nicholas Spenser, Aspinall said his name was. He's also on the list to be interviewed.' Oldroyd finished his coffee and summed up. 'Thank you, Andy. We've managed to acquire a lot of information quite quickly, though I can't say I think there's a front runner from those suspects. It may be someone else entirely who we haven't heard anything about yet. It's still very early days, but at least we've made a start.'

'Isn't it likely that the killer was someone who knew Shipton was leaving the basin early, sir?' suggested Jav. 'And that suggests a member of the group in the pub that she told her plans to.'

'She could have told other people,' ventured Steph. 'Or it may have been a chance encounter on the canal which led to the murder.'

'All possible,' said Oldroyd. 'Maybe she invited someone on to the boat further upstream. The problem with all these ideas is that we keep coming back to the fact that there doesn't appear to have been anyone else on the boat at the time of death.' He frowned as he considered this, then stood up, smiling and rubbing his hands together. He enjoyed it when there was plenty of material to get stuck into. 'Anyway, let's get on with the second round of interviews. You're right, this case is a challenge, but we can't fail to crack it when the chief inspector has such a good team around him.'

'Thank you, sir,' said Steph with a little bow. 'And we feel the same about you.'

They all laughed.

Two

Saltaire was built between 1851 and 1872 as a model village by Sir Titus Salt, a philanthropist and mill owner in the Yorkshire woollen industry. The name of the village combines his name with that of the local river. Salt moved his business from Bradford and constructed a massive textile mill near the river, canal and railway on a site near Shipley. He built robust stone houses for his workers much superior to the slums of Bradford, wash-houses with tap water, bath-houses, a hospital and an institute for recreation and education, which had a library and a reading room. There was also a concert hall, billiard room, science laboratory and a gymnasium. The village had a school for the children of the workers, allotments, a park and a boathouse. Saltaire is now a UNESCO World Heritage Site.

Rowan had a very similar interior to *Meg* – decorated in bright colours, with lots of memorabilia on shelves, tables, and even fastened to the walls.

Walking past the kitchen to the narrow lounge area, Oldroyd noticed a fierce-looking set of kitchen knives held on a magnetic strip, with their sharp blades on display. He also saw some old photographs of the folk group Rowan performing in various venues. Oldroyd was able to pick out the younger Bob Anderson in the background on the drums. Anderson had dark hair in those days, and a luxuriant ponytail. Bridget Foster, with long wavy hair, could be seen playing her flute.

Oldroyd turned to the couple sitting opposite him and Steph. These days, Bob Anderson was paunchy and bald at the front of his head with his now wispy and grey ponytail still present at the back. Bridget Foster, meanwhile, had lost the long locks, and now had short greying hair and a face lined with age.

Oldroyd thought of his own receding hair and tendency to be overweight, and reflected on how no one escaped the ravages of time.

'So you were both in Rowan with Annie Shipton for a number of years?' he asked.

'That's right,' replied Bob.

'And how would you describe your relationship with her?'

Bob and Bridget exchanged glances. 'Good on the whole,' replied Bridget. 'You have to get along with each other in a group like that or it wouldn't work. We all agreed about what kind of folk music we wanted to write and perform.'

'Liz Aspinall told us a little about that when we talked to her earlier,' Oldroyd said. 'You sang about the hard lives of ordinary people in the north, didn't you? I do remember you vaguely, though I've always been more of a classical music man myself.'

Bridget smiled and continued. 'Annie was a good singer, and she was excellent at organising our schedule. Of course, she could be difficult – a bit abrasive and argumentative. She wanted her own way on things and was like a terrier until she got it. Everyone in the group had their fall-outs with her, but they always made up. If we hadn't stayed friends, we would never have come to live here together.'

'Liz also mentioned your brother Simon's death. Can you tell me about that?'

Bob glanced at Bridget and licked his lips nervously. 'Look, I knew this would come up, but it was a long time ago and—'

'It's better if you just tell us what happened,' interrupted Oldroyd with a friendly but firm look.

Bob took in a deep breath. 'Simon joined the group when he was only nineteen. My parents and I thought he was too young, but he was very keen and a good fiddle player. The others wanted to give him a chance, so I went along with it. Of course, I've regretted that ever since. He'd been with us touring for about a year and we were in the north-east, somewhere south of Newcastle. The schedules we had were tight – we left one venue after a gig in order to get to another to perform the same evening. It could be a longish distance between the two.

'We had a big van which carried some of us and all the equipment. The others went in a car which belonged to Alan Sotherby, who was our technical person.' Bob spoke slowly, as if carefully remembering each detail. 'It was a winter evening – dark and raining hard when we left this pub at about eleven o'clock to drive down to Leeds. We were all tired. Simon and I got into the van and Annie offered to drive.'

Bob stopped and shook his head. 'I shouldn't have let her.' The detectives saw that there were tears in his eyes. The memories were still painful. 'We went down the A1 with the wipers swinging across the windscreen. The road was quiet. The others were in the car right behind us the whole way. Then, suddenly, a deer ran across the road in front of us. Annie swerved to try to avoid it and the van came off the road and hit a tree. Simon was sitting by the passenger door, and he took the full force of the crash.'

He stopped and shook his head. Bridget put a hand on his arm and continued for him.

'I was in the car behind the van and saw what happened. Everyone saw it. I spotted the lights of a farmhouse nearby, so I ran over and called 999 from their landline while the others went over to help.'

Bob continued. 'Simon was unconscious. The ambulance came and they took him to hospital back in Newcastle. He died the next day. I had to face our parents and tell them what happened. It was horrible. To die so young – and he was such a talent. Me and Annie only had minor injuries.'

Oldroyd was silent for a moment. 'I can see that this is still difficult for you, and I don't want you to have to relive all the awful details. You understand that we are conducting a murder investigation, and in the circumstances, this could give you a motive for killing Annie Shipton. So the question is: did you blame her for your brother's death?'

Bob shook his head. 'It wasn't really her fault. What she did was just instinctive, but as she was the person driving, you obviously think maybe it wouldn't have happened if someone else had been behind the wheel.' He looked at Oldroyd. 'But I didn't kill her nearly thirty years later in revenge, if that's what you're thinking. Why would I wait so long?'

Oldroyd nodded. 'Sorry for bringing up painful memories. There is just one more thing I need to ask, however. I understand you left the group at about the same time as Liz Aspinall. She said that was because you fell out with Annie Shipton. Is that true?'

Bob replied, 'We didn't have a blazing row or anything, though I think Annie felt let down because it wasn't long after Liz and Roger also left. The thing was, Bridget and I didn't like the way the group was going in terms of the music. New people joined, and they wanted to play different stuff – more rock than folk. Louder electric guitar and drums, and fewer vocals. Annie agreed with them, but we were used to something quieter, more traditional and lyrical, if you like. When we played the new stuff, Bridget's flute was completely drowned out. It didn't sound like the folk music we love.'

'We were also tired of constantly being on the road,' continued Bridget. 'We went to live in Chapel Allerton in Leeds. We managed to rent a small, terraced house.'

Oldroyd nodded. He knew the area well. His ex-wife lived there – still alone as far as he knew – and could access yoga, sourdough bread, cocktails and all the rest of life's essentials within a ten-minute walk of her tiny, but very expensive, terraced house.

'I gave flute lessons and Bob got a part-time job at the School of Music teaching percussion. We never managed to earn a lot of money and what we did earn was swallowed up by our rent, even though the house was tiny. It was one of the reasons why we eventually came here – it's a much cheaper way of life.'

'Yes,' said Oldroyd. 'Liz Aspinall said the same. We understand that there was a dispute between you and Shipton at some point regarding copyright issues.'

The couple exchanged another glance.

'I heard from Liz that she'd mentioned this to you,' said Bridget. 'I don't think it was her place to say anything about it. But, anyway . . . she's right.'

'Tell us all about it,' said Oldroyd.

'OK,' said Bridget, who paused before beginning her story. 'You have to understand that in the early days of the group everything was very informal. We were just kids having a good time and we never thought about money. It was all very exciting and creative. Bob and I and Annie wrote most of the words and composed the music of the songs; we performed them but never bothered to copyright or anything. We never considered it. It was only later when the band got a little more famous that we started to register things formally and the issue of copyright and royalties came up. There was no problem with it until we left the group and they continued to perform our songs, including some of the early ones. I found out that Annie had copyrighted a number of these early songs in her name, even though Bob and I had actually written them.

'When I confronted her about it, she said she'd done all the paperwork, and we'd shown no interest, so why shouldn't she get the revenue? She also claimed that we wrote the songs together. Which was true of some of them, but not all. A number of the ones she'd claimed under copyright were definitely our work. It was typical Annie at her most dismissive and stubborn. She wouldn't give way. We had a pretty furious row about it.'

'Was it ever resolved?'

'Not properly. We didn't have the money to employ lawyers in those days, and it would have been risky. How could we prove which of us wrote certain songs without her help, when other songs were clearly a joint endeavour? In the end she agreed to let us share some of the royalties, but we've never had the money we think we were owed. It would have been a useful bit of income. Bob and I have never been very well off.'

Oldroyd was sitting back in his chair, listening to Bob's story. 'If your relationship with Shipton broke down, how come you came to join her here on the canal?'

Bob again exchanged glances with Bridget. 'To be honest, I didn't want to, initially. But Bridget persuaded me. She said it wasn't just Annie. Liz, Ben and Roger would be here too, and it would be great to be together again. I wouldn't have to spend much time with Annie if I didn't want to, so I agreed. As Bridget said, it was cheaper, and we were short of money.'

'And how has it been? How did you feel about her after you all moved to the area?'

Bob shrugged. 'We sort of forgot about the copyright business. I don't think there was ever much money involved. Annie was perpetually short of cash. It's not like she swindled us out of a fortune.'

Oldroyd turned to Bridget. 'How did you feel about Shipton after she behaved like this?'

Bridget had picked up a pen from the table in front of her and was nervously fiddling with it. 'As I said before, Annie could be difficult. You had to accept the rough and the smooth with her. Obviously, I thought she behaved badly. It hurt that we had created those songs together while she claimed the credit and the money for them. But there was not much we could do about it.'

Steph was making notes. 'Can you tell us where you both were and what happened this morning?' she asked.

Bridget dropped her pen, and it rattled as it landed on the floor. She was afraid of telling the truth but remembered Liz Aspinall's warning that she'd shared with Bob. She turned to him now to encourage him to speak.

Bob said, 'I got up early and, as it was a lovely morning, I went for a walk downstream.'

'That's towards Shipley?' asked Oldroyd.

'Yes.'

'Did you see anything unusual here in the basin or anywhere else?'

'No. I walked for a couple of miles then doubled back to the shops to buy some groceries. The first time I was aware that something had happened was when I got back and saw the police cars and the tape around Annie's boat.'

'How about you?' asked Steph, turning to Bridget, who hesitated. She was going to give an honest account but not tell the police that she was worried about where Bob was and what he might have done.

'I got up a little later, and, when I looked out the windows, saw that something was wrong. I walked over to *Moorhen* and spoke

61

to the police who told me that a woman had been found dead on the boat. Someone else confirmed that it was Annie. Then I came back to wait for Bob to return and tell him. It wasn't long before he arrived.'

There was a pause as Oldroyd considered these accounts with an inscrutable expression on his face. 'So,' he said at last, 'do you know of anyone who would want to kill Annie Shipton? We already know about her debts, and her conflicts with a cyclist, with the director of the Mill Centre and with her estranged husband.'

'I can't think of anyone, Chief Inspector,' said Bridget. 'Can you, Bob?'

'No,' Bob said. 'As you've discovered, Annie tended to rub people up the wrong way, but I can't see any of the people you've mentioned wanting to kill her.'

'Maybe not,' said Oldroyd. 'But someone did. Anyway, we'll leave you for now. An officer will be round later to take a statement.'

When the detectives left, Bridget and Bob said nothing to each other. After a while Bob went out to the tiller and smoked a cigarette as he looked across to Annie's deserted boat.

At the Mill Centre, the reception was quiet. Julie Wilton took the opportunity to make herself a coffee at the large bean-to-cup coffee maker, which Julie thought looked good but her mocha pot at home made better coffee.

The walls were white, decorated with arty black and white photos of the mill before and after the conversion. Furniture made from dark reclaimed wood completed the industrial-chic look. As she sipped her coffee, Julie reflected on how lucky she was to work in such a nice space.

Just as she was relaxing, Bert Marshall approached the desk. *Damn,* she thought. Bert was quite a character, but he could be a nuisance – always hanging around, as though he didn't have much work to do. And of course, when you actually needed him for something, he could never be found. He was always dressed in grubby overalls, which wasn't a good advert for the centre if he was the first person that visitors saw. He also had a tendency to leer and to get a bit too close to you, especially if you were a woman. His age was difficult to determine but he was probably not as old as he looked. Julie felt a bit sorry for him, in a way.

He smiled when he saw Julie. 'How's it goin', love?' he asked, leaning over the desk.

His language grated with Julie, who moved her chair back a little. However, she was eager to find out more about the murder, and he was always a good source of gossip about what was going on in the area, so she humoured him.

'OK, thanks. A pretty normal day . . . apart from what's going on outside. Have you found out anything else about what happened down at the canal?'

He glanced around melodramatically to see if anyone was listening, leaned a little further forward and spoke in a low voice. 'No one has told me anything, but I've seen things, Julie – very important things.'

'What do you mean?'

He winked at her. 'I couldn't possibly say, love, but put it this way . . .' He paused and then spoke in a whisper. 'I've a good idea what happened and who was involved.'

'Really? What?' exclaimed Julie, drawing back. He was far too near to her, and she wanted him to leave, but what he was saying was too interesting. 'Shouldn't you go to the police, then?'

He shook his head again and put on a wise, knowing expression. 'I can't be sure yet. Can't make accusations without evidence, you know.'

Julie knew he was trying to impress her and was sceptical about his claims. 'What are you going to do then?' she asked.

'Just you wait and see,' he said, nodding enigmatically before heading further into the building, in the direction of his little cubbyhole where he kept all his supplies and equipment.

He laughed to himself as he opened the door into the dirty little room which stank of oil and disinfectant. He had indeed been trying to impress the pretty receptionist, but he hadn't told her the full story. He was going to use what he knew to his own advantage before he went anywhere near the police. But only when the time was right.

~

The detectives were eating sandwiches for lunch in their room at The Navigation. Oldroyd had been sorely tempted to go into the bar and order something there, along with a nice pint of bitter. Being on duty, however, it wasn't an option. But this didn't prevent him from looking towards the bar with a certain longing.

Jav had got the sandwiches from a local bakery. He and Andy were eating ham and cheese while Jav and Steph enjoyed hummus and red pepper.

'We tried the boat called *Gypsy*, sir,' said Jav between mouthfuls, 'but there was no answer. The Wards may be at work.'

'Yes, it's possible. And the same will probably go for Sam Wallace. Did you manage to find his address?'

'Yes, sir. Andy and I will go down later.'

'Anderson and Foster were interesting, weren't they, sir?' said Steph.

'They were,' replied Oldroyd, pulling a face as he drank from his glass of water. He would have preferred a pint of beer . . . the bar was so close! 'There's a lot of history between the former members of that folk group. It might have been a long time ago, but there are clearly still some long-held grudges. In Anderson's case, the fact that Shipton was driving the van that crashed and killed his brother must have been very difficult to come to terms with. Then, Shipton claiming copyright on songs that Anderson and Foster had written really cut deep.'

'I agree, sir,' said Steph. 'Anderson tried to play it down by saying that there was not much money involved, but it's not just that, it's the fact that someone has taken ownership of something you created. All artists hate that.'

'Yeah, they do,' added Andy. 'There have been some ding-dong battles in the rock music world about people allegedly stealing stuff.'

Steph turned to Oldroyd. 'Also, sir, did you notice how nervous Foster was when you asked her about their movements this morning? I think she's anxious about Anderson. Maybe she thinks he could have done it.'

'I agree. I didn't push it because sometimes it's better if they think you just suspect. Then they're not sure, get anxious and make mistakes. We don't know how Anderson really felt about Shipton. He had two reasons to wish her harm, so he's definitely on the list – as is Bridget Foster.'

Andy said, 'Does anyone else feel that it's a bit strange that these old hippy folk groupers all came to live here together after so many years apart, and when they didn't get on all that well in the past? I wonder if the killer is one of them. Could they have moved here simply to find an opportunity to kill Shipton?'

'In that case, it took them a long time to do it. They've all lived here several years, haven't they?' said Steph.

'True. Though it wouldn't have been easy. Someone put a lot of planning into this,' said Jav.

'I think I can buy their story about it being cheaper living on a boat and amongst a group of people you know and have a lot in common with,' said Oldroyd. 'It's not as if they're all living in the same house. Anyway, another person we mustn't forget is Shipton's husband. Estranged partners always high on the list of suspects. What's the situation with him, Jav?'

'He and the daughter have been contacted. Apparently they are both on their way here. They want to be with their close friends and each other after what's happened. I think we will be able to question them if we do it sensitively.'

There was a knock on the door, and one of the forensic team entered to say that they had finished examining *Moorhen*. They would submit a full report as soon as they could. Their preliminary conclusion remained that there was no evidence of anyone having been on board the boat except the victim.

'OK,' said Oldroyd. 'I think it's time we had a look at that boat ourselves.'

~

An officer remained on guard by *Moorhen* as the detectives arrived. The exterior of the boat was worn and quite dirty. There were some old plastic flowerpots on the main deck, with greyish soil inside and the remains of dead flowers. They made their way on board, putting on their plastic gloves and carrying plastic evidence bags. They carefully stepped over the bloodstains by the tiller and went down the wooden steps into the boat.

The inside of this narrowboat was much more spartan than the others, and had a desolate atmosphere now that its occupant had been removed in such terrible circumstances. There was a strange quietness below deck, punctuated further by the usual poignant signs left by a person who intended to return: an unwashed cup and plate by the sink, clothes strewn on a chair. The furniture was worn, and there was little in the way of decoration. The whole interior needed repainting. It also smelled of tobacco and weed. Annie Shipton must have been a regular smoker.

Oldroyd looked out of the dirty windows, which afforded a rather blurred view of the canal and its charms. The condition of the boat inside and out suggested that Shipton had indeed been short of money, so it was no wonder she'd got into debt. Maybe her husband had been much better off, and she had started to struggle when he'd left her. Aspinall said the victim never had a job. Had she wanted the others to join her here so she could cadge off them, get them to support her?

There was an untidy pile of papers on a table. Oldroyd had a quick look through them, before putting them into a bag to be taken away for a more detailed examination. He found the letter from Ros Collins threatening Shipton with eviction. It appeared that she hadn't paid her mooring fees for a considerable time. There were other bills for repairs at a boatyard down towards Leeds, just past Shipley. If these were also unpaid it would explain why she had been heading up to Skipton boatyard which was much further away. She had exhausted her credit elsewhere.

'Sir, look at this,' said Andy, who had found a photograph in a kitchen drawer.

All the detectives gathered round. The photograph showed Shipton in a bar somewhere with her arm around a woman. Both were smiling into the camera.

'Jav,' said Andy, pointing to the image. 'This is definitely Shipton. I got a good look at the body when we first found her. And isn't this other woman Ros Collins from the Canal and River Trust, who we were talking to earlier?'

'You're right,' said Jav. 'She didn't tell us that she knew Shipton that well. They look quite intimate here. It looks as if it was a few years ago, though.'

'Well, that's interesting,' observed Oldroyd. 'You'd better go back and speak to her again. Take the photograph with you.'

Andy placed it in a bag.

'There's another photograph here, sir,' said Steph, who had been into the bedroom. She held up a framed photo she'd taken from a dressing table. It showed Annie with a man and a teenage girl between them. Again, the photograph appeared to have been taken some time ago. 'I would think this is with her husband and daughter,' added Steph.

'More than likely,' said Oldroyd as he examined what looked like a family group at a birthday party. It was a happy picture with everyone smiling, dressed in smart casuals and with neat hairstyles. His brow furrowed as he looked closely at the image. There was something about it that was ringing bells for him, but he couldn't decide what.

Oldroyd went back up to the tiller and then rummaged around the boat. 'Well, that's very peculiar,' he said at last.

'What is, sir?'

'Has anyone seen a windlass?'

'A what, sir?' asked Jav.

'It's the tool you use to open and shut the sluices on the big gates at a lock,' said Andy, proudly parading his recently acquired knowledge.

'Oh.'

Nobody had seen one on the boat and a further search revealed nothing.

'Hmm, that's strange – you can't get through a lock without a windlass. No canal boat is usually without one.'

'It could have fallen overboard in the struggle, sir, like her phone,' suggested Andy. 'It's usually kept by the tiller, isn't it?'

'Yes. But what struggle? The evidence suggested there wasn't one.'

'True.'

Oldroyd thought for a moment and then continued. 'Has anyone seen anything else interesting?'

Jav had gone back to the small deck by the tiller, part of which was still covered in bloodstains. 'I don't know, sir,' he called. 'If Forensics confirm that there's no evidence that anyone came on to the boat, how on earth did the killer manage to commit the crime?'

Oldroyd shook his head. 'We're no further on with that mystery, either.'

~

As the detectives walked back towards The Navigation, Jav exclaimed, 'Look at that boat over there – it's absolutely filthy.' He pointed up the towpath, away from the basin and several boats up from where Andy and Steph were moored. 'Who on earth lives in that?'

Oldroyd smiled. 'Let's go and have a look,' he said to Steph.

'I'll go and put the kettle on, sir,' said Andy.

'I'll check on the team,' said Jav. 'I'll be back soon.' He strode off to where a group of officers were gathered near the police cars.

Oldroyd and Steph approached the old boat. It had a metal chimney coming out of the roof from which smoke was drifting.

'Oh, I love the smell of wood smoke,' said Oldroyd. 'It reminds me of Bonfire Night. I quite fancied getting a wood-burning stove for our new house, but my partner was dead against it. She said the smoke is dangerous – full of harmful particles, and that the stoves emit a lot of CO_2.'

Steph laughed. 'Well, she's right, sir. Some local councils have banned them.'

Oldroyd shook his head. 'Amazing, isn't it? That the middle classes embraced real fires because they thought they were more natural and looked good, and now they're having to beat a hasty retreat since we've realised stoves and fires aren't good for the environment or health.'

They reached the boat, but could see no sign of life. The vessel was in a much worse state than Shipton's. The metal parts were rusting, and the hull was covered in a layer of grime. There were no flowerpots or any other decorations, and the windows were either boarded up or covered in dirt. If it wasn't for the smoke, it would have had all the appearance of an abandoned boat.

Oldroyd tapped on one of the opaque windows. 'Hello!' he shouted. There was no response, so he tapped again.

'Hold on!' a man's voice roared from within. Seconds later an outlandish figure appeared by the tiller. He was portly, with a huge beard and a bright blue bandana tied around his hair. He wore a grubby checked shirt, and baggy corduroy trousers.

'Who are thi and what does thi want?' he said, looking suspiciously at the two detectives.

Oldroyd smiled. He loved encountering old-school Yorkshire eccentrics who spoke with broad accents. They were a dying breed unfortunately. He showed his warrant card and introduced himself and Steph.

The man scowled. 'Police?' And then repeated his question. 'What does thi want?'

'Are you aware of what's been happening here?'

'No, ah've been busy all day. Whatever it is, it's nowt to do wi' me. Ah've got work to do.'

'Someone's been murdered on one of the boats,' said Steph.

He screwed up his face. 'Murdered? Bloody hell! Whatever next? Summat like that would never have happened in th' old days.'

'Her name was Annie Shipton. Did you know her?'

'Was she one o' them hippies taking up t' basin?'

'Yes.'

'They're a nuisance that lot. They're not real boat people; they just push up t' price o' moorin' till folk like me can't afford it.'

'Have you lived on the boats a long time then?' asked Oldroyd.

'Aye, nearly all my life. Me dad had a job on t' Aire and Calder Navigation. He worked a tug pulling Tom Puddings dahn t' canal.'

'What were they?' Oldroyd laughed. He knew that people like this man responded well if you showed interest in their past and way of life.

A crinkly smile came to the man's face. 'They were coal tubs that were filled up near Wakefield and pulled dahn to Goole. Then t' coal were put on ships.'

'I see.'

'Then he got his own boat and we lived on it for a while – four kids and me mum and dad. There wa'n't much space.'

'I'll bet.'

'This wa' t' last boat he 'ad.' He put his hand affectionately on the tiller. 'Ah've kept it goin' all these years. Come in and have a look.' He beckoned to them. Oldroyd smiled at Steph. The man's initial hostility had melted away.

They went down the now familiar steps into the living quarters, but this boat was very different from what they'd seen before. It was like stepping back in time. There were lacy curtains and peg rugs made from pieces of old rag. Once upon a time the interior had been nicely painted, but everything was now faded and absolutely stacked with stuff.

Near the tiller were plastic containers and bundles of rope. Further in were piles of paint pots and metal nameplates with rounded corners There was a large, roughly made easel that had one of these plates placed across it. It was in the process of being painted in the bright reds and greens typical of narrowboats. There was scarcely anywhere to sit except some dusty, rickety-looking

71

chairs, and a threadbare sofa. Oldroyd and Steph decided to remain standing.

'What's your name, by the way?' asked Oldroyd.

'Len. Len Nicholson. And ah paint stuff for the boats.' He pointed with pride to his work. 'Ah used to be a sign writer for shops and stuff. T' wife and ah lived in Bradford but when she died, ah decided to come back to live on t' boat. Ah make a bit o' money doin' this.' He laughed. 'It's amazin' what folk'll pay these days for summat ornamental like that. Ah paint th' outsides o' boats too and put little pictures on o' castles and flowers and stuff like that.'

'People want all the traditional things.'

'Aye, they do, but they don't have to live like we did when ah wa' a nipper. It wa' all cramped up inside and we had a coal-fired stove. It got freezin' in winter.' He nodded to an ancient stove on legs, the flue going out of the ceiling. 'Ah've kept t' stove but ah burn wood now.'

'Yes, we smelled it on the way down,' said Oldroyd. He was fascinated by all this history and had to force himself to return to their purpose. 'So . . . did you notice anything unusual this morning, Len?'

'Not really. Ah get up early but, as ah say, ah've got work to do. But ah did hear a boat goin' past when ah was getting up at abaht quart' to six and that's unusual. There's usually never anybody abaht at that time.'

'Which way was it going?'

Len pointed. 'Towards Skipton.'

That was almost certainly Annie Shipton, thought Oldroyd.

'You didn't see the boat?'

'Naw. Ah was down in 'ere makin' some tea. Just heard it go past.'

'Do you ever have anything to do with those people you called hippies?'

'Naw, not my type. Ah see 'em in t' pub now and again. Someone told me they were in a folk group.'

'They were.'

'Anyway, ah'm not here all t' time. Ah can't afford t' moorin' fees so ah have to keep movin' on. You're allowed to stay for free in most places on t' canal for a day or two. Ah go between here and Gargrave and back again. Ah know folk all up an' down t' canal. There are still one or two of us old 'uns left.'

Oldroyd asked Len a few more questions about his life on the canal, but most of the answers didn't seem to relate to the case at hand.

Afterwards, they left the boat and walked along the side of the canal.

'Well, that was an experience, sir,' said Steph with a smile.

'It was, indeed. Very interesting about the history of boats and the canal, though I'm not sure we learned anything about the case except that the boat he heard must have been Shipton's.'

'Unless there was someone else on the water at that time, sir. And if so, they might have seen something.'

'That's true. We'll get Jav and his team to investigate. In fact, we must extend the search for possible eyewitnesses. This murder was committed in the open, so someone may have seen something. I'm expecting the press tomorrow and we can put out a request through them.' He yawned. 'It's been a busy day, hasn't it? Even more so for you and Andy.'

'It has, sir. It seems so long ago that I saw that boat drifting down that I can hardly believe it was this morning.'

'I can imagine,' said Oldroyd, as they reached the pub. 'Anyway, Andy was going to put the kettle on a while ago. He'll have to make us a fresh pot and then we'll see what else we need to do before we call it a day.'

~

When Laura Ward arrived home from work, she found Jav and Andy waiting for her. She'd been dreading this and would have to face them alone – Darren wouldn't be home for a while yet. The detectives showed their warrant cards and Laura led them down into the boat. Inside, everything was basic and functional without much attempt at decoration. A dog with shaggy black hair, which had been lying on a grubby mat, growled at the sight and smell of strangers.

'Sorry it's not very tidy in here – didn't have time to clear up very well this morning, what with everything going on. Shut up, Ivan!'

The dog slunk down on its mat.

'Don't worry. I'm sure you know why we're here,' said Andy.

Laura nodded, but didn't say anything else.

'What happened this morning? How did you find out about the murder of Annie Shipton?' asked Jav.

Laura frowned. She felt very claustrophobic facing two detectives in the narrow compartment. She wished Darren was here.

'We got up at the normal time. We were having breakfast when we noticed the police were around. Darren went up and found out what was going on, then he came back to tell me. That was it, really. Shortly after that we both had to leave for work.'

'Where do you work?'

'I work as a waitress in Bradford and Darren's a window fitter. He works all over the area. I think today he said he was going over to Wibsey.'

'OK. We understand that you and Annie Shipton didn't get on very well, and that last night you had an altercation with her in The Navigation?' said Andy.

Laura took a deep breath. 'I would be lying if I said I liked the woman. I thought she was a stuck-up old middle-class hippy who thought she owned the canal. Her and her friends are all the same. Weren't they all in some kind of crappy folk group in the nineties?'

'Something like that. Was it just that you didn't like her, or was there more to it than that?' asked Jav.

'What do you mean? I would never have physically attacked her.'

'That argument you had with her in the pub was witnessed by a number of people. What was it about?'

Laura's face darkened at the memory. 'She wrote this blog about living on boats here. I'll give you the URL. Last week she wrote some nasty stuff about people she thought shouldn't be living on her precious canal – chavs, she'd probably call them – and it was obvious she was talking about me and Darren.'

'Why?'

'She mentioned a dog fouling the towpath, and obviously meant to imply it was Ivan, which is a complete exaggeration. It only happened once when he ran off, but we cleared it up. We always clear up after him. And she went on about music. We've played stuff a bit too loud at times, we had a party here once, but we turned it down when they asked us. The problem is they just don't like our music.'

'It made you very angry, this pattern of harassment?'

'Yes. I saw them going into the pub and I went in and had it out with her. Darren stayed outside. I admit I went a bit over the top, shouting and stuff, but I didn't attack her. Not then, or at any other time.'

'What did you do after the confrontation?'

'We came back here. Darren told me off for losing it with Shipton. Then we went to bed.'

'And stayed there until this morning when you both got up for breakfast.'

'Yes.'

'Neither of you got up early and went out walking?'

75

'No, we're not early risers, and we both had the morning off, so we had a lie-in.'

'OK, we'll need a statement from yourself and Mr Ward about the events of last night and your movements this morning. An officer will come round to take those.'

Laura nodded, looking relieved as they left.

Outside, Jav turned to Andy. 'What do you think?'

'I think the motive is there and she can obviously be hot-headed. Whether she could plan something like that, I don't know.'

'The problem for them is that they are backing up each other's alibis. But they could have worked together,' said Jav.

'True. And the same could be said about some of the other narrowboaters.'

'Yes,' said Jav, shaking his head. 'The victim had plenty of enemies who were in the vicinity of the murder scene. Evaluating them is going to be difficult, never mind the question of how the murder was committed. I'm glad we've got DCI Oldroyd on the case with us.'

Oldroyd and Steph followed the canal towpath downstream to the address of Sam and Janice Wallace. As they knocked on the door of the terraced house, they could smell cooking. Janice opened the door, and when the detectives showed their warrant cards she frowned.

'I knew you'd be round here at some point, but not as soon as this. Someone's been telling you stuff about Sam. Anyway, you'd better come in. I hope it's not for long, our tea's nearly ready. I'll call Sam.' She went to the door and shouted upstairs for her son to come down.

Oldroyd and Steph sat on chairs by the kitchen table. The smell of frying bacon and sausage was making Oldroyd hungry.

Janice turned to the detectives. 'I know Sam's been in trouble before, but it was only silly, young lad's stuff. He has a bit of a temper, but he wouldn't do anything very bad. He's a good lad really.'

Before Oldroyd said anything, Sam appeared. He looked suspiciously at the detectives before he sat at the table opposite them.

'I take it you know what happened early this morning,' Oldroyd said. 'That a woman called Annie Shipton was murdered.'

Sam nodded.

'I also understand that you knew her and that you were not on the best of terms.'

Sam looked at his mother as if for help, but he had to answer for himself.

'She hated me – she hates all people who bike on the towpath. She wanted to stop us, but we have a right to do it.'

'So, you argued with her about that?'

'Yeah.'

'We've been told that you recently had to be prevented from attacking her during an argument.'

Sam hung his head and avoided eye contact. He was rubbing his big hands together nervously and he didn't reply.

'Sam, answer the question,' said Janice.

'She were saying bad stuff about me. I was going a bit fast on my bike, I admit, but she called me a yob and said I should be locked up. I called her . . .' He paused. 'I called her a fucking bitch and I stood close to her. People came and pulled me away, but I wasn't going to hit her or anything. I've been in fights before, but I wouldn't hit an old woman like that.'

'Right,' said Oldroyd. 'Have you had any contact with her since that happened?'

'No.' Sam glanced at his mother. 'Me mother told me to keep away from her. But I still cycle on the towpath, and nobody can stop me. I don't go fast any more.'

'Did you go out cycling early this morning?'

'Tell the truth, Sam,' said Janice.

'Yes. I cycled up beyond the lock above Saltaire and back.'

'Did you see Annie Shipton on her boat?'

'I didn't see her. I don't know which one is her boat. I saw a boat coming down to the basin when I was cycling back.'

'I saw you pass me,' said Steph.

'Oh!'

'Did you see the same boat when you were on the way up to the lock? We're pretty sure that she didn't make it past the lock so you should have seen the boat on your way up too,' continued Oldroyd.

Sam looked a little bewildered. 'I . . . I can't remember,' he said. 'I don't think I saw it. I was looking over at the fields more than at the water. There were some horses by the hedge. I . . . I like to watch 'em.'

'So you only noticed it on the way back. Did you see anything strange about it?'

'Not really. It was just going slowly down the canal.'

'What about at the tiller? Did you see anyone steering?'

Sam looked uncomfortable as if he thought his story didn't sound convincing. 'No . . . I mean, you don't really notice, do you? And I've seen people leave the tiller to pop down quickly into the boat to get something if there are no other boats around they could bump into, you know?'

'Annie Shipton was slumped on the deck by the tiller, Sam, but you didn't see her?' asked Steph.

'No,' replied Sam and looked anxiously towards his mother again.

'It's OK,' said Janice.

'And you cycled straight back here?'

'Yeah. I had to get my breakfast and get off to work.'

'That's what happened,' added Janice. 'He was back here by quarter past seven. After breakfast we both went to work.'

'OK,' said Oldroyd. 'We'll be sending an officer down to take statements from you both.' He got up. 'We'll leave you to get your tea.'

Janice closed the door behind them and turned to look at Sam. 'Are you sure you've told the truth?'

Sam was exasperated. 'Yes, Mum, don't you believe me?'

'You definitely didn't see Annie Shipton?'

'No! How many more times?!'

'Even to speak to? I don't think you would do anything nasty, Sam, but if you saw her and spoke to her, someone might have seen you. And if that gets to the police, they'll be back here, and you'll be in trouble. And the last thing we want is more trouble with the police, isn't it?'

'Yes, Mum, yes, Mum. God, I don't know what else to say!'

'All right. Well, sit down and let's have our tea.'

~

'What do you think, sir?' asked Steph as they walked back up the towpath. 'He was very nervous and edgy, wasn't he? Do you think he was concealing something?'

'I don't know. He's a young chap, not very articulate, and wary of the police after his past involvement with us. I can imagine him hitting someone in a fit of temper, but I don't know about planning an attack and taking a knife. And how would he have known that she was going to be there?'

'He seemed very confused about what he saw on the canal, sir. You were right that he must have seen the boat twice.'

A barge puttered slowly past them on its way up to the basin. Water lapped slowly against the bank and a blue tit sang among a clump of reeds moved gently by the wind. The murder also seemed a brutal desecration of the peaceful life of the canal, mused Oldroyd.

'Yes,' he said to Steph. 'It wasn't very convincing, but it is amazing what you can miss when you're concentrating on something else. I can believe that he didn't notice a boat on the way up if he was looking over the fields, and when he saw it on the way back, he didn't register any detail. If he wasn't the murderer, he could have been a vital witness. But it seems Shipton was murdered while he was cycling further up the canal.'

They could see the basin ahead now, and another barge coming down towards them.

'We don't know for certain that she ever made it as far as the lock, sir,' said Steph.

'You're right. That is an assumption we've been making. Well done for questioning it. If she didn't make it to the lock, that makes the murder even more difficult to explain. Who else was physically on board with her? My thinking is that something must have happened at the lock, although what it was, I still have no idea. Tomorrow, we need to walk from the basin up to that lock and see what we make of it.'

'Right, sir.'

They arrived back at The Navigation, where they met with Jav and Andy. After everyone was debriefed, Oldroyd summed up.

'Well, we've got quite a list of suspects now and it's only day one. Some are more likely than others. There are more people to interview and track down tomorrow. One is this person at the Mill Centre who came up against Shipton. What's his name?'

'Nicholas Spenser, sir,' replied Andy.

'And we need to interview Shipton's daughter and her husband. OK for now. It's been a long day so let's go home – or back to the narrowboat, in your case,' he said, nodding at Andy and Steph.

'Yes, sir. This is not exactly how we thought our holiday would work out,' said Steph, grinning.

'No. You could go back to your holiday at any time, you know. Jav and I can get support from someone else.'

'No way, sir,' replied Andy. 'We're not abandoning this investigation now. It's fascinating stuff. But I wonder if, when it's all over, we could take our leave straight after the case, so that we can finish our trip?'

'I'm sure that can be arranged. It wouldn't be fair otherwise.' Oldroyd got up. 'Well, I'll see you all tomorrow. I might have to see DCS Walker before I get here. He likes to be kept informed. Also, we'll need to deal with the press. Jav, can you arrange a briefing for late morning tomorrow – say, eleven thirty?'

'Of course, sir. I'll be here early. I imagine Andy and Steph might be even earlier as they just have to step off their boat.'

Everyone laughed and Oldroyd left to drive home to New Bridge.

Jav drove from Saltaire to his home in Allerton, Bradford. He and his wife, Nadia, had a new-build three-bedroom house in this prosperous suburb of what, since the decline of the textile industry in the 1960s, had been a struggling city.

Jav had been brought up in Manningham, one of the poorest parts of Bradford. He'd had the ambition to work in the police force as a detective since he was a young child. Some people in the local community were suspicious of the police and of his decision to join the force when he left school after acquiring good A levels. Many expected him to follow a more lucrative career path into medicine, pharmacy or accountancy, but he was lucky that his family supported him.

He started as a police constable in Bradford before joining CID, and then moved to Harrogate station as a detective sergeant. He had very fond memories of his time there, but he knew it was right, when the opportunity came, to return to Bradford. He wanted to serve in his home city and felt that it was important that people of his heritage were part of the local police.

When he arrived, he parked his car in the drive and burst into the house in his usual cheery fashion. Inviting smells of a spinach and potato curry drifted into the hallway. Nadia was in the kitchen preparing dinner.

'Have you had a good day?' he asked as he embraced her. Nadia was a teaching assistant in the primary school where their two daughters, Fatima and Aleena, were in year 3 and year 5.

'Yes, one of the kids brought in a small piece of volcanic rock, so "volcanoes" was the theme for the day. We ended up making our own with papier mâché and plastic bottles. Oh, it's great fun in reception – no boring SATs!'

'Do I sense a rant coming?' asked Jav.

'Ha, ha,' she said, smiling and placing a finger on his lips. 'But don't be so loud. I've got them doing their homework in there. If they hear you, they'll come in here and won't want to go back. I don't like them staying up late to finish their work.'

Jav was desperate to see his girls. 'OK, I'll just go in quietly and see what they're doing.'

'Well, make sure they get on with things and don't interrupt them for too long. Tea will be ready in half an hour.'

Jav crept into the hall and slowly opened the door to the dining room. The two girls were working at the table.

'Hi, Dad!' called Aleena as she caught sight of him, and rushed over to hug him. The younger Fatima followed her.

'Hey! I'm so pleased to see you . . . but Mum says you must get on with your work, and she's right. You can tell me about your day later.'

Dutifully the two girls sat back on their chairs.

'Where've you been today, Dad?' asked Aleena.

Jav found it difficult to resist chatting to the girls when he hadn't seen them all day. 'Down at Saltaire, by the canal. And I've met up with friends I used to work with at Harrogate. It was really good to see them again.'

'Did somebody get murdered?'

'I'm afraid they did.'

'On the canal! Oh, how exciting!'

'Aleena, that's not very nice. I've told you before. It's a very bad thing when someone is killed.' Jav frowned. It was always a problem knowing what to tell his daughters about his work. Like most kids they were fascinated by gory details, which he tried to avoid telling them. He knew they had some status among their friends for having a dad who was a detective and would find it hard not to pass things on, however much he told them not to.

'But, Dad . . . I meant it's exciting because we're going on a school trip down there tomorrow.'

'What?'

'We've been learning about canals in history and we're going there to see how a lock works.'

Jav was not keen on the idea. 'Do your teachers know what happened there today?'

'I don't know . . . but we won't interfere with your investigation,' she said in a droll, adult way which made him smile. He knew that she would take tremendous pride in explaining to her friends that her dad was solving a murder on this very canal.

'I wish we were going,' said Fatima.

'I bet you do,' said Jav. 'But I'm sure you'll get the chance in a couple of years.' He thought maybe he should contact the school and get them to postpone the visit, but he wondered if Aleena would ever forgive him if he did that.

'OK, well, I'm going to speak to your teacher early tomorrow morning and—'

'You're not going to get Miss Hopkins to cancel it, Dad!'

Jav held up his hand. 'No . . . listen . . . I'm going to remind her of what's happened and that she must keep the school party away from certain areas. If she agrees to do that, then the visit can go ahead.'

'Hurray!' Aleena ran over and hugged him. Fatima continued to look disappointed. Jav glanced at the door hoping Nadia wouldn't come in and find him talking to the girls when they should be working.

'And now I really think you should both get on with your homework before tea,' he said.

'OK, Dad, we will.'

∽

At six o'clock, Nicholas Spenser drove across the Aire Valley to his modern detached house in Baildon, a small town on the edge of the moors. It was stone, built in a modern style, and was surrounded by lawn and low-maintenance shrubs. He liked to think of it as an executive-style house. He parked the white Audi in the drive and went inside.

'Hi, Sam, I'm home!' he called.

'In here,' came a reply from the kitchen. His wife, Samantha, ran a small beauty parlour in the town centre. The aroma of cooking greeted him. The kitchen was very orderly, and his wife was immaculately turned out as usual, wearing a cotton shirt dress with a belt emphasising her slim figure. She was stirring a pan and he put his arms around her from behind.

'Hi, darling . . . Wow, that smells good!'

'Chicken in mustard sauce. It'll be ready in fifteen minutes. I just need to get the veg on. What happened with the police?'

He was used to this brisk manner from her when she was stressed, and knew that he needed to tell her the truth as straightforwardly as possible. 'They didn't come to see me today, but they probably will tomorrow, or when they find out more about Shipton and her antics. It had to have been her out of everyone . . .' Then he noticed that the house was quiet. 'Where are the boys?'

They had two sons in the lower years of a local high school. Nicholas would have liked to send them to a private school, but they couldn't afford it.

Samantha turned round. 'They're having tea at their friends'. Can you pick them up later?' She returned to questioning him. 'So, the woman who was killed was the leader of that group opposed to the extension?'

'Yes.'

Her face clouded over. 'That will make you a suspect, then.'

Nicholas sat down at the kitchen table. He saw there was a bottle of wine already open and he poured himself a glass. 'Why? Don't jump to bad conclusions.'

Samantha took a drink from her own glass by the cooker. 'The police always suspect anyone who had a bad relationship with the murder victim. You know that.' Samantha's uncle had been in the police and what she'd seen and heard about his work had given her an insight into policing. 'What happened anyway?'

Nicholas explained how Shipton had been found dead on her narrowboat. 'Why would anyone think I'd kill her just because she was campaigning against me?'

'You're a bit naïve when it comes to this sort of thing, aren't you? Let's assume she was killed earlier today.'

'I think she was. Julie said that Shipton had been at the pub last night and she wouldn't be cruising on her boat after dark.'

'OK. So what's your alibi for this morning?'

'Sam!'

'I'm serious. The police will ask you. What are you going to say?'

'I left at the normal time. Twenty minutes past eight. You were still in bed.'

'That's no good. Tell them you said goodbye to me, and I'll back you up.'

'You mean you want me to lie?'

'Yes. Then you should be off their list. Without anyone to support your story, you'll stay a suspect. You could have left here early and murdered her before going into work.'

'What? You don't think . . . ?!'

'No, you idiot. But look at it from their point of view. They don't know what a harmless thing you are. And you had a motive however much you deny it. Oh shit!'

She leaned over the cooker, on which the sauce for the chicken was burning.

Nicholas drank some wine and shook his head. 'OK, but it's not going to be easy lying to the police.'

'You'll manage. And it's only a white lie,' she replied as she tried to salvage the sauce and then began to prepare the carrots and peas.

Nicholas was glad her gaze was not on him at that moment, as she might have suspected there was something else bothering him. She didn't know the full story. It wasn't just a question of an alibi; there were other things that could implicate him in the murder. Things that he had not told her about. Things that were beginning to look like mistakes.

~

'It's ready!'

Andy and Steph had finally returned to their narrowboat, where Andy had made a meal of sausages, mash and peas. They sat at the table.

86

Andy sighed. 'It's good to relax, isn't it, after all that? It seems ages since you woke me up to tell me there'd been a murder.'

Steph laughed. 'I know . . . and here we are meant to be on holiday! We haven't seen anything here yet as visitors. Not the art gallery, the park . . . nothing.'

Andy bit into a thick Cumberland sausage. 'Wow, that's good, even though I say so myself! Never mind. It's exciting, isn't it, being on a case like this with the boss? I wouldn't swap it for anything. We can catch up on the sightseeing later.'

'I know.'

'What about tonight? We can have a walk round that park while it's still light and then we could go up into the village. I don't fancy going back to The Navigation – too much like work – but there should be some good pubs up there.'

'There aren't any, I'm afraid.'

'Why's that?'

'Sir Titus Salt, who built the village for his workers, banned public houses in Saltaire as he'd seen workers in Bradford wasting their wages on drink. There was a library, allotments and a concert room but no pubs.'

'Bloody hell! Isn't that unknown in Yorkshire?'

'Pretty much, but anyway we just need to go beyond the old village, and we'll find some pubs if you're so thirsty.'

Andy grinned. 'Surely you wouldn't deprive me of a pint or two after such a hard day? And, as you just said, we are on holiday.'

'Yes, but you know I don't like you drinking too much . . . and you had a bit of a skinful last night.'

Andy put his hand over hers. 'I know, but you don't need to worry. My hard-drinking days are over. I'm too old now. How is your dad, by the way?'

Steph's violent, alcoholic father had had a terrible effect on her early childhood, and had left her with a strong sense of caution concerning alcohol. He'd disappeared back to London when his daughters were young, but had recently reconnected with Steph and her sister Lisa. He was no longer a drinker, but the scars of his years of alcoholism were still there.

'He's OK. He's got a better job and he's no longer in that horrible shared house. I know he feels a lot more positive about life now that he sees me and Lisa more regularly.'

'Well, that's good for everyone, isn't it? You've got a dad again, and he's got his daughters, which should help him keep off the booze.'

'Yes, and Mum's happy about it too. She's been so good throughout, when I think of what she went through when we were little. She left it for us to decide whether we wanted to see him again. And I'm glad we did.' She yawned. 'Do you know what? I'm really tired. I was awake at half past six this morning. Let's just go for a quick drink, and get an early night.'

Andy also yawned. 'I think you're right. It's been a long day.'

The atmosphere in The Navigation that evening was very subdued. Groups of regulars sat together, talking in lowered voices and occasionally glancing across at the table where Liz Aspinall, Bridget Foster and Bob Anderson sat looking rather morose.

Bridget and Liz had not really wanted to come to the pub, but Bob had persuaded them. He said it was better than mooching around in the boats and that it was good to be with other people.

'I can't believe it was only last night she was in here with us,' said Bridget, shaking her head. 'It seems a long time ago somehow.'

'It's the shock,' observed Bob, taking a sip of his beer. 'It distorts your perception of time – slows it down or speeds it up.'

'Maybe we should have gone somewhere else,' said Liz, looking furtively around the room. 'I feel like people are watching us. They probably think we killed her.'

'They're bound to speculate, but it's best to just ride it out. That's another reason I wanted to come in here. The longer we avoided it, the more it would become a barrier, and the more it would look like we may have something to hide.'

Liz didn't reply. They were all quiet for a while, looking down at their drinks.

'Do you think it was that bloke on the bike? He had a nasty temper,' asked Bridget at last.

Liz shrugged. 'Maybe. But let's face it, she had a lot of enemies.'

Bridget put her hands to her head. 'Oh, I don't think we should go on like this, trying to work out who might have done it. It's driving me mad. Let's leave it to the police.'

Bob put his hand on her shoulder. 'I think you're right. But we're also bound to wonder about it, aren't we?'

'Yes, but does it get us anywhere? Tomorrow, we need to go somewhere and get away from here for a while.' She turned to her partner. 'Let's get the train into Leeds. It'll be nice to be in the bustle of the city. It feels claustrophobic here at the moment.'

'OK,' said Bob. 'Do you fancy coming, Liz?'

'No. I'm going to stay here. I've spoken to Ben on the phone. He's coming here tomorrow with Brittany. Obviously, the police want to speak to Annie's husband and daughter, and I'd like to be here for them.'

'Bloody hell, I'd forgotten about them,' said Bridget. 'It shows the stress we're under. Let's stay here in the morning and go to Leeds in the afternoon. I just don't want to stick around all day.'

'OK, that's fine,' said Bob.

Liz finished her drink. 'Right, I'm off to bed. I'm absolutely exhausted. I'll see you both tomorrow morning, then.'

'Yes,' said Bridget. 'I hope you sleep well.'

'You too,' replied Liz and she went back alone to her boat, just as Annie Shipton had the previous night.

∾

'Jim . . . ? Jim, are you awake?' whispered Deborah. It was very dark in the bedroom.

Oldroyd grunted and turned over in bed. 'What is it?' he mumbled.

'Can you hear that noise?'

'What?'

'It sounds like something behind the skirting board.'

Oldroyd sat up and listened. He heard some tiny scratching noises. 'What about it?'

'I think it's a mouse.'

Oldroyd slumped down again. 'Oh, bloody hell! Is that all? You're not frightened of mice, are you?'

'Jim! No, I'm not . . . but I don't want them in the house.'

'Well, you wanted to come and live out in the countryside. This is what you get.'

'We need to do something about it.'

'I'll get a mousetrap,' murmured Oldroyd.

'Not one of those horrible things that smashes their spine.'

'OK, a humane one.'

'How do they work?'

'The mouse is trapped alive in a box and then you take them somewhere and release them.'

'But that sounds as if they'll just come back again.'

There was a pause before Oldroyd replied, 'What do you suggest, then?'

Deborah sat up in bed. 'I think we should get a cat. I said so when we were looking at this house . . . and, besides, it already has a cat flap.'

Oldroyd turned to face her. 'A cat to control mice? They don't exactly kill them humanely. They toy with them and batter them for ages before they finish them off.'

'I know, but at least it's more . . . natural. And I think if we had a cat the mice would keep away in the first place.'

'And who'll look after it when we go away?'

'We can put it in the cattery. Didn't you have any pets when you were little?'

'No, my mother didn't like animals in the house.' He paused. 'And I tend to agree with her . . . but if you want to get a cat that's OK. They're clean, and they don't take as much looking after as dogs, do they?'

'No, especially when you have a cat flap. I thought we could get a nice black and white kitten from the rescue centre.'

'Oh, you seem to have got this all worked out. I think the mouse is just an excuse for you getting a cat. Am I right?'

She was gently massaging his arm and shoulder, which he always found relaxing. 'Maybe,' she said. 'But it will help with the mouse problem. I've seen droppings in the kitchen too.'

'I see. Well, fine, then, I suppose.'

'You'll get attached to it as soon as it arrives. Kittens are some of the cutest things in the world. I remember all the cats we had when I was growing up. One only had three legs. It lost one in an accident. How sad is that? Jim . . . ? Jim?'

She heard snoring. Oldroyd had gone back to sleep.

Three

I'll tell the tale of Mary Flint,
She worked at Shuttle Eye –
A weaving mill
In a Yorkshire town,
But she was doomed to die.

She was doomed to die, O Lord!
She was doomed to die.
Cast from the fold
To bitter cold
Where she was doomed to die.

Mary had a pretty face,
The master's son thought so.
They met at night,
By a silvery light
And Mary couldn't say no.

By the dark of winter-time,
She was great with child.
Her father cast her
Out of doors.
The snowstorms they were wild.

She was doomed to die, O Lord!
She was doomed to die.
Cast from the fold
To bitter cold
Where she was doomed to die.

From 'The Ballad of Mary Flint' performed by Rowan
© 1994 lyrics by Liz Aspinall, music by Roger Aspinall

The next morning, Oldroyd called in to report to his boss, DCS Walker. Walker was in his sixties, but showed no sign of wanting to retire, despite being in an almost constant state of outrage and contempt for his superior – the young chief constable of West Riding Police, Matthew Watkins – who took a managerial and jargon-laden approach to his role and the way he communicated.

Oldroyd and Walker were on good terms as they shared the same values and attitudes – mainly that policing was about what was done in the field and not the office. Unfortunately, Oldroyd frequently ended up as the person on whom Walker unloaded his anger and frustration.

'Nah then, lad, come in,' said Walker. He and Oldroyd, being die-hard Yorkshiremen, liked to use the odd bit of dialect to each other in private and were on first-name terms.

'Mornin', Tom, how are thi?'

'Well, I'd be a lot better if it wasn't for this pile of rubbish.' He held up a document and Oldroyd's heart sank. He was going to be subjected to one of Walker's rants.

'Do you know what this is? It's that idiot's vision of the future of policing.'

Oldroyd knew who the 'idiot' was without being told.

'Apparently, police officers will sit in "surveillance centres", as he calls them, watching live CCTV footage all day and recording crimes that take place. Then they'll send out robots to arrest people. Marvellous, isn't it? No need for expensive cars, uniforms, equipment or even training. And policing can be done by anybody watching a screen.' He held up the document with a look of contempt and dropped it into the wastepaper basket. 'He wouldn't survive as a second-rate science fiction writer, and he has about as much knowledge of the reality of policing as a child at primary school. You see . . .'

And so he went on for several minutes, stroking his moustache and getting redder in the face, while Oldroyd waited patiently for him to get it out of his system.

Oldroyd had found that the best way of dealing with Walker when he was in this mood – which was most of the time – was not to agree with him or to ask any questions, but just to wait until his anger subsided.

Eventually Walker looked at Oldroyd with a small jolt of recognition, as if he'd forgotten that he was there. 'Anyway, Jim, how are you getting on over in Saltaire? The victim was killed on a narrowboat, you say?'

'That's right, Tom. And in strange circumstances too.' He explained how the body had been found.

'And no evidence of anybody else being on board?'

'No, but we've already got a string of suspects with motives.'

Walker grunted. 'Good. Well, it sounds as if it's right up your street then. You like the ones that are a puzzle, don't you? The Bradford people are very fortunate to have you advising them. I know you'll acquit yourself well, and it'll be a feather in our cap. David Haigh's OK. Good detective, but a bit of a big-head, you know? It'll be good to get one over on him. It's a bit of luck they're short-staffed.' He winked at Oldroyd. 'It was nice to hear from

Javed Iqbal, though. He was a good lad when he was here. I thought he would go far. He always wanted to go back to his hometown. Nothing wrong with that – policing is best done by local people. Or maybe robots,' he said sarcastically, glancing at the wastepaper basket. 'Haigh's lucky to have him.'

Oldroyd explained about Andy and Steph. He knew it was a devotion-to-duty story that Walker would love, and he was right.

'That's wonderful, isn't it? There they were on leave, but are still ready to help when they see the need. People like that are the bedrock of policing and worth fifty of that useless, petty bureaucrat who's supposed to be leading us all. I tell you, if he saw the body of a murder victim, he'd probably pass out.'

Oldroyd quickly intervened to thank Walker for his time and made his escape before the old boy got wound up again.

~

When Oldroyd arrived at the crime scene, the press were already waiting for him. He'd told the other detectives to leave the media to him. He was very experienced at dealing with them, and enjoyed the joking and banter.

He got out of his car and the reporters who had gathered around the basin and by The Navigation immediately came over when they saw who it was. In truth, he hadn't expected them to be here quite so early, but he could handle it.

'Detective Chief Inspector Oldroyd,' announced one reporter, thrusting a microphone in Oldroyd's face. 'This must be a very serious case if they've brought you in. Can't the Bradford police cope?'

There was some laughter at this as reporters crowded around his car. He would have to conduct the press briefing from here. There was no chance of arranging anything more formal.

'Yes, it is a serious case, but I've been brought in because of staffing problems at the Bradford station and not because the detectives there are unable to deal with the case. The facts are as follows: that the body of Annie Shipton was found in her narrowboat early yesterday morning. She had suffered a stab wound to the neck. She was a resident on her narrowboat here at the Saltaire basin. The investigation is still in its early stages, but we already have a number of lines of enquiry.'

'Is it true she was found dead on the boat as it floated downstream?'

'Yes.'

'That's a bit spooky, isn't it, Chief Inspector?'

'Spooky? I'm not sure about that. We're not thinking that she could have been killed by a ghost. Would a ghost be able to stab their victims anyway?'

This produced some more laughter and Oldroyd smiled. Humour and ridicule were the best methods of dealing with their more outlandish theories.

'Do you think she was stabbed by someone who had hidden on board?'

'That's a possibility. Or the suspect is someone who boarded the boat later.' He didn't say that they hadn't found any evidence of anyone else being on board at the time of death. That would only lead to headlines of the 'Police Baffled by Case of Dead Woman on Boat' type, which made the police look stupid. 'We know that she was heading upstream towards Skipton, but we think she only made it as far as the first lock above the basin here. So I would ask you to stress in your reports that we want to hear from anybody who was near the canal, and that lock in particular, yesterday morning between about six and seven a.m., and who might have seen something either on the canal or on the path.'

'Could this be anything to do with drugs, Chief Inspector? We've heard rumours of drug dealing in this area,' asked a large and sweaty reporter. He thrust a microphone at Oldroyd, who resisted the urge to step away from the man's body odour.

'That's not featured in the case at all so far, but we're not ruling anything out at this stage.'

'We've heard that the victim and her friends were hippie types, and they performed together in some kind of folk group in the nineties,' said a young female reporter to whom folk music of the nineties probably seemed as remote as Bing Crosby or Frank Sinatra did to Oldroyd.

'It's true that they were in a folk group, yes.'

'Could it be about settling old scores, Inspector? People in groups and bands are always falling out, aren't they?'

There was an uncomfortable level of truth in this, but Oldroyd would not be drawn into providing any detail. 'I'm not going to comment on that other than to repeat that we are investigating a number of lines of enquiry, though I don't expect to make an imminent arrest. This is only the second day.'

'Some of those hippies were a bit pagan, weren't they? You know, human sacrifice and stuff. If the body of the victim covered in blood was in the boat floating down the canal, could it have been some kind of ritual killing?'

'Oh dear, I think you've read too many horror stories. Or are you confusing it with Boromir's funeral boat in *The Lord of the Rings*?'

There was laughter at this, which again performed its role of dismissing the ridiculous idea.

'I think it's important that we keep to the facts and don't get carried away by our imaginations.'

'Do you think the killer will strike again, Chief Inspector?'

This question was always asked and Oldroyd often felt that they hoped he would say yes because that would lengthen and sensationalise the case. He gave his standard reply. 'At this stage we have no reason to believe that anyone else is at risk, but I would ask people to be vigilant as a dangerous person is at large. Again, I would ask for anyone with any information, however trivial it may appear, to come forward. So thank you, that's all I've got time for at the moment.'

After this Oldroyd strode off towards The Navigation. The reporters followed, trying to ask him some more questions, and then scattered around the basin, no doubt attempting to find out more information from anyone who would give them a quote, whether it was true or not.

~

The detectives met in the back room of The Navigation. Oldroyd told them about the impromptu press conference and Jav delivered a report on what the forensic investigation had discovered.

'Dr Coates confirmed that a stab wound was the cause of death – a stab wound inflicted from behind the victim. She also says that the wound was made from above at an angle, through the neck at the base of the skull and out lower down near the sternum. It appears as though the assailant was somewhat taller that the victim.'

'Possibly,' said Oldroyd and paused. 'Are the forensic team still saying that there is no evidence of anyone else having been on board the boat?'

'Yes. The only blood found belonged to Shipton, and there was no sign of a struggle. There were no traces of anyone else having been on the boat recently, including a lack of footprints in the blood. So if someone did hide onboard and then attack her, they made an excellent job of covering their tracks,' said Jav. 'We've looked through all the paperwork that was recovered from the boat. She didn't have a computer on board. There was nothing that adds to what we already know.'

'Good work.'

'We've also analysed Annie Shipton's blog – the one that offended the Wards. The entry was very provoking, but contained no material that seemed to be relevant to our investigation. If there was anything threatening going on, she concealed it very well.'

'OK. As we seem to have a long way to go, we'd better get cracking. We've got to interview this chap at the Mill Centre about Annie Shipton and her opposition to his plans, and I want to go up the canal to the lock, have a look round and see if it gives me any ideas about how this crime might have been committed.'

'Ah,' interposed Jav. 'While you're up there, sir, you might encounter a school party on a day out.'

'Oh?'

'Yes. It's from my daughter's school. Aleena will be there. Her class is doing a project on canals. I contacted the school to tell them to keep well away from the basin here. They're going up to the lock to see how it works.'

'Good, we'll look out for them. Anyway, you and Andy need to go back to the Canal and River Trust office and ask that woman . . . what's her name again?'

'Ros Collins, sir.'

'Yes . . . Ask about her relationship with Annie Shipton. Then I think—'

At this moment there was a knock on the door and the landlord Phil Cunliffe came in. 'Sorry to interrupt, but Ben Shipton is here. Annie's husband. I thought you would like to see him.'

'Yes,' said Oldroyd, 'send him in.' He turned to the others as Phil left the room. 'OK. Jav and Andy stay here and talk to

Shipton. Steph and I will go to the Mill Centre. We'll meet back here later.'

Ben Shipton came into the room as soon as the two detectives had left. He was tall with a shock of hair, now mostly grey, and he was wearing jeans and a leather jacket. He wore an earring in one ear.

'Take a seat,' said Jav. 'I'm sorry for your loss.'

Shipton blinked at Jav and Steph as if he could still scarcely comprehend what had happened. 'I . . . I can't really believe it. Phil Cunliffe told me what happened. Who on earth would want to kill Annie? I know she could be difficult, but to be murdered on her boat?' He shook his head as if this were an act beyond words.

'We intend to find out who did it,' said Andy. 'We understand that you were separated from your wife. How would you describe the relationship between you recently?'

Shipton's demeanour changed, and he looked up at the two detectives. 'I hope by that you don't mean you think that I had anything to do with it.'

'Just try to answer the question, sir. I know it's difficult but we have to ask you these things,' replied Andy.

Shipton sighed. 'Annie and I were married for a long time, but our relationship was always up and down. We both had firm ideas about the group and what we should play. And, well, we used to argue about it.'

'We've heard that there were some rows between the pair of you. Loud enough to be heard in some of the other boats.'

Ben frowned. 'Who's been telling you that?' He looked round but saw that neither of the detectives was going to answer. 'Yes, we did row about things now and again. We're . . . We were . . . both strong-willed and stubborn.'

'What made you finally separate?' asked Jav.

'It was Annie's idea that we should move on to the canal when Brittany – that's our daughter – left home. But I never liked it.

100

It's too cramped on a boat. We got on each other's nerves. After a while, I'd had enough, so I moved over to Haworth. I rent a small cottage there.'

'We hear that you still visited Saltaire,' said Jav.

'Occasionally, but I never stayed overnight. Annie and I were on reasonably good terms, and of course we needed to talk about our daughter. I also came to see the others – you know Liz, Bob and Bridget. We had a lot of good memories of our time in the group.'

'Were all the old members of the Rowan group friendly with each other?' asked Andy.

'Yes. We always got on well, otherwise there wouldn't have been a group. Of course, we didn't always see eye to eye. That's inevitable when you're performing – people have different ideas. It wasn't just Annie and I who disagreed now and again.' He looked at Andy. 'Anyway, if we'd all had enough of each other, why come to the canal to live together in our later years, so to speak?'

'OK, so where were you early yesterday morning?'

'At home in bed. Alone. I'm not an early riser.'

'So no one can vouch for you?' asked Jav.

'I'm afraid not, but I certainly didn't come down here to murder my wife. She was stabbed in the neck, wasn't she?'

'Yes.'

Shipton grimaced. 'That's just horrible. Who would do that?'

'That's what we wanted to ask you. Were you aware that your wife had any enemies? Anybody who would want to harm her?' asked Jav.

Ben shrugged. 'I'm sure everyone's told you that Annie rubbed up a lot of people the wrong way, but I don't know of anyone who'd want to kill her. Can I go now? I really want to see Liz, Bob and Bridget. I know they'll be really upset too.'

'OK. I'll get an officer to take your statement when you're ready. Also, I know you'll want to go on to her boat to sort everything out, but that's not possible yet, as it is a crime scene and may yield some clues as to what happened.'

'And what about . . . ?'

'Your wife's body will be released to you when Forensics have finished their investigations. Again, the body may contain vital evidence.'

'I see.' He closed his eyes for a moment, as if it were all too much to take in. 'I've spoken to my daughter on the phone. She's devastated, of course. Her school is allowing her some time off, and she'll be here this afternoon. I'm going to wait for her to arrive. In the meantime, I'll call on the others and see how they are. To be honest, I'd prefer not to be here at all. I like this place even less now.'

'Did you get the impression that he wasn't telling us everything?' asked Andy after Shipton had left. 'The boss always tells me to watch carefully for a reaction when you ask a key question of a possible suspect. When you asked him if he knew of anyone who would want to do her harm, he seemed to hesitate slightly.'

'Yes, I noticed. Maybe there is some conflict or grudge between the members of that folk group that we've still not been told about. It could go back a long way.'

'He could be remembering the things that affected Anderson and Foster. But I really wonder . . . If this is to do with something that happened such a long time ago, why have they waited all this time to take action? They've been here on the canal for years and had plenty of opportunity for revenge.'

Jav shrugged. 'I don't know. But it suggests there's much that we don't yet know about this particular group of people, and whether they really might be capable of murder.'

~

Oldroyd and Steph walked across the bridge near the huge mill. Wide stone steps, up which the mill workers of the past would have tramped in their clogs, now led them to the shop and exhibitions. Huge doors opening on to massive rooms with metal ceiling supports were a reminder of the large and heavy machinery that had once operated throughout the building.

'Have you been to any of the exhibitions here?' asked Oldroyd. 'They've got some wonderful David Hockney paintings.'

'Yes, sir. I hope I'll get the chance to come with Andy when all this is over. I saw that collection of Hockney's paintings of springtime on the Yorkshire Wolds, although it was a few years ago now.'

'Yes, I remember it. So many old West Riding mills have been demolished or are lying empty – it's good to see one like this refurbished and given a new purpose.'

The conversation stopped as they entered the building by a more modern entrance. They presented their warrant cards to Julie Wilton, who contacted Nicholas Spenser.

'Through this door, up the stairs and it's the first door on the right. He's expecting you.'

As the detectives went off, Bert Marshall appeared in reception like the proverbial bad penny. 'Is that the police?' he whispered to Julie.

'Yes. I wonder if they've come to arrest Mr Spenser,' she whispered back.

'What? They can't do that, it wasn't—' He stopped abruptly.

Julie burst out laughing. 'I'm only joking.' She looked at him with her head on one side. 'What did you mean by that, anyway? "It wasn't . . ." *It wasn't* Mr Spenser you saw committing the murder?' she asked melodramatically.

'Oh, I know you don't believe me.' He nodded his head at her. 'But mark my words: the truth will come out in the course of time.' He turned away as Julie tried hard to suppress further laughter at this portentous little speech.

Upstairs, Nicholas Spenser welcomed Oldroyd and Steph into his office and invited them to sit down. He occupied a seat behind his stylish modern desk. Oldroyd noticed the lovely view over the waterways and the park. A colourful narrowboat full of pretty red potted geraniums was gliding slowly upstream. A collie dog sat at the front, its intelligent face scanning the water. Another boat passed on the way down and it looked like the man and woman at the tillers had a brief chat.

'I take it this concerns yesterday's awful murder?' asked Nicholas.

'Yes. We understand that you were not on good terms with the victim, Annie Shipton,' replied Oldroyd, coming straight to the point as usual.

Nicholas frowned. 'Well, I hardly knew the woman. The disagreement was all to do with our plans for the building here. We've got some exciting ideas for the expansion of the centre. They involve the construction of a new wing on to the old mill, which will provide a new exhibition space, a lecture theatre, café and a visitors' centre for the whole of the Saltaire Village World Heritage Site.'

'It sounds good.'

'Yes. And it's very imaginatively designed in steel and glass, which lets in lots of light. Unfortunately, some people take the view that the style clashes with that of the old stone of the mill and also that it will bring in more visitors to a place that is already overcrowded, as if it's a bad thing to generate more revenue for the area.' He spoke enthusiastically, with copious use of arm gestures.

He really believes in the scheme, thought Oldroyd.

'What part did Annie Shipton play in all of this?' he asked.

Nicholas sat down. When he continued, his bright tone had disappeared. 'She took on a leadership role in the opposition group and organised a petition. I met her once and she was quite abusive

– accused me of trying to ruin the area. She brought up all sorts of ridiculous objections: the building work would be noisy; the canal towpath wouldn't be able to cope with all the additional visitors; there would be more cars and more air pollution. I don't know how much she believed in even half of it. She struck me as someone who likes a fight, and once she gets an idea into her head, she won't relinquish it.'

'What's the situation now regarding these plans?'

An angry expression passed over Nicholas's face. 'We did have outline planning permission from Bradford Council, but Shipton's campaign persuaded them to call in the plans again to reconsider them. I wouldn't care if that group – Save Saltaire, they call themselves, as if we are going to start demolishing the village – had a lot of support, but they don't. It's just a few activists who I believe have spread lies about our proposals to get people to sign their petition.'

'And you seem very angry about it.'

'Yes, I am. We've put a lot of work into those plans and spent a lot of money on consultants and architects. It would be tragic if that was all wasted, and the town didn't get this development, which I – and most people – believe would be so beneficial. If only . . .' Nicholas seemed uncharacteristically at a loss for words.

'Do you mean if only Shipton and her crew would disappear?' asked Oldroyd.

'Something like that, I suppose,' replied Nicholas, then he seemed to realise the implications of what he had said. 'But of course I had nothing to do with her murder. That's absurd.'

'But the progress of your scheme will be more assured now that she's not around, would you agree?'

'Well, yes, maybe, but—'

'And where were you yesterday morning?'

Nicholas was flustered. He realised his wife had been right when she said the police would consider him a person of interest.

'I live in Baildon. I left home at the normal time, about twenty past eight and was here by a quarter to nine. The traffic's always bad.'

'Can anyone verify your movements?' asked Steph, who was making notes.

'My wife was still in bed when I left. But I popped in to give her a cup of tea and say goodbye. Then I came straight to work, and Julie on reception here saw me arrive.' Nicholas seemed a little sheepish. Was it guilt for lying? He got to his feet. 'You're not seriously suggesting that I would murder someone so that our scheme could get through?'

'Stay calm, sir, and sit down,' said Oldroyd firmly. 'We're investigating everyone who might have had a motive for killing Annie Shipton. We're not making any accusations. It's all just routine. How well do you know the canal?'

'You mean the one that goes between the mill buildings?'

'Yes.'

Nicholas shook his head. 'I see the boats passing by, but I don't know much about it all. I don't come from this area. I was brought up in Sheffield and I moved here when I got this job.'

'Have you ever been on a narrowboat? Do you know how they operate?'

'No, I don't. It's not really something that interests me.'

'Fine.' Oldroyd got up. 'Well, we'll leave it there for the time being.' He smiled at an uneasy-looking Nicholas. 'And I hope your plans for the centre come to fruition. They sound excellent to me.'

Nicholas smiled and showed them politely to the door. He was relieved to see them go. He didn't want the police sniffing around. You never knew what they would uncover. The fact was that if you believed fervently in what you were doing, it was sometimes necessary to take unusual steps. He went back to his desk and thought for a moment. Then he decided it was time to give someone a call before the police got too close.

When Andy and Jav presented the photograph they'd found on board Shipton's boat to Ros Collins at the Canal and River Trust office, she admitted that she'd not told them everything about her relationship with Annie Shipton.

She sat at her desk, looking at the photograph, and smiled. The image seemed to bring back some fond memories.

'Annie and I were in a relationship a few years ago. I'm gay, and she was bisexual. We met at a gay bar in Bradford.'

'Why didn't you tell us this before?'

Ros shook her head. 'I know I should have, but I thought it might give you a reason to suspect me if you knew I was Annie's ex-girlfriend. Also, in the past I have had homophobic remarks from police officers.'

'Maybe some police officers still think that way, and the force is continuing to address and improve things,' said Andy, who never failed to be surprised by how some outdated attitudes persisted in the world. 'I'm sorry you were treated like that. Many of us are trying to change the force's culture for the better and root out these dinosaurs.'

'It was a while ago and I'm glad things are changing,' said Ros.

'How did the relationship end? Did you remain on good terms with her?' asked Jav.

Ros smiled again. 'Annie was always changing and doing something different; she was never dull. That's one of the things I liked about her. After a while she moved on to someone else. I was upset, but I had no choice but to accept it. When I got this job, I was surprised to find her here, living with her husband on a narrowboat. I was always aware that she was married while we were together. It was just a shock to see them there together.'

'It must have been awkward having to ask her for mooring fees, and more so when she didn't pay.'

'Yes. Annie was difficult. She seemed to think that because we'd had a relationship, I would somehow let her off without paying. But I couldn't. She was always like that with money: lax and irresponsible. And she expected things that were just unreasonable.'

'When you sent that letter – which we've seen now – was she angry?'

'Yes.' She looked uncomfortable. 'I didn't tell you the truth about that either. She came over and was really affronted that I could send a letter like that to someone I'd been close to. I told her that I would lose my job if I didn't collect the money.' She paused and looked at the detectives again. 'We had a row and she used emotional blackmail – asked me if I would actually evict her from the marina. But it wasn't a violent confrontation, and I would never have killed her, certainly not because she didn't pay her mooring fees. I still had affection for her.'

'Tell us again about your movements yesterday morning.'

'OK. I live nearby. I walked here and arrived at half past eight. Then I heard that Annie had been murdered.' Stating this seemed to remind her of the awful truth of her former girlfriend's death. She lowered her head, apparently on the verge of tears. 'Despite everything, I really am going to miss her. But I didn't kill her.'

'What do you think?' asked Andy as he and Jav made their way back to The Navigation.

'Thwarted love and jealousy are powerful motives for murder, but I don't sense they were that strong in her case. But she knows the canal well, which might prove to be significant in relation to how the crime was committed. So I think we have to keep an open mind.'

❦

Ben Shipton met with Liz Aspinall as well as Bob Anderson and Bridget Foster on their boat, *Rowan*. The atmosphere was tense. The coffee they were drinking failed to relax anyone.

'I still can't believe she's gone,' said Bridget at last. 'There we were with her in the pub that evening and the next day she's dead.'

'In a way I'm glad that she spent the last evening in the pub with you all,' said Ben.

'Yes,' said Bob. 'It wasn't a bad evening. We were listening to a folk group, which led to some reminiscing about the old days.'

'And they found her on her boat, floating down the canal?' asked Ben, still incredulous.

'Yes. Slumped against the tiller apparently,' replied Bob. 'As luck would have it, she was found by a policewoman. The police-woman and her boyfriend – also a police officer, can you believe it? – were moored just outside the basin, and she was the one who saw the boat drift past. They must have been on holiday originally, but they seem to be taking part in the investigation along with two more detectives. One of them is that Chief Inspector Oldroyd from Harrogate. I've heard about him – famous for solving difficult cases. I think he'll get to the bottom of what happened.'

'The sooner the better,' said Bridget. 'I've had—'

'Oh! Look, she's here! Brittany!' cried Liz Aspinall who had been silently watching the basin through the window during this exchange. She instantly rose and ran up the steps and out of the boat.

Brittany – in her mid-twenties, her jet-black hair long and loose – was walking down towards the boats from the car park. She was wearing black skinny jeans and an oversized linen shirt, which seemed to dwarf her slight build. She caught sight of Liz running towards her.

'Oh! Auntie Liz!'

They hugged, and both women burst into tears.

'It's so nice to see you,' said Liz. 'And look at your hair! You've changed it again. You look great. I'm so sorry this has happened.'

They were joined by the others. 'Dad!' exclaimed Brittany when she saw Ben coming to greet her.

Ben said nothing, but hugged his daughter for a long time as he too shed a tear. Bob and Bridget waited at a distance before offering their condolences to Brittany. After this, they returned to the boat.

Brittany was desperate for information about what had happened. They told her what they knew, careful in how they phrased it, knowing that although Brittany was strong, she had to be upset over her mum's death.

'I can't believe she's gone,' said Brittany, echoing Bridget's earlier reflection. 'And I'll never see her again.' This shocking realisation caused her to burst into tears again. Liz put an arm round her shoulder. 'Who was it? Who would want to kill Mum?'

'The police are conducting a thorough investigation,' replied Bob. 'We'll just have to leave them to it.'

Brittany got up. 'I must go to the boat and sort out Mum's stuff. I—'

'Sit down, love,' said Bridget. 'You can't go on board *Moorhen* – the police have taped it off. It's a crime scene. Stay here, try to relax a bit, and have a drink. Tea? Or coffee?'

Brittany put her hands to her face and sank back into her chair. She accepted a cup of tea.

'You'll be able to go in when they've finished,' said Bob. 'In the meantime, Bridget and I are here to help you and your dad with everything.'

'Thanks, Bob,' said Ben. He looked weary. 'There's a lot to do. We've got to register the death and think about the funeral.'

'Oh God!' exclaimed Brittany. 'I hadn't even thought of that.'

'Never mind about it just now,' said Liz, who was sitting next to Brittany and holding her hand. 'Just take things steady, a day at a time.'

'I don't know what to do about the boat,' said Ben.

'Plenty of time to sort that out later,' said Bob. 'Once the police have finished, we'll keep an eye on her. You can take your time clearing her out.' He glanced at Brittany. 'I think when you're both ready, the best thing to do would be to report to the police. They'll want to speak to you, Brittany, and you'll save them a journey out to see you in Oldham. They always appreciate a cooperative attitude from people.'

'What will they want to talk to me about?'

'Your mum – do you know of anyone who would want to harm her, was she having any problems, things like that.'

'Right. I've no idea who could have done this. It's just awful.'

'Never mind, just answer their questions as fully as you can and don't conceal anything. They always find out everything in the end.'

'OK.' Brittany looked down, and seemed to be thinking about the last thing she had said to Bridget.

It was pleasant autumn weather as Oldroyd and Steph walked up the canal towpath in the direction taken by Annie Shipton the day before. In the distance they could see the hills above Skipton, the blue sky above broken by fleecy white clouds. Cattle were grazing in the peaceful fields either side of the canal. To the right there were woods, which led up to the cliffs above Shipley Glen.

'A canal is a wonderful thing, isn't it?' remarked Oldroyd. 'I remember when I did a trip along one years ago. You see the landscape in a completely different way and at times you escape from the roads completely. You're there alone on the quiet water, the overhanging trees and the birds paddling up and down.'

'That's quite poetic, sir,' replied Steph with a smile. 'Andy and I were just getting into it when all this happened, so we haven't experienced much of the peace yet.'

'No. But you must continue on your journey after the case. As I said earlier, you can take the time as leave. Walker was very impressed, by the way, that you broke your holiday to help with the investigation.'

'To be honest, sir, we wouldn't have missed it for anything.'

Oldroyd laughed. 'There's nothing quite like a mystery to solve, is there? It's like Sherlock Holmes' famous statement. *Come, Watson, the game's afoot.* It really gives you a buzz.'

As Steph and Oldroyd enjoyed their walk, Aleena's class, equipped with clipboards and dressed in hi-vis jackets, accessed the towpath above the basin via a footpath through the woods. The first thing they saw was Len Nicholson's boat. Smoke was again rising from the chimney.

'Aw, miss, look at that boat! It's really dirty,' said one of the kids. 'I wonder who lives in there!'

Some of the other kids were laughing and trying to peer through the windows.

'Come away,' demanded the teacher, feeling harassed, as most teachers did on field trips when so many things could go wrong. The potential for injury or for a child to go missing was high in this area, but she also knew the educational value of this trip was worth the risk. 'It's rude to look through someone's windows like that.'

Suddenly the door opened, and Len Nicholson climbed noisily on to the small deck by the tiller. 'Nah then,' he bellowed. 'What are you lot up to?'

At the sight of this huge and bearded intimidating figure, the children jumped back wide-eyed from the boat and ran off up the towpath, followed by the teacher, who hastily apologised to Len as she did so.

He smiled and said, 'Never mind, love. Ah like to see kids enjoying 'emselves but it looks as if ah've scared 'em off. Ah didn't mean to. Ah wa'n't cross. Ah wa' only joking.'

Oldroyd and Steph were almost at the lock, which was not far upstream, when they heard the sound of excited children's voices on the other side of the water. It was Aleena's class running away from Len's boat.

'Well, here are the kids Jav told us about,' said Oldroyd with a smile. 'It's not going to be quite as peaceful as it has been.' He watched the children with a fondness, remembering his son and daughter at that age, when they had been full of enthusiasm for everything.

The children were excited as they could see a narrowboat coming upstream from Saltaire behind Oldroyd and Steph, ready to pass through the lock. Some of them started to run the last stretch so they could get a closer view. The harassed-looking teacher shouted at them to stop and keep away from the edge.

The boat was just entering the empty lock by the bottom gates. Oldroyd's curiosity was alerted by the behaviour of some of the children, and he watched them as a crew member from the narrowboat closed the gates at the bottom and opened the sluice gates at the top.

The anxious teacher ushered the children away from the edge, though many were keen to look down into the scary, dark depths of the lock and watch as the water churned at the bottom of the gates and then rose, bringing the boat up as it did so. Some of the children were asking if they could have a go with the windlass. The teacher explained what was happening as the raised boat proceeded through the upper gates, reminding them of what they had seen on a video at school. It was clearly not as good as seeing the whole thing live, however! The children were entranced.

'So,' said the teacher. 'You can see how much higher the boat is now, and that is how a boat can go up or down using the locks. Any questions? William?'

'Has anyone ever fallen into this lock and drowned, miss?'

Oldroyd, overhearing this, thought, maybe not drowned but someone had probably died here not long ago. Maybe it was a good thing they didn't know about that.

'I don't know about this lock,' answered the teacher, 'but people have drowned in locks, which is why we have to be very careful not to go too near the edge.'

There were cries of 'Oooh!'

Another child had her hand up. 'Yes, Millie.'

'Miss, if you left all the gates open all the time would all the water drain away?'

'That's a very good question. Yes, the water would drain away. Which is why it is important for people to keep the gates shut when boats are not going through. Water for the canal comes from reservoirs, but they can become empty in dry weather. Then there wouldn't be enough water for a boat to sail on the canal. Last question?'

A smirking boy put his hand up. 'Can you go to the toilet on a boat, miss? And does it go into the water if you do?'

There was a chorus of 'Ugh!' and 'Yuk!' Some of the children looked into the water as if expecting to see turds bobbing around.

The teacher gave the boy an icy stare. 'Yes, you can go to the toilet on a boat, David, but everything goes into a holding tank. And then the tank is pumped out into the mains sewage system, maybe at a marina, when it's full.'

Cries of 'Ugh!' again, and 'Oh, I wouldn't like that job, miss!'

'No. Well, I think that's enough for now. It's time to complete your worksheets.'

After a while, the school party moved on to the path back to the village, leaving Oldroyd and Steph alone as the narrowboat chugged away upstream.

'Well, they seemed to enjoy that, sir,' said Steph.

'Yes, and so did I,' replied Oldroyd as he examined the lock again. 'I liked those kids and their questions.' Then he turned to Steph. 'I'm sure now that this is as far as Annie Shipton got on her boat. We need Jav to get his team to do a search around this lock. After watching those kids, I'm beginning to get an idea of how her murder might have been committed without leaving a trace at the scene of the crime.'

∾

'How are you all doing?' asked Gary Wilkinson, who was serving Bridget Foster in the shop. She put some milk and some teabags on the counter.

'It's a shock. I don't think we've taken it in yet. We all knew Annie for so long. Since we were students, you know. And then there was all that time we were in Rowan together.'

'Yes.' Gary took the money from her and rang up the till.

'Ben arrived today and then Brittany. She had to drive over from Oldham, and she's distraught, poor girl. It's one thing to lose a parent when you're still young, but quite another for that parent to be murdered.'

'I know. Bloody hell! It doesn't bear thinking about.' Gary shook his head. 'Is she going to stay here with one of you?'

'No. She's going to check in with the police and then go back to Haworth with her father.'

'Right. Do you think the police have any idea who did it?'

'I don't know. Annie being the person she was, I'm sure there's no shortage of suspects. But who wanted to *kill* her? I can't see it.'

'Well, offer my best wishes to everyone, especially Ben and Brittany. I don't expect they'll be coming in here – too much on their minds.'

'OK, I will.' Bridget collected her groceries and walked out of the shop, leaving Gary deep in thought.

It wasn't long before another person entered the store: Bert Marshall from the Mill Centre.

'What're you doing here, Bert?' said Gary, looking at his watch. 'Don't they give you enough work to do down at the centre?'

'Nearly dinner time, Gary. Just popping out for a bit of air. It's terrible in that boiler house; hot and stuffy.'

'I see.' Gary could not keep the sceptical tone from his voice.

'I'll have a packet o' those mint imperials. I've always liked them.'

Gary reached into the glass display cabinet to pick out the sweets.

'What do you think about it all, then?' asked Bert in the same *sotto* voice he'd used to Julie.

'I take it you mean the murder. I don't think much of it, like everybody else round here.'

Bert nodded. 'No. It's a bad do. But some of us know a thing or two, you know. We saw things.' He tapped his nose in a silly manner.

'I take it you mean *you* saw something.'

'Yes. It's another reason why I'm here. I'm hoping to bump into somebody.'

'Are you?' Gary couldn't take Bert seriously. 'Well, I hope they don't come in here. I don't want you pulling out your gun and making a citizen's arrest.'

Bert laughed. 'Oh no, I don't want to arrest them. I've got other ideas.'

'Have you? Well, I don't want to hear about them. Off you go, Bert.'

Bert laughed again as Gary waved him towards the door.

Outside, Bert looked around and smiled to himself. Yes, he would come back another time. And maybe people might start to respect him.

~

Sam Wallace sped on his bike down the towpath past the basin and then off on to a path that led into Roberts Park. It was Friday afternoon. The roofing job they were doing on a nearby building was finished, so the boss had given them permission to knock off early. He was good like that.

Sam, still dressed in his dirty work clothes, cycled through the park, across a road and then a field. He looked around a number of times, as if not wanting to be seen by anyone he knew. Ahead was a wooded slope. He got off his bike, hid it behind a tree and then took out his phone. Earlier he had made some arrangements for that afternoon, and was checking that everything was going according to plan.

If his mother could see him now she would be less than pleased. He'd kept the truth from her – that his cycling had another purpose other than wholesome recreation.

His call was answered quickly. 'Hi, everything OK?' he said. 'Right, see you soon, usual place.'

He looked around again to see if anyone was watching and then walked off into the quiet autumn woods.

~

'Thank you for coming over to Saltaire so promptly in the circumstances,' Jav said, as he and Brittany took a seat in their room at The Navigation.

Jav asked the questions and Andy wrote her responses in his notebook.

'Did you have a good relationship with your mother?'

'Yes. We had the usual kind of arguments when I was a teenager, but we got on well.'

'I assume you are aware that your parents had disagreements.'

'Yes, but not when I was living with them as a child. They fell out after I'd left home.'

'Would you say you were closer to your father than your mother?'

'I don't know. Maybe? My mother didn't always find it easy to show affection.'

'Did you take your father's side when your parents split up?'

'Not particularly.'

'And can I ask you where you were yesterday morning?'

Brittany bridled. 'Why on earth are you asking me that?'

'I'm sorry, it's just a routine question that we have to ask everybody who's connected to a murder victim.'

Brittany sighed. 'I was getting ready to go to work. My husband was there.'

'OK. Did you know of anyone who would want to harm your mother?'

'No.'

'Alright, we'll leave it there. I'd like to say again that I'm sorry for your loss.'

'Can I go now? I want to go back to my aunts and uncle. They're not really my relatives but I grew up with them. They were all in Rowan together, you know.'

'Yes, we understand. Can you tell your father that we need to speak to him again?'

'OK.'

~

Ben Shipton returned to face more questions.

Andy began. 'There are some more things that we need to ask you in the light of what we've discovered this morning. I'm sorry to have to raise this question but Ros Collins at the Canal Trust has confirmed that your wife was bisexual, and that she and Annie had an affair.'

Shipton looked sheepish. 'It's true. She did have an affair with Ros.'

Andy spoke to Ben. 'I have to bring this up, I'm afraid. We were wondering if this affair was the reason you had the big arguments that people heard, and why you finally left.'

Ben looked down. 'Yes. It was a factor. I could accept that she was bisexual, but an affair is an affair, isn't it? Whatever the sex of the people involved. We rowed about it, and she wouldn't promise me not to have any kind of affair again. She said she needed to express that side of her identity. I found that very difficult.'

'Had you always known that she was bisexual?'

'Not when we first met and when we were married. She told me a few years later and I resented that. I felt like she had deceived me, but I was OK with it until she started having affairs.' He glanced at his daughter. 'It wasn't just Ros Collins. She had several relationships. They were all brief flings, but they hurt.'

'Was this hurt deep enough for you to wish her harm? Get revenge?' continued Andy.

'No. I would never have harmed her.'

'OK,' said Jav. 'Thank you for your help, that's all we need for now. Feel free to go.'

Ben nodded and left the room.

At that moment, Oldroyd and Steph arrived back at the basin. They saw a man embracing a young woman.

'That must be Ben Shipton and Brittany,' said Oldroyd. 'I recognise them from the photograph in *Moorhen*.' They went into The Navigation where Jav confirmed that they had just questioned the father and daughter. Inside, Oldroyd sat down and his brow furrowed as if he'd witnessed something that didn't sit right for the second time that day.

Tea was brewed and the team began to compare notes on the interviews they'd conducted.

'Nicholas Spenser has a motive all right,' began Oldroyd. 'He's passionate about his plans for the expansion of the Mill Centre and he must have hated Shipton for leading opposition to those plans. I think he's staked a lot of his reputation and his future career on the scheme going ahead. We need to check his alibi with his wife.'

Oldroyd drummed his fingers on the table, which was full of mugs of tea that gently rippled as he did so. 'The problem is that the murderer must have some knowledge of the canal and narrowboats. Spenser said he knew nothing about it, and I'm inclined to believe him. He just doesn't strike me as the type to plan to kill someone on a canal boat . . . or anywhere else for that matter.'

'He could be lying, sir, or there may be more than one person involved,' suggested Jav.

'Yes,' replied Oldroyd. 'You could be right, but as you'll remember, I'm not a fan of theories involving more than one murderer unless there's clear evidence. It makes things more complicated.' He took a drink of tea and looked around. There were no biscuits in sight; Steph was on guard. 'How did you get on with Collins?'

'She confessed immediately that she'd had a relationship with Shipton, who apparently was bisexual, and that she'd kept it from us for the usual reasons – frightened that we might suspect her, distrust of the police in the gay community, stuff like that,' said Andy.

Jav continued. 'There's clearly the rejected lover motive there. She seemed very calm about it all, but she may have concealed her real feelings about her ex-girlfriend. She may have felt very angry at being rejected.'

'She's very familiar with boats and the canal, so she would be able to plan the attack.'

'OK,' said Oldroyd.

Andy took over. 'You got back here, sir, just when we'd finished talking to the Shiptons.' He looked at his notes. 'Brittany Jenkins, as she is now. She and her husband, Harry, live in Oldham. She's in a bit of a state about her mother's death, obviously. We went through the usual questions, and she said she didn't know of anyone who would want to kill her mother. She has a good alibi for yesterday and the only motive I can think of is that maybe she did actually know about her mother's behaviour, and held it against her somehow. She may have wanted to get revenge on behalf of her father.'

Oldroyd was leaning back in his chair with his hands behind his head and his eyes closed, as he often did when the team were conducting a review of the investigation.

'Good work,' said Oldroyd. 'I think it's more likely that Annie Shipton's affairs provided the husband with a motive rather than the daughter. Anyway, we need to leave them in the mix. At this stage I never completely eliminate anyone who had a relationship with the victim. Otherwise you tend to start focusing too intensively on your main suspects and don't leave your mind open to other possibilities. Even worse, you start to believe a certain person

121

is the guilty party without enough evidence and the history of the darker side of policing shows us where that leads.'

'Fitting people up and miscarriages of justice,' said Jav.

'Exactly. And there were some horrendous examples of that in the seventies.' Oldroyd took a deep breath. 'So, who else have we got?'

Andy looked through his notebook again. 'There are the people who had money issues with her: Collins on the mooring fees, the copyright dispute with Foster and Anderson, and Gary Wilkinson at the shop to whom she was in debt. Their motives don't strike me as very strong, especially Wilkinson, but as you say, sir, it's very early to eliminate anyone.'

'Yes, it's not always the strength of the motive that's crucial. People can get into arguments, and that can result in unintended violence.'

'A stronger motive for Anderson, it seems to me, is the death of his brother in that crash. He might well have never forgiven Shipton for that.'

'I agree,' said Oldroyd. 'Even though it was a long time ago.'

'There's Sam Wallace, sir,' said Steph. 'He was definitely near the crime scene yesterday morning. I can imagine him having another altercation with Shipton and then attacking her. He probably didn't expect to see her there; it was just chance, and his temper got the better of him. There's been some previous allegations about him flying off the handle.'

'Then, finally,' continued Andy, 'Laura Ward, and maybe her partner, who hated Shipton and had a row with her the night before, witnessed by many people, including me and Steph.'

Oldroyd dropped his arms to his sides. 'Blimey, what a list! On most of these investigations it seems we're either struggling to find any suspects at all, or we're inundated with them. But even this list of suspects feels a bit long for my comfort!'

Jav grinned. 'I prefer it this way, sir. At least we've got plenty of avenues to work. I hate it when there's nothing to go on, and you have to wait for something to turn up.'

Oldroyd frowned. 'Yes. The problem is that by now I usually have a front runner among the suspects, even if I change my mind later. But this time . . . I've still no idea.'

'Maybe we'll discover more suspects, sir,' suggested Steph.

'I'm not sure I could cope with any more,' said Oldroyd, shaking his head. 'The better news is that I've had the beginnings of an idea about how the murder was done, but I'm not sharing it yet. It may come to nothing.'

The other detectives said nothing. They were familiar with this quirk of their boss: sometimes he wouldn't share the details of an idea or theory until he was reasonably sure that it was correct. They knew that he did this partially to train and test them – could they work something out given that they had the same information as he did?

Oldroyd continued, 'Also, I wanted to ask if any of you noticed anything significant about Brittany Jenkins.'

'What kind of thing, sir?' asked Jav.

Oldroyd shook his head. 'I don't know. When I saw her, she reminded me of something or somebody, but I'm not sure what.'

No one else had noticed anything.

'Never mind. I might be just imagining it. I'm desperate for a lead.' He got up. 'Jav, if you can get your team to make sure the statements are collected and checked through to see if we've missed anything. I'm going to call it a day here. I need to go home, get some peace and quiet, and think.'

Steph often came back at her boss with the same teasing joke when he said something like this. 'Right, sir. Sherlock Holmes again, is it? Well, remember what I always say: you can play your violin long into the night, but no drugs.'

'It'll be neither, I'm afraid,' replied Oldroyd with a laugh. 'I wish I could play the violin, and I've never fancied any drugs other than alcohol.'

~

It was a warm but overcast evening when Laura Ward arrived home from work. They usually went out to eat or had a takeaway on Fridays, so there was no food to prepare. After recent events, she felt uncomfortable being in the boat by herself. She was still edgy after the murder of Annie Shipton, and, despite Darren's reassurances, still thought the police regarded her as a prime suspect due to the row she'd had with Shipton the night before. If only she'd not lost it and stormed over to The Navigation. Her temper had got her in trouble before.

She decided to go for a walk up the towpath and call on Len Nicholson. She liked Len, who was an ordinary person like herself, and not one of those hippy types who got on her nerves.

As she walked along, she could hear the sound of the heavy late Friday afternoon traffic passing along the road at the top of the village, but it was quiet by the canal. She reached the dilapidated narrowboat, stepped aboard, and knocked on the door. Smoke was billowing from the chimney as usual.

She heard Len's voice shouting, 'Who is it?'

'It's Laura. How're you doing?'

'Aye, wait a minute.' Laura heard Len's clumping footsteps. The door opened, and his grubby, bearded face smiled at her. 'Ah wa' just abaht to knock off for t' day. Come in.'

Laura followed him back into the boat, which smelled of paint. There were a number of signs drying on easels, which Len had obviously spent the day painting. They sat on the dusty sofa, and he opened a couple of bottles of beer. He passed her a glass that was almost as dusty as the sofa itself.

'I'll be fine with the bottle, Len.'

On one of the walls was a very old black and white photo of a smoky industrial scene. Barges were being loaded with coal.

'Are you in that picture, Len?'

Len looked over his shoulder at the photo. 'Nah, yer cheeky bugger. That's a very old photo. That's me grandad wi' that shovel.'

'Yeah? It must have been a hard life.' Laura looked at the man holding the shovel. He was wearing dark trousers, heavy boots, a baggy shirt with a waistcoat and a cap. He had a droopy Victorian moustache and, like most men in pictures from that era, he wasn't smiling.

'Aye it wa', but his cousin 'ad it tougher.'

'How's that?'

'He wa' a legger.'

'A what?'

'He worked in t' tunnels lyin' on a plank on top of the boat, his feet on t' wall, walkin' t' boat through. There's no towpath through t' tunnels.'

'Bloody hell!'

'Aye, now that wa' hard. Anyroad, how're yer getting on dahn there wi' t' police around all t' time?' asked Len.

Laura took a swig of beer. 'OK. They've got a job to do, I suppose, but I'll be glad when they've gone. Have they been up to see you?'

'Aye, yesterday afternoon. Wanted to know if ah'd seen owt, but ah haven't, though ah might've heard her boat going past. It wa' very early.'

Laura shuddered. 'I don't like thinking about it. I didn't like that woman and I had a row with her the night before. Do you know what she said about us?' She told him about the blog.

'The snooty bugger,' said Len, as he drank his beer. 'They think they bloody own t' canal, that type, and they don't know owt abaht it. Wi' all their pretty boats that've never seen any work. They don't know what canal life used to be like: hard, dirty and cold, just like that on t' photo.' He laughed. 'But ah'm not complaining. They keep me i' work makin' their nameplates and paintin' nice pictures on t' boats. They lahk me to do it cos they think it's more real if it's me. And they'll pay me good money.'

'I know.' Laura took another swig. 'Anyway, Len . . . I'm worried that the police might think I murdered Annie because I had that row with her.'

'Huh! Never in all this world! Thi'd never kill someone just cos thi didn't like 'em. Even though she wa' an awkward so 'n' so.'

Laura smiled. 'Thanks. I'm glad you've got faith in me, Len. But who do you think might have done it?'

'Me? Ah've no idea.' He paused. 'Ah've known one or two other people get done in on t' canal over t' years. It's usually one o' two things. Either there's a row and a fight and sumdy ends up fallin' in to t' watter, or there's some feud been goin' on a long time and sumdy plans to do their enemy in. In this case, it could be either.' He finished his beer and leaned over towards Laura. 'Thi don't get away wi' it,' he said, shaking his head knowingly. 'T' canal and t' boats always give up their dead. Those folk are allus caught. It's a peaceful place, t' canal, and it won't put up wi' owt that upsets it. Thi always 'as to respect that.'

They chatted on for a while. When Laura finished her beer, she thanked Len for his hospitality and for listening to her before she left. She felt reassured by his faith in her. It was nice to feel that other people didn't suspect her. But the other stuff he'd said about the canal giving up dead people sounded a bit spooky.

Outside, the sky had darkened. It was cooler and it looked like rain. She turned up the collar on her jacket and walked quickly down the towpath.

～

Sam Wallace arrived back home later than he intended. He got off his bike, put on the lock and checked a few things before going inside.

'Where've you been? Tea's been ready for ages – I thought you were going out tonight.'

Sam hated it when his mother monitored his movements and wanted him in for set mealtimes. It made him really wish he could get a place of his own, but he couldn't afford the rent.

'Been out cycling up through the woods – we knocked off early at work. Just went a bit further than I thought.'

She looked at him suspiciously. 'You haven't been seeing that lot again, have you? Ryan Nelson? Barry Hainsworth?'

'Stop treating me like a teenager! What if I have? It doesn't mean I'm goin' to do owt stupid, does it?'

'So you have seen them recently?'

'You can't choose me friends for me! I'm twenty-two!'

She came towards him, and he shrank back. 'No, I can't choose your friends,' she said in a menacing voice. 'But you seem to forget all the bother you got into, and I don't want to go through that again. They'll send you down next time – you know that, don't you? If there's any more fights or smashing things up . . . Then you'll be out of work. And I can't support you for ever.'

He couldn't face her. 'I'm not goin' to do owt like that. I'm not a daft teenager any more. I'm not in any gangs or owt like that.'

She wasn't reassured but decided not to press it any further. 'OK. Sit down, then.'

Without a word, Sam sat at the table and his mother filled his plate with a meat pie, chips and peas.

~

When Jav arrived home, feeling weary after a long day, Aleena ran out to meet him before he'd even left the car.

'Dad!' she cried as he opened the car door. 'We had a great time by the canal, but where were you? We never saw you! My friends were disappointed. I said you'd be there.' Aleena got a lot of status from having a father who was a detective. She often regaled them with tales of his exploits, most of it made up.

'Don't you remember? I said you wouldn't be allowed where we were doing our work. Only the police can go there.'

'Is that because evidence could be continated?'

Jav laughed. '*Contaminated*, yes, that's right. I think I saw your class in the distance, but I couldn't pick you out.'

'We watched a boat go through the lock. It was scary when the water was down and you could see the wet walls. Miss Hopkins had to get cross with Peter Spicer for going too close to the edge. I think she thought he was going to fall in. I wish he had.'

'Aleena!'

'Him and his friends are such a pain. I hate boys. They spoil things for everybody else. Like, some of them ran over a little bridge without asking and she shouted at them to come back. Because of that she made everyone stay on one side, and me and Philippa wanted to go over and look down into the water from that bridge. It's not fair!'

'Oh dear,' replied her father. 'What if we go back sometime, and you can go over the bridge with me?'

'Hurrah!' Aleena jumped up and down. Then she remembered something. 'Oh, on the canal, there were two people watching us at

128

the lock: a nice-looking blonde lady and an old man. I think they were detectives. Do they work with you?'

Jav recognised the description of Steph and Oldroyd and had to laugh. 'Well, I think you're right. They are detectives. That man is Detective Chief Inspector Oldroyd and he's quite famous, although he's not that old. Remember he was on telly a while ago, and I told you who he was? I used to work with him.'

Aleena put her hand to her mouth. 'Oh! I thought I'd seen him before! Wait till I tell Philippa tomorrow!' She ran back into the house crying, 'Fatima! We saw a famous man at the lock!'

Jav smiled and shook his head. Wasn't it great to be young and full of energy and enthusiasm!

~

The sky was dark over the canal basin and the rain that Laura Ward had seen approaching had started to fall heavily on the narrow-boats. Inside their boat, Andy and Steph listened to the drumming of the rain on the roof as they drank some wine. They'd lit their wood stove for the first time, and the warm glow made them feel safe from the weather outside.

'Are you still enjoying life on the canal now that it's not so sunny?' teased Andy.

Steph looked out of the window. Raindrops were splashing into the water and the mallards and coots had sought shelter among the reeds and under the trees which swayed in the wind.

'Yes, I am. It's nice to see the canal in all its moods.'

Andy looked out across the marina towards the brightly lit windows of The Navigation. 'It looks very inviting over there in the pub. Do you fancy going later? There might be music on again. It's Friday night.'

'Maybe, but we've got to eat first. Can't have you drinking on an empty stomach. I was wondering if you fancied a pizza? We could get a delivery.' She began to search on her phone.

'Will they deliver to a boat?'

'Why not? You've seen how many people live on the canal. The takeaway places must be used to it. I've got one here.' She was scrolling through the menu. 'What do you fancy?'

'Just the usual – ham and mushrooms.'

Steph placed the order using an app. 'Thirty minutes, it says. It is Friday night. Imagine getting pizza delivered to a narrowboat!'

They settled down to wait.

'It's really cosy in here, isn't it?' Steph said, and grinned at Andy.

'Yes, I am really enjoying it,' he said. 'It's very different from any holiday I've ever had . . . and we've only just started. Or rather, it will be once we wrap this case up!'

'Do you think we might get fed up of going through locks before we get back?'

'Naw, we'll get used to it. And we're not rushing, are we? We'll be able to show people what to do on the way back.'

'Anyway, how do you think we're getting on with this case?' asked Andy.

Steph rolled her head. 'Well, it's early days. I think the boss has a few ideas about how it was done, but you know what he's like. He doesn't like sharing things until he's fairly sure. As far as who did it, I think he's in the dark as much as the rest of us. Basically, there are a lot of suspects, but the motives don't seem strong enough for any of them. It's always a sign that he's a bit stumped when he says he has to go home and think.'

'Yes, I suppose that's what he's doing now.'

〜

Oldroyd was in fact having a quiet meal with Deborah. Once they were finished, they watched some TV together, and just relaxed.

Later when Deborah went to bed, he went back into the sitting room, put on his headphones and played a Beethoven String Quartet. He'd been a lover of classical music, and particularly chamber music, since his father, an amateur cellist, had taken him to concerts in Leeds, Halifax and Huddersfield. He selected Opus 132, a titanic and profound late composition by the then completely deaf composer. Beethoven's late quartets always put him in the mood to think, especially when he had a difficult case to consider.

When the music finished, he felt more focused and sat in the dark listening to the rain outside while he gave his mind to the case and its details. Some things had rung bells, but he couldn't, as yet, make sense of them; the puzzle wouldn't fit together. He couldn't help thinking that some parts were still missing and that there could be more traumatic events and revelations to come.

Four

The Rochdale Canal was officially opened in 1804 and runs for 32 miles from Castlefield Basin in Manchester to Sowerby Bridge in Yorkshire where it joins the Calder and Hebble Navigation at Tuel Lane Lock, the deepest in Britain with a fall of six metres. The canal's route was surveyed by the famous engineer James Brindley. The canal rises to 183 metres as it crosses the Pennines. There is no tunnel under the highest part and the canal has a total of 91 locks.

Early Saturday morning found Liz Aspinall in running gear and trainers, jogging up and down the towpath next to the canal. There were a number of puddles to stride over after the previous night's heavy rain. It was overcast and a little misty, although the sun was trying to break through.

She liked to run several times a week in the morning. It was part of the structure she had adopted in her life after her husband had died and she was left alone. She enjoyed the buzz that running gave her; it helped her to fight the negative feelings. Unfortunately, recent traumatic events had disrupted everything, but this morning she finally felt like resuming her routine. The towpath was generally quiet during the week but today was Saturday and there were more dogwalkers and early-start ramblers around.

She reached the lock where Oldroyd and Steph had watched Aleena and her class the day before. It was empty, and its stone edges were damp and slippery. She kept well back from the sides and ran on a little further before turning round.

She smiled as she remembered seeing Brittany the day before. This had improved her mood a lot, even in such tragic circumstances. She had always been very fond of the girl, and had watched her grow up with interest. Brittany had been the only young person among their group after Megan died. Unfortunately, now that she was in Oldham, Liz saw very little of her and she missed her a lot. Brittany gave her a link with the younger generation that she'd always valued. She didn't want to end up like many old people who spent all their time with those of their own age and went on about how awful the modern world was and how things were better in the past.

She put on a little sprint as she arrived back at the basin. As she stood, panting and recovering before making her way back to *Meg*, she saw two people in conversation on the other side of the basin near the marina. They were some distance away, but she thought one of them was Bert Marshall, the caretaker at the Mill Centre, who often stopped for a chat with anyone who was up early on his way to and from work.

Back on board *Meg*, she had a shower and then sat eating some muesli for breakfast, wondering how she was going to spend the day. It was always a difficult moment. She found it difficult living alone and often felt on the brink of depression. The disruption to her small circle of friends wasn't going to make it easier.

∽

It had been decided that Andy, Steph and Oldroyd would take a break on Saturday and Sunday, leaving the detective constables who worked for Jav out of the Bradford station to follow up on alibis and check statements in the case of the murder of Annie Shipton. They were all glad of the break and it would enable Oldroyd to keep his promise to Deborah about working in the garden and making the spare room ready for Louise's visit.

Jav took his daughters for swimming lessons in Bradford, while Andy and Steph took the opportunity to come off duty and temporarily resume their holiday.

It was now a bright morning after the rains of the previous night. Steph had planned a walk from Saltaire through Shipley Glen up on to Ilkley Moor, so after breakfast they put on their shorts and walking boots, picked up their rucksacks and set off. The walk was described in a small guidebook that Steph had brought with them. They followed the route through the park and across the road that Sam Wallace had cycled along the previous afternoon, and eventually found themselves facing the same wooded slope. At the bottom was a white building with a green corrugated iron roof.

'Ah,' said Steph, consulting her book. 'That must be the Shipley Glen Tramway. Have you ever heard of that?'

'A tram right out here? It sounds like some quirky thing the boss would know about.'

'Yes. It says here that it's a "cable-operated funicular railway" – whatever that is – and it was built in 1895 to give access to a funfair at the top. It was later taken over by the council, and now it's run by volunteers.'

'A funfair! I'll bet old anti-public houses Titus what's-his-name wouldn't have liked that. I'm sure he was a good bloke in many ways, but he sounds a bit of a Victorian killjoy.'

'This was well after his time. But it's interesting to think of the mill workers escaping from the sedate park and the library and going up the hill for a bit of lively entertainment at the top. Come on, I think it's open. Let's have a ride.'

There was, in fact, a big sign that confirmed her hopes: 'Open Today'. They walked past it, and into the little station.

The bearded and rather oily-faced man who sold them the tickets looked at them curiously. 'Aren't you two of the detectives on this case down near t' marina?'

'Yes,' replied Andy. 'We're off duty today . . . but if you know anything that's relevant to the case, maybe you should tell us.'

The man laughed. 'No, it's not that. It's just I saw you down there with that Chief Inspector Oldroyd. He's famous round here, isn't he? Everybody's been sneaking down for a look. I know it's a bit ghoulish, but we don't get stuff like this happening much in these parts.'

'That's a good thing, isn't it?' remarked Steph.

'I suppose so. The worst we get is drug dealing. When it does happen, it usually goes on in these woods.' He pointed over the wooded hillside. 'A few of us have seen groups meeting and they leave stuff behind . . . you know, stubs of joints, bits of tin foil.'

'I presume that's been investigated by the local police,' said Andy.

'It's definitely been reported, but I've not heard that anyone's been arrested. Anyway, there's a queue forming . . . Better get on.' He handed them a couple of old-fashioned card tickets, slightly smudged with oil. 'It should be a smooth journey up to the top today. I've been here for a while this morning, greasing and oiling.' He grinned. 'We volunteers do all the various jobs.'

Andy and Steph took their seats at the front of the narrow wooden carriage, which started to fill up behind them. A bell sounded, the tram set off with a jerk, and steadily made its way up the steep trackway. Halfway up, the other carriage passed them on its way down.

'Do you think this drug thing could have anything to do with our case?' asked Steph as they rattled a little unevenly through the woods.

Andy shrugged. 'You never know, I suppose. But there's no evidence that Annie Shipton was a dealer is there?'

'No. But you know how many violent crimes are linked to drugs these days. It's very rural here, but we are surprisingly near to the tough urban areas of Bradford . . . not that rural areas are immune from such things.'

'Right.' The tramway reached the top. 'That wasn't far!' exclaimed Andy. 'You mean to say that people in Victorian times couldn't walk that stretch up to the funfair?'

'Ladies in their long skirts were not expected to exert themselves very much.' Steph consulted her guidebook again. 'Now, if we walk straight up here, we'll reach some cliffs, and more woods. And then eventually we'll get up to Dick Hudson's.'

'Whose?'

Staph laughed. 'It's a famous pub which was run in the nineteenth century by a landlord called Dick Hudson. A well-known walking route over Ilkley Moor to Ilkley starts there.'

'Listen to you. You sound like the local guide . . . or the boss giving one of his little talks about something in Yorkshire.'

'Well, I'm standing in for him as he's not here. Come on, it's a distance up to the pub from here and the reward is a pint and a sandwich at the bar.'

The prospect of this put a spring into Andy's step.

Saturday morning was the time when Bob Anderson cleaned *Rowan* while Bridget went into Shipley to do the big weekly shop. The interior of the boat was very compact, which made cleaning relatively easy once you learned where all the nooks and crannies were.

Bob put an old CD into their sound system. It was one of two recordings that Rowan had made twenty years before. As he dusted and wiped the surfaces and mopped the narrow floors, he listened to the songs and looked at the stuff they had on the walls – posters advertising their gigs and photographs of them performing. He heard their voices and their instruments, and nostalgia flooded over him for the time they'd all been young together. It had been such a fun life on the road, and they'd taken it for granted.

When you were young it seemed that the happy times you were having and the carefree attitudes you had would last forever. Now Rowan was over, and Roger and Annie were dead, one of them murdered. Liz and Roger had lost their daughter. Naïvely, you thought that tragic things would never happen or, if they did, that they wouldn't be followed by other incidents. Looking back, maybe the death of his brother had foreshadowed the awful things that had happened later. It was ironic that a lot of their songs had been quite downbeat in the folklore tradition, and now tragedy seemed to be happening to them.

Bob shook his head as he cleaned the sink and the kitchen area. What happened to that youth, its innocence and hopefulness? It seemed to pass so quickly, especially once life's difficulties kicked in: money, arguments, relationship difficulties, finding somewhere to live when you finally had to settle down.

One of his favourite Rowan songs, 'Under the Autumn Trees', came on. It was a melancholy song and he found he had tears in his eyes. It was unlike him to cry, but the shock of Annie's death in such terrible circumstances was overwhelming.

He sat down and took a little time to recover as he listened to the rest of it. A young-sounding Liz was doing the vocals and he could hear himself on the drums. He remembered the day of the recording well. It had been so exciting to go down to the studio in London. But the song was a sad one, like many folk songs, about a girl whose young lover dies. It made him reflect on the fact that he was in the autumn of his life.

Bridget came back with the shopping to find him sitting with the duster in his hand and a gloomy expression on his face.

'What's the matter?' she asked as she put down the bags. The music was still playing.

Bob stretched his arms, shook his head and sat back in his seat. 'Nothing really, just listening to this, and getting lost in all sorts of melancholy thoughts about getting old. I can't believe that two people who performed these songs with us are now dead.'

Bridget sat down and reflected as she listened. 'No. It is sad, but there's nothing we can do about it, is there? Old age comes to us all in the end, and there's only one way of avoiding it: what happened to Roger and Annie.'

Bob smiled. 'I know. I'm being silly, but I think what happened with Annie is only just properly registering with me.'

'That's not surprising. It was a big shock and people do have delayed reactions to things like that and it causes some to have odd thoughts.' She looked at him. 'When the news came that Annie had been murdered and you were still at the shops, I started to get panicky thoughts that maybe you could have done it.'

'Really!'

'Yes, because of what happened with Simon, and all that trouble about the copyright. But now I've calmed down I'm not worried at all. I trust you. I know you would never do anything like that.'

'I certainly wouldn't.'

'That's why I was so nervous when the police were here. I didn't want to tell them about your row with Annie, but they knew about it anyway from Liz. I was going to say something to her about it, but there's no point. The police would have found out anyway.'

'What are your thoughts now? About who might have done it, I mean?'

Bridget shook her head. 'I don't know. I think that cyclist would be capable of doing something violent and I still worry about Ben.

Annie could drive anyone to distraction, and I wonder if he lost it with her. It would be terrible for Brittany if that's what happened.'

'Oh God, that would be even worse – one of our group murdering another member.' He put his head in his hands. 'But, yes, it was so good to see Brittany yesterday. I realised that she's the only bit of continuity our group has going into the future.'

Bridget looked at him. 'Does it make you wish we'd had kids?'

'No, I still don't think it was for us. I suppose I'm just finding it hard to accept that everything comes to an end, that's all.'

Bridget leaned over and gave him a big hug. 'Never mind. We've still got each other and we're a lot better off than many people. I'll put the kettle on, and we'll have a cup of tea. I bought some scones at that lovely bakery. That'll cheer you up.'

Bob laughed. 'It will,' he said.

Janice Wallace was suspicious of her son's behaviour recently. He had been out late the previous night and had come home in a strange state. It was mid-morning, and he was still in bed, which was unlike him, even on a Saturday when he wasn't working. Something was going on and she didn't like the feel of it.

She decided to investigate, and quietly ascended the narrow and steep flight of stairs. She would have been happier if he'd smuggled a girlfriend into his room. Not that he really needed to do that as she was broad-minded about such things. But this secretive stuff worried her, especially after what had happened to him before with the police.

She entered Sam's dark room stealthily. It had the usual young man's smell of sweat and unwashed clothes, but he kept it reasonably neat. She peered over him in his bed; there was no movement, just the sound of a gentle snore. She crept round the bed and picked up his clothes, which had been abandoned on the floor. She felt carefully in the pockets of his jeans and took out keys, money and a small plastic bag.

The bag contained some white powder. She frowned. It was what she had suspected: drugs.

She knew very little about drugs but knew that bags of white powder were rarely innocent.

'Sam! Sam!' she said loudly and shook him.

'What? Aw, Mum, get out! I'm trying to sleep.' He turned over and pulled the duvet around himself.

She grabbed it and yanked it off him.

'Mum! What the hell are you doing?!'

'Waking you up. It's not far off dinner time. But no wonder you have to sleep if you've been taking this stuff.'

He sat up and looked at her with bleary eyes. 'What? Have you been going through my bloody things?'

'Yes, and I don't want this in my house, thank you very much.' She held up the bag of powder.

He made a grab for it. 'That's mine. Give it me.'

She held it behind her back. 'Not until you tell me what it is and what you're up to messing about with this stuff.'

'Why should I? It's nowt to do with you.'

'Oh, isn't it? So if the police suspect something and they search here and find this, who's going to be in trouble then?'

Sam hung his head.

She raised her voice. 'What is it?!'

'It's just coke,' he mumbled.

'"Just coke." That's all right then. Just an illegal class A drug that you've brought into my house.'

He looked at her. 'How do you know about coke?'

She laughed scornfully. 'You think because I'm over forty I don't know anything. People were taking this before you were born.'

He peered at her more closely with eyelids still droopy from drug-induced sleep. 'Did you ever do drugs, then?'

She swatted him over the head. 'No, you cheeky bugger. If you want to know, we used to smoke weed. But that's as far as it went.'

Sam now regarded her with some admiration and curiosity. 'Who's we?' he asked.

'Never you mind. It's a long time ago. You need to get rid of all this and don't you dare bring it in here again. And where did you get it anyway?'

He shook his head.

'Sam, you either tell me or I'll tell the police.'

'You wouldn't.'

'Why not? Now I know this is going on, I have a duty to report it, otherwise I could be seen as condoning it.'

He looked away from her, embarrassed. 'It's just this bloke. We meet him in the woods near the tramway.'

'Who's we?' she asked, mimicking him.

'It's just Terry and Liam.'

'I might have known,' she scoffed. 'So, you meet this dealer in the woods and buy cocaine with your hard-earned money, you fool? And then do you sell some of it on? Are you a dealer too?'

He looked outraged. 'No, I'm not. We just buy it for ourselves. That's it.'

She frowned. 'Well, I don't want to know how much you spend on it. It would upset me too much. I think you're completely stupid. It's addictive, you know.'

'I know. We don't take much.'

'Huh. That's what they all say.' She shook her head at him. 'Anyway, as long as you don't bring it in here, I can forget it's happening. I can't control you at your age, but if you get hooked on it, or the police find out, you'll most likely lose your job, and then what are you going to do? Be a layabout like that Danny Worthington?'

'He's all right, is Dan. He's a laugh. But stop worrying about me. I know what I'm doing.'

She snorted with contempt and was about to leave the room when she thought of something. 'That woman who was killed didn't know about this drug dealing, did she?'

'Why would she know? Aw, you're not still thinking I had owt to do with that?'

'Well, I don't know if I can trust you after this. Maybe she stumbled on your den in the woods, or whatever it is, and saw you. Then she could have blackmailed you, so you all decided to get rid of her.'

Sam looked shocked. 'Bloody hell, Mum, who do you think we are? Gangsters?'

'There are plenty of those around not far from here in the cities. Drugs are their speciality.'

'You don't believe I would do that, do you?'

She looked at him with suspicion. 'No, I don't. You're not a complete idiot. But I don't know what the police might think if they find out about it. Anyway, get dressed, you big stupid oaf, I need you to come to the supermarket with me. It's a big shop this week and I'm not carrying it all myself.'

She left the room and Sam cursed his carelessness. Although, once again, he hadn't told her the full truth.

⁓

Nicholas Spenser had decided to come into work, even though he normally took the weekend off to be with his family, mainly because a detailed model of the Mill Centre extension and an exhibition explaining the plans was opening to the public. He wanted to be there and say a few words of introduction and promotion. He had also invited someone along with whom he hoped to have a conversation. He had been unable to contact this person on the phone.

Spenser arrived in good time, and said hello to Julie on reception before heading off to the large meeting room on the first floor. In the centre on a big table was the model of the planned works. It showed clearly the existing sandstone mill and the new glass and steel building attached at the end, extending the building alongside the canal. Around the room, information panels explained the different parts of the project. Nicholas couldn't help smiling. It conveyed vividly how light and airy this new space would be, ideal for art exhibitions. In addition to a modern gallery space, there were smaller rooms, workshops and a new café and restaurant. Who could see this and fail to be impressed?

By ten thirty, people were starting to gather outside the room. The galleries were open and, as it was Saturday, visitor numbers were high. At ten forty-five, Nicholas invited them in, including Alistair Crompton, who was a local councillor for Saltaire. A portly man with a fat face and small, piggy eyes, he always dressed in a shabby suit.

Once everyone was settled, Nicholas said a few words about the proposals: how they would make a great project of which he was sure Titus Salt would have approved, how it would enhance the Mill Centre and make it a nationally known gallery and centre for art, and how Saltaire and the whole of the Bradford area would benefit from increased tourism.

This short speech, delivered with his usual enthusiasm, was greeted with a smattering of applause and then people were left to examine the model and read the information boards. Nicholas was glad there appeared to be no one present from Annie Shipton's group opposed to the plans. They were probably still too shocked by her death to plan any action today.

After a few words with members of the public, he and Councillor Crompton left the room and sat down in the nearby café. Nicholas had already spoken to Crompton about a delicate matter, and he hoped to resolve it today. But as soon as he saw Crompton's face take on a sour expression, he knew things were going to be difficult.

A waiter brought them two coffees, and they set to discussing business.

'Let's keep this brief, shall we?' said Crompton, looking around to make sure no one was listening as he took a sip of his coffee. 'I shouldn't be spending too much time with you. It could be compromising, especially if there are any of Shipton's group here.'

'I don't think there are,' replied Nicholas, also looking round and then dropping his voice. 'Anyway, you're here as a representative of the council, attending the launch of our exhibition, on the invitation of the Mill Centre. Look, all I'm asking is that you don't say anything to the police about our little arrangement. If they find out, it will draw their attention to me. They'll start to wonder whether Shipton knew about it and whether I got rid of her before she could say anything.'

'Did you get rid of her?' asked Crompton abruptly.

'What?' Nicholas's mouth dropped open.

'Well, she was a thorn in your side, wasn't she?'

'Yes . . . but of course I didn't. What do you think I am? I know I've offered to give you money to try to get this voted through the council, but I'm not a murderer. I just don't want the police to get suspicious. And it will be very bad for the scheme if it's found out that I've tried to bribe someone.'

'Why would I tell them anything? I'd be confessing to doing something illegal.'

'No, I didn't think you would. But I wanted to make sure you were going to stay quiet now that there's a murder inquiry. You know, just keep your nerve. It will all blow over when they've found out who murdered her. I haven't given you any money yet so nothing can be traced. We'll sort it all out when everything's settled.'

Crompton nodded but he was frowning. 'I just don't like the police sniffing around. It's very bad for my image, especially if the press get hold of it.'

'Why would they? They're more interested in the murders at the moment. The police can't say or do anything unless they've got evidence, which they haven't.'

Crompton nodded but he still looked unconvinced. They finished their coffee without saying a great deal more and then left. They had not noticed that a person on the table behind them was smiling. It was a member of Annie Shipton's group. He had been tipped off that this meeting was going to happen, and had managed to get close enough to overhear everything without being noticed. He had even taken a photograph of the pair with his phone. This was gold for the group. They had long wondered if Nicholas Spenser was involved in something nefarious concerning the council, and now they knew for certain.

Instead of simply strolling across The Stray, Oldroyd and Deborah had to drive to the Harrogate parkrun now that they had moved out of the town. Much to Oldroyd's annoyance, this meant getting up earlier on Saturday morning. However, he made the effort because he knew that running had made a big improvement to his fitness.

After the run they usually had breakfast somewhere in Harrogate, but today they came straight back home, showered, and did a couple of hours' work in the garden. Oldroyd found it a bit of a strain after completing the parkrun, but Deborah seemed to have endless energy as she dug, pruned and weeded the untidy borders.

Oldroyd was finally having a rest when Deborah suggested that they go to a cat rescue centre on the outskirts of Harrogate. She was on a roll today, getting things done she'd been planning for a while.

'At least we have a cat flap already,' said Oldroyd as Deborah drove through the suburbs north of the town.

'Yes, but we don't need it yet. The cat won't be allowed out for a while, especially if we get a small kitten. We've got all we need: cat box, litter tray, basket, food. You don't mind clearing out the litter tray, do you?' She laughed.

'I suppose not,' replied Oldroyd, who was now actually quite looking forward to getting a cat. His ex-wife, Julia, hadn't liked the idea of having animals in the house and he couldn't look after one by himself in the flat overlooking The Stray.

They drove from New Bridge across to Harrogate and soon found the street, where there were neglected-looking houses and unkempt, litter-strewn gardens.

'I think that's it,' said Deborah as she pulled up outside a small, detached bungalow.

'Good Lord,' exclaimed Oldroyd. He had imagined a smart, clean, organised place. Here, the rundown building had a wooden sign fitted to a wall saying, 'Harrogate Cat Rescue'. The ragged lawns and shrubs were completely enclosed with high fencing and cats could be seen sitting on the ledges of every visible window.

'Oh dear,' said Deborah. 'It's not exactly what I expected, but let's not be judgemental. Apparently they do a wonderful job saving cats that have been abandoned or treated cruelly.'

'It looks to me like someone else then has to come and rescue them from the Cat Rescue.'

'Jim! That's unfair. Let's go in and see what they have.'

'I'll bet the smell will be *formidable,* as the French say,' replied Oldroyd.

He was right about the smell of cat litter and urine, which hit them as soon as they entered the house. They were met by a long-haired woman dressed in shabby jeans. She was carrying two cats and was being followed by two more. They were all meowing in different ways. Above the din, Deborah explained that they were looking to adopt a kitten.

'The ones under a month old are in here,' said the woman. She led the way into what would once have been a sitting room. There was a large metal cage containing about a dozen tiny kittens. Some were trying to climb up the wire mesh, others were huddled together to make a large furball.

'Most of these were abandoned – some in a dustbin.'

'Oh, that's shocking!' exclaimed Deborah.

'Yes, we care for them as well as we can but it's not as good as a nice home.'

Deborah and Oldroyd looked at the kittens and decided on a cute black and white one, which seemed to be straining to get to them. The woman got it out and the little creature immediately climbed on to Oldroyd's shoulder.

'That's his sister, there,' said the woman cunningly. 'Their mother couldn't feed them.'

The sister was all black, fluffy and just as cute. 'She's adorable!' said Deborah, who picked up and stroked the black kitten. Oldroyd mouthed the word 'two' to his partner and shrugged. Deborah, however, was already completely smitten. 'We couldn't possibly separate them, could we, Jim?'

Oldroyd sighed. 'I don't suppose so,' he said with feigned reluctance. He liked to tease her but in fact he already felt bonded to the two kittens. Soon, after arrangements had been made for the cats to have some inoculations at the local vets', they were on their way back to New Bridge with Oldroyd driving and Deborah nursing the cat box and making reassuring noises to the two tiny, furry creatures inside.

∼

Gary Wilkinson and Ros Collins were enjoying the busy day around the marina. Gary's shop was full, while Ros was doing well in recruiting people to become members of the Canal and River Trust.

They met outside as they both took a break in a lull over lunchtime. From the number of people sitting and standing by The Navigation, it seemed as though Phil Cunliffe was also doing a good trade today.

Gary smoked a cigarette as he looked across the marina. Shipton's boat and the area around it were still cordoned off. There was a line of people by the tape staring at the deserted and rather ghostly-looking *Moorhen*.

'Amazing, isn't it?' said Gary. 'The ghoulish side of people comes out at a time like this. They can't resist gawping at where a murder took place. They'll be snapping shots with their phones as well, no doubt.'

Ros was sitting on a concrete bollard. 'Yes, well, at least it brings people in. I've recruited ten people this morning and sold a pile of guidebooks.'

'Good for you, and long may it continue. Actually, it'll all die down again when the investigation's over.'

'Up to a point, although the extra publicity might give us a boost for longer. Have you any idea where the police are with it?'

'Not really. They were up at the lock yesterday apparently. I presume they think that's where she was murdered. And they were keen to talk to Ben Shipton and his daughter when they turned up. Maybe they think it's a family affair.'

Ros shook her head. 'The idea of the daughter, Brittany, coming over in the very early morning to kill her mother on a narrowboat seems completely bizarre to me.'

Gary laughed sardonically. 'I agree. My money's on that young cyclist who has a temper or one of the people who were in that group with her. There could have been a long-standing grudge.'

'Clearly the police need to recruit you.' She got up. 'I'm off back, I've just seen some people go in. See you later.'

'OK.' Gary stubbed out his cigarette and walked back to his shop too.

It was Saturday evening, and Oldroyd and Deborah were relaxing at their New Bridge house with Oldroyd's sister Alison. The original plan had been to meet in Leeds, but neither Oldroyd nor Deborah could leave the kittens on their first night at the new house.

Alison was a few years older than him. A now retired vicar, she had finally decided to leave the parish of Kirby Underside out in the countryside between Leeds and Harrogate. Oldroyd had expected that she might retire to a quiet neighbourhood in Harrogate or Knaresborough, but true to her feisty, strong and unpredictable character, she had bought a flat in a modern development in the centre of Leeds near the Corn Exchange. She attended and helped at an inner-city church, which ran a hostel for homeless people. She said that she'd enjoyed her 'sabbatical' in Kirby Underside but needed to leave comfortable, middle-class rural life and return to the realities of life for many people in urban Britain. Social action to help others who were poor and struggling had always been at the centre of her faith.

Oldroyd found it difficult to share her religious faith, but regarded Alison as his mentor: wise, tolerant, progressive and deeply spiritual.

'How are you finding living in the centre of Leeds?' asked Deborah. 'It's very nice in our village, but it can all get a bit twee at times. I can see the attraction of being in the city.'

'Leeds is great now,' said Oldroyd. 'Forty years ago, there were four or five pubs in the centre where men went to get drunk and then start fights in the street. There weren't many restaurants or cafés either. Basically, there was nothing to do except the cinema and the theatres. How's the flat?'

'Oh, I love it. I wake up in the morning and there's such a buzz outside. It's so interesting being at the centre of things. And St Oswald's is doing such good work – I really feel privileged to be part of it,' replied Alison. 'And before you say anything, Jim, I don't work there every day. I spend a lot of time lounging in cafés reading, going to galleries and walking in Roundhay Park. I have retired.'

'Well, I'm pleased to hear that,' replied Oldroyd. 'But I'll believe it when I see it.'

Alison laughed. 'And how's it going with your house? It's interesting, isn't it, how you have gone further into the countryside, while I've gone into the city?'

'Yes,' said Deborah. 'We just felt we wanted to live in a peaceful village. It'll take a while to get everything in the house as we want it, but we'll get there. And it's so nice to have a garden again.'

'And you, Jim? Are you missing your flat overlooking The Stray?'

He put down his beer glass. 'Not particularly. I never thought of that place as permanent. It was just somewhere I found after Julia and I had split up.' His eyes twinkled mischievously. 'Anyway, Deborah hasn't told you about the terrible infestation.'

Alison looked alarmed. 'Of what?'

'She thinks she heard a mouse behind the skirting board. She'd have jumped on to a chair if she hadn't been in bed. But I still reckon it was just an excuse to get a cat.'

Deborah laughed. 'I'm sure there are mice in there. And our cats will deter them when they've grown a bit.'

'Oh, so you've persuaded him to get more than one?' said Alison.

'Yes, we went to the rescue centre and came away with two – a brother and sister, Jack and Luna, we've called them,' said Oldroyd. He went out and came back holding the two kittens.

'Oh, they're lovely!' exclaimed Alison as she stroked them. 'But watch out when they're big enough to go outside. The last cat I had used to bring mice into the kitchen – dead, alive, and sometimes just bloody bits and pieces.'

'I hope not,' said Deborah. 'You'll have to clear it up, Jim. I wouldn't touch anything like that. Anyway, that's better than a trap. I couldn't stand the idea of that metal bar coming down and smashing their spine.'

Oldroyd was quiet for a moment then suddenly and forcefully declared, 'Yes! Of course! I'll bet that was how. It's obvious!'

Alison and Deborah would have been surprised if they hadn't been used to Oldroyd retreating into reveries about his work in the middle of a conversation. This usually happened when he heard or saw something that gave him an insight into whatever case he was currently working on.

'Oh no!' said Deborah. 'Not again. I think we should be getting some credit for solving his cases. We always seem to be giving him ideas. I take it that's what's going on, Jim?'

'Yes, sorry,' said Oldroyd, coming back into the moment. He was still holding the kittens absent-mindedly. 'You did give me an idea then, but it was something I should have thought about a while ago.' He turned to Alison. 'I'm on a murder case at Saltaire. I was going to mention it to you, in fact. Do I remember you going

151

to folk music gigs and talking about a group called Rowan?' Alison had always enjoyed folk music, especially if it had a northern feel to it.

'Oh, yes. Rowan. They were really good. They sang some lovely ballads about northern life. They never reached national importance, but around here they were very popular – Annie Shipton, Bob Anderson, Bridget Foster.'

'It was Annie Shipton who was murdered.'

'Really!' exclaimed Alison. 'That's terrible.'

'I know. The former members of the band are living on narrowboats at the basin in Saltaire. Including Liz Aspinall, if you remember her too?'

'Liz Aspinall, of course! I think I read that her husband died.'

'Yes, that's right, and their daughter unfortunately. Both of cancer.'

Alison shook her head. 'Awful. It's so sad when people like that who were so talented and made lovely music come to such a tragic end.'

'Yes,' said Oldroyd. 'Anyway, another drink, anyone?'

'Before that, Jim,' said Deborah with a smile. 'Please take those poor kittens back to their basket. They've been crawling over you for long enough.'

～

There was a chill in the air as Bert Marshall walked quietly down the towpath towards Saltaire on Sunday night. The canal was not lit, but he was very familiar with this route and was not afraid of falling into the water. Traffic droned on the distant main road through Saltaire, but the canal and the adjacent fields were silent and still, with the black shapes of cows and sheep watching him as he passed.

He was very pleased with himself, smiling as he walked. He was sure that the person he was about to meet would be amenable to paying for his silence. And not just once, either. This could become a nice little earner.

In the distance he could see the basin and the marina where there were a few lights and the dark masses of boats moored on the towpath. What he didn't see was the figure that crept up behind him and delivered a blow to the back of his head. He fell to the ground.

The assailant looked around before pushing the body with their foot. It rolled into the water with a gentle splash. Bert Marshall drifted out into the centre of the canal and was then pulled gently downstream by the current. There was another splash as the murder weapon was thrown in after the body.

Monday morning dawned cool with a mist over the canal and the fields nearby. It was a reminder that autumn was progressing. A little below Saltaire and the basin, an early dog walker was on the canal towpath. The dog was a little ahead of him when it started to growl.

'Freddy? What's wrong? What have you seen there?'

The walker caught up with the dog, which seemed to be worrying an old coat that had been floating in the water. Then with a gasp, he saw that there was a body in the canal. It had been caught in a patch of reeds at the side. It was face down, the hair matted with blood around a large wound to the head.

The man called emergency services, who arrived promptly and removed the body of Bert Marshall from the Leeds and Liverpool Canal.

'This could up the ante a bit, couldn't it, sir?' said Andy.

The four detectives were at the scene where Bert Marshall's body had been found. The towpath was cordoned off with blue and white incident tape. The wet and weed-bedraggled body now lay on a stretcher, and was being examined by Miriam Coates.

'It could,' replied Oldroyd laconically. He frowned as he looked at the body. The truth was he had not expected another murder, and was unsure whether or not this was linked to the death of Annie Shipton. 'Do we know who he is?' he asked.

'We've retrieved his wallet. His name is Robert Marshall. That's all we know at the moment,' said Jav.

'Dead for several hours. Cause of death most probably this severe head wound,' said Dr Coates. 'He was hit with something pretty heavy. The skull is crushed. It's possible he could have been alive but not conscious when he went into the water so he could have drowned. I won't know until I get him back to the lab.'

'OK,' said Oldroyd. 'It's up to your team to follow this up, Jav. The killings may be pure coincidence. This bloke might have been drunk and got into a fight. Then his assailant dumped him in the canal, hoping the body would travel downstream away from the area. The problem is that the current in canals is slow moving and anything floating tends to drift to the side and get caught up in weeds, which is exactly what happened here.'

'But you're not a great believer in coincidences, are you, sir?' said Steph.

'Not in a context like this. Two murders within three days is very suspicious. We'll see what Jav finds out. In the meantime, I think we're a bit in the doldrums waiting for a breakthrough. And the media will be on to this latest killing in no time.'

Andy and Steph knew that despite their boss's skill in solving almost impossible cases, he often became anxious when he hit a difficult patch. There was always so much pressure on him, the great detective, to come up with the answer quickly.

'Don't worry, sir, we'll crack it.'

Oldroyd smiled. 'Your faith is very touching, but there's always the first time.'

At the Mill Centre, Julie Wilton was wondering why she hadn't seen Bert Marshall on this Monday morning. He was usually around early in the day. She saw another member of the caretaking staff, who said Bert hadn't turned up and they'd had to wait until another keyholder arrived. This was very unlike him but she got on with her work and forgot about it until a shocked-looking colleague called Yvonne arrived at reception.

'Have you heard?' she asked in a faltering voice.

'No, what?'

'Bert Marshall's been found dead in the canal. It's awful, isn't it?'

Julie's face drained of colour. 'What happened?'

'I don't know, but Anne, who works in the bookshop, said she spoke to someone who knew the person who found the body and he said there was a lot of blood. So it looks like Bert was murdered too. He wouldn't kill himself, would he? Isn't it awful after that other murder? What's going on round here? I don't feel safe any more.'

Yvonne was beginning to sound hysterical, and Julie didn't quite know what to make of her second- and third-hand accounts of what had taken place. How much of it was true? But she knew that if Bert had been murdered, she needed to talk to the police. When Yvonne left, Julie immediately reached for the phone.

At the basin, the news was filtering through the local community that there had been another body found in the canal. Len Nicholson was talking to Gary Wilkinson about it as he was buying some cigarettes and a few provisions at the shop.

'Ah think this 'ere part o' t' canal's cursed,' he pronounced, nodding his head sagely.

Gary humoured him. 'Oh, and why is that, Len?'

'Well, yer see, sometimes there's a stretch o' watter where bad things keep 'appenin' and nob'dy can explain it. Ah've seen it before. There wa' a place on th' Aire and Calder, near a lock it wa' – people drowned, had accidents, boats sank. It wa' terrible. Folk started avoiding t' place if they could.'

Gary looked at the old narrowboater with wry amusement. 'Don't you ever take coincidence into account?'

Len shook his impressive head and beard. 'Too many things 'appen together sometimes. Mark my words.' He pointed at Gary. 'T' canal never forgets. If summat bad goes on, t' spirits are angry and other bad things can 'appen.'

'What spirits?' asked Gary, trying not to laugh.

'Ah told thi – t' spirits o' t' watter and t' spirits of all t' folk that've lived on t' watter like me and me family. Sometimes when a boat goes past, ah could swear ah 'ear me dad's voice and ah've seen me mam more than once walking down t' towpath.'

'Right, well, if you think the whole place seems to be haunted, I'd pack it in if I were you, and go and live in a house.'

'Get away wi' thi, ah could never live away from t' canal now. It's in me soul. Ah couldn't live agean in a house that couldn't move. T' spirits look after me cos ah'm one o' their own. Ah've lived most o' me life on t' watter.'

'I see. I'm very pleased for you.'

Len paid and put all his purchases in a threadbare shopping bag that he pulled out of his pocket. 'See yer, then.' He ambled out of the shop and Gary burst out laughing. He was still laughing when the door opened and Darren Ward slouched in, looking very pasty-faced.

'Something's tickled you,' he said to Gary.

'Oh . . . yes,' muttered Gary as he tried to stop laughing. 'I've just had Len Nicholson in here.'

'Is that the old bloke who lives on that crappy old boat?'

'Yes. You've heard that they've found another body?'

'No! Where?'

'Just down past the mill, in the canal amongst some reeds.'

Darren grimaced. 'Bloody hell.'

'Yes. Well, in comes Len talking about the spirits of the water and that the canal is cursed.' He changed his voice to imitate Nicholson. 'T' canal never forgets, tha knows.' He collapsed in laughter again and Darren grinned. 'I wish you could've heard him.' He shook his head and looked at Darren. 'Anyway, what are you doing here? Not going to work today?'

'No, I'm lousy – I've got flu or summat. I've only just got out o' bed and I'm off back. Have you got any paracetamol or anything?'

Gary pointed to a small range of cosmetics and health products. 'We've got some paracetamol, but you can only buy two packets. That's the law. If you want more, you'll have to go to a pharmacy.'

'OK, I'll take one. It'll keep me going until Laura gets back.'

Gary fetched the pills for him. As Darren was paying, he asked, 'Another body, you say?' He shook his head. 'Who was it?'

'I've not heard anything yet, but whoever it was, I think it's going to make everybody round here feel nervous.'

'Is it to do with the other murder, then?'

'Who knows? We'll just have to wait and see.'

～

157

'It's awful. He could be a nuisance, the way he hung around talking to you, but he was a character, you know. He always had some interesting gossip.'

A tearful Julie Wilton was talking to Oldroyd and Steph in an office behind reception at the Mill Centre. She had phoned the police, who had confirmed that they had found Bert Marshall in the canal.

'How much did you know about him?' asked Oldroyd.

Julie dried her eyes on a tissue. 'Not much, really. He never mentioned a partner or family. I think he was probably very lonely. He was a bit odd, and his social skills were poor. I suppose deep down I felt sorry for him.' She looked at the two detectives. 'The reason I wanted to speak to you was that . . . well, he'd told me things.'

'What kind of things?' asked Oldroyd, instantly on the alert.

Julie frowned and nervously twisted the tissue in her hand. 'He wouldn't give any details. He wanted it to stay sort of dramatic and a secret. He said he'd seen things and had a good idea of what had happened – with Annie's death.' She said this carefully, making a big effort to remember his words accurately. 'I'm not a detective, but Bert lived above Saltaire and he walked down the canal towpath every morning from the direction of the lock to get to work – always early because he had to open the place up. I think he saw something that day. Maybe he even knew who—' She stopped. 'I know I should have told you this before, but I didn't take Bert seriously, so I didn't think it was important. I'm sorry.'

'Never mind,' said Oldroyd. 'Go on.'

'He said that he was going to sort it all out soon. Do you think he went to the person he saw and tried to blackmail them?'

Oldroyd exchanged glances with Steph and smiled. 'Well, if you ever get tired of your job here, we'll employ you at West Riding Police. I think you're most likely right.'

'And then they killed him?' Her eyes filled with tears again.

'I'm afraid that's probably what happened. Thank you, you've been—'

Oldroyd was interrupted as the door was abruptly flung open.

Nicholas Spenser stood in the doorway looking very angry. 'Julie? What on earth's going on? Who gave you permission to call the police?'

'Oh, I'm sorry, Mr Spenser. I didn't think you'd mind. There was something very important about Bert Marshall that I had to tell the police.'

'"I didn't think"? You certainly didn't think! And I do mind! Now we've got a police car outside and the place is swarming with detectives! What do you think this does for our image?!'

Julie started to cry again.

Oldroyd stepped in and fixed Nicholas with the hawkish expression and penetrating grey eyes he used when questioning recalcitrant criminals. 'Mr Spenser, I think that's an unnecessary exaggeration.' His voice was like a razor. 'There are precisely two of us here. Your employee has performed her duty in speaking to us and has given us vital information which will be very valuable in our investigation – an extremely serious investigation, I might add. Beside which considerations about the image of this centre – which is not going to be compromised in any event – pale into insignificance.' He nodded towards Julie. 'I advise you to cherish an intelligent and brave employee such as Julie in case you lose her to an organisation that will value her more highly. She is a credit to you.' He stopped speaking but was still staring at Nicholas as if to dare him to argue.

Nicholas wilted. 'Oh, I see. Well, yes, er, well done, Julie. I didn't realise . . .' His voice tailed off.

'That's more like it,' said Oldroyd. 'Ms Wilton has had a shock in losing a friend and colleague in the victim Bert Marshall and she is very upset. I suggest that you send her home early today in order to rest. She is a very important witness, and we may need to speak to her again in the forthcoming days.'

Nicholas was open-mouthed. 'Well, er . . . yes, if you say so, Chief Inspector. I'm sure we can organise something.'

'Excellent. We'll leave it there for today, then. Thank you once again,' he said to Julie, and winked at her when Nicholas couldn't see his face.

Outside Steph burst into laughter. 'Oh, sir, that was vintage stuff. You reduced him to a quivering wreck.'

'I punctured his damned pomposity, alright,' replied Oldroyd, still quite angry. 'I don't like that man – he's a bully and I'm very suspicious about the fact he doesn't like the police around because it damages the image of this place. Is there more to it than that?'

'OK, sir, you may be on to something. But you'll need to calm down and assess it later.'

'You're right,' said Oldroyd and smiled. He'd worked with Steph for many years, and she knew that occasionally he allowed his feelings about a suspect to get a little out of control, and that he welcomed a word from her in those situations.

'It certainly looks like the latest victim saw something and was killed because of it.'

'Yes, the question is, what? I'm convinced more than ever that Annie's murder must have happened at that lock. And I think I know how it was done.'

～

Bridget Foster walked across to *Rowan* to speak to Liz Aspinall, who hadn't appeared so far that morning. She knocked at the door and called her name.

'Come in, Bridget. The door's open.'

Bridget went down the steps and into the main room. Liz was lying on the sofa. 'Are you OK, Liz?'

'No, I'm a bit off it. I think I've got a cold. No energy.'

'There must be something going round. Gary at the shop said that Darren Ward came in for some paracetamol, and he looked terrible. He hadn't gone to work.'

'Oh, dear.'

'Can I make you a cup of tea or anything?'

Liz sat up, looking very peaky. 'That would be nice, thanks. I was just about to go outside for some fresh air.'

Bridget put the kettle on and made a pot of tea. As she brought it over to Liz, she said, 'You won't have heard the news.'

'What?' said Liz, accepting her mug.

'We think there's been another murder.'

'No!'

'A body's been found in the canal just downstream. Apparently, there was a bad head wound, so it seems as if someone bashed him and then dumped his body in the water.'

Liz turned away in disgust. 'That's awful. Who was it?'

'The police haven't confirmed anything, but rumour has it that it was one of the caretakers at the Mill Centre. If it's who I think it is, you'll have seen him around. Wears an old-fashioned donkey jacket. He walks down past here every day on his way to and from the centre.'

'I think I know who you mean. I've seen him when I'm out running.'

'You didn't see anything strange this morning? Oh, I don't suppose you went running?'

'No, I really didn't feel like it.' Liz lay down on the sofa again and put her hands to her head. 'What's going on? First Annie and now this.'

'I know. It's creepy and it makes you feel unsafe, doesn't it? Is there some crazed serial killer around? Make sure you lock up properly at night, Liz. I don't like to think of you by yourself here in this boat. If you ever feel scared, come over to ours. We've got a spare room.'

Liz gave her a weak smile. 'Thanks, but I'm sure I'll be OK in here. I shan't be opening the door to strangers or wandering around in the dark.'

'OK, but please come over to us for tea tonight. Bob's making a vegetarian lasagne.'

'Oh, the famous veg lasagne! Does he still put carrots in it?'

'He does. He likes controversy.'

Liz smiled and some of the tension left her face. 'I know, I've had it before. Thanks, it'll be good to come over. I certainly don't feel like cooking today.'

'Great. I'll leave you to rest, then.'

'Thanks. Are Brittany and Ben coming over today?'

'I'm not sure. I don't know whether the police want to talk to them again.'

'OK.'

Bridget left the narrowboat as Liz closed her eyes again and fell into a light sleep.

~

'Two murders now, Chief Inspector. Things are hotting up, aren't they? Are the crimes linked? Is a serial killer at large in Saltaire?'

Oldroyd and Steph had arrived back at the basin from the Mill Centre, only to be met by a group of reporters who swarmed around them, notepads and microphones at the ready again. Oldroyd wasn't surprised. He knew the media people had amazing sources and were on to stories with incredible swiftness. He was ready for them. He positioned himself with his back to the boats and cleared his throat.

'Whoever provides you with your information is jumping the gun a little. We don't know for certain that the person recovered from the canal today was murdered. It's true that he had received a head wound, but that could have been caused by a fall. Neither do we know where he entered the water, as his body could have been carried a distance downstream.'

In fact, he was satisfied that Marshall had been murdered, but he liked to toy with the reporters.

'Is that right, Chief Inspector? We were told he'd definitely been done in.'

'Who told you? This person sounds as if they know a lot about it. Maybe I should be talking to them?'

This produced laughter, which Oldroyd savoured. He was just too clever for them.

'Now, as far as the facts go,' he continued, 'the victim has been identified as Robert Marshall, known locally as Bert. He lived in this area and worked as a caretaker at the Mill Centre.' He pointed in the direction of the gallery. His eyes twinkled. 'And I've been teasing you. It's most likely he was murdered. His death could be connected to the fact he knew something about the murder of Annie Shipton.'

This produced a reaction.

'Oh, you mean he was silenced, Chief Inspector! Was it blackmail?!'

Oldroyd smiled; he'd thrown them some red meat and they would feast on it.

'We don't have any details yet . . . and I said it *could be*. We are interested in talking to anyone who might know something. Did they know Bert, and did he say anything to them? We are also keen to talk to anyone who may have seen anything happening in this area last night: people walking, a conversation between two people, a stranger. It could seem quite trivial but may turn out to be important. I'm sure you will report my request in your usual helpful way. But sadly, from your point of view, I don't think we're talking about the Saltaire Serial Killer, though I concede that would make a good headline.' Oldroyd drew more laughter at this. Then after the usual warning that people should take care and stay on the alert, he announced that he had to go and refused to answer any more questions.

~

Inside The Navigation, the detectives held another case meeting while they drank coffee.

'There's a very good chance the latest victim was killed because he saw something, and perhaps decided to try a bit of blackmail,' said Oldroyd as he explained what Julie Wilton had said to him and Steph. 'I'm not sure it tells us very much about who the killer is, except that it must have been someone Marshall recognised, and that means he witnessed Shipton's murder. As it seems he was a bit of a busybody, that still includes a lot of people in this area.'

'We heard something yesterday that might be relevant, sir,' said Steph and she told Oldroyd and Jav what the tramway operator had said about drug dealing in the woods. 'I suppose there's just a chance that Shipton could have had something to do with it, sir – you know those old hippies and their drug-taking.' She gave Oldroyd a mischievous smile.

'I hope you're not including me in that group,' said Oldroyd with a sniff. 'It seems unlikely that she would, but it's something to bear in mind.'

'If she did get involved,' said Jav, 'the drug business in Bradford is big, and it can get violent between rival gangs.'

'Yes, though I don't know whether I can see a drug gang planning an unusual murder like Shipton's.'

'No,' conceded Jav. 'I'll get some officers to have a look around in those woods and see what they can find.'

'Good. Now,' announced Oldroyd with a gesture, 'I've got a firm idea about how the murder of Annie Shipton was done and I'm going to demonstrate it soon.' His audience was unsurprised. They knew about their boss's taste for the dramatic. 'Have there been any developments with any of the other suspects?'

'No, sir,' replied Jav. 'I've checked through all the statements, and there are no inconsistencies and nothing new has come to light. Dr Coates confirmed all the details about Annie Shipton's body, including time of death, and the cause being that unusual neck wound. She's now working on the body of Robert Marshall. We've confirmed that Annie Shipton did have a booking with Benson's boatyard at Skipton on Thursday at ten a.m., so she was heading there when she was murdered. Forensics have been working up at that lock where you think the murder took place, but haven't found any significant evidence.'

'Good. Well, if you'll just excuse me for a few minutes,' said Oldroyd and he left the room, leaving the others to decide what needed to be done in relation to Marshall's murder. When he returned, he had a smile on his face and was carrying a bag. 'OK, follow me.' He turned to Andy and Steph. 'We're going to go upstream on your narrowboat.'

~

'This is very intriguing, sir,' said Jav as they rode on the narrowboat up to the lock where Aleena's class had been on their school trip.

Oldroyd wouldn't say anything.

When they arrived, luckily there were no other vessels around. They moored the boat at the side of the canal just below the lock and they all got off and walked up to the bottom gates, which were open.

Oldroyd stood near the huge balance beams. 'OK,' he began. 'I'm pretty sure that this is where the murder took place. If Annie Shipton had gone through this lock and up towards Skipton and was killed further on, how could the boat have got back through this lock with only a dead person on board? There's no evidence that anyone boarded who could have steered the boat and got it through the lock. And Shipton's body was by the tiller with blood all around it. And, if the murder had been committed downstream before she got to the lock, that would have involved her being killed by someone on the bank. We've speculated about people throwing knives from the bank, but not only would it have been very difficult to hit her, the lack of weapon and angle of the wound suggests that she was stabbed from above and not the side. I did think about a passing boat. But, Steph,' he said, turning to her, 'you didn't see one pass when you were watching the canal that morning. Also, the angle of the wound is still wrong even if someone managed to hit a moving target from another boat. So, the killer would have to be stationary and the boat moving slowly beneath them. It all suggests this lock.' He turned round and pointed.

'Now this particular lock is a little unusual because normally people go from one side of a lock to the other on footboards attached to the balance beams and the gates. These can be dangerous if they get slippery, and can only be used when the gates are closed. This lock, however, has a narrow footbridge over the bottom entrance.' He indicated a footbridge with some wooden railings. 'When Steph and I visited, a small group of the children ran on to this bridge to watch a boat pass underneath. That made me see that the bridge was a good position from which to commit the murder.'

'I'll bet Aleena was at the front of that group!' said Jav with a smile. 'She's a feisty character.'

'Maybe . . . but seeing them gave me another part of the answer.' He suddenly walked off to the side and picked up something from the long grass by the towpath. It was a long wooden pole. 'I got Gary Wilkinson from the shop to cut this for me and place it here.'

'What exactly is it, sir?' asked Jav.

'It's that very common device – a bargepole, similar to those carried on all boats, to pull and push things. They have a hook on one end. The other night my partner said that if we had a cat and it brought in a dead mouse, she wouldn't touch it. I found myself continuing an old saying in my head, you know – wouldn't touch it with a *bargepole* – and I realised that is what the murderer could have used.

'Now this one's been shortened a little at the bottom end. The murderer probably concealed this on the bank very much as I've done. Now I just have to tie this on.' He produced a narrow piece of stiff cardboard from the bag, cut in the shape of a long knife and fastened it with strong twine to the end of the pole.

'So Shipton's boat arrives at the bottom gates, which are open, and the killer moves on to this little bridge. Let's demonstrate. Steph get back on board and steer the boat into the lock.'

Andy untied the boat and Steph reversed it a little before heading slowly to the lock.

Oldroyd raised his voice so that everyone could hear. 'Now, boats go slowly into locks so as not to hit anything, and the throttle is turned off once they get in. Annie would have been completely focused on steering the boat into the lock and the killer would have concealed the bargepole until Annie was under the bridge and facing away from them.' The boat with Steph reached the bridge and glided underneath. Oldroyd raised the pole and suddenly brought it down at a steep angle.

'Ow, sir!' called Steph. The cardboard knife had hit her on the back of the neck. Steph rubbed the impact point.

Oldroyd laughed. 'Good! I managed to get it right. You really have to time it properly. I bet the killer practised this. I partially got the idea for this from my partner when she was saying how awful it was when the snapper arm of a mousetrap smashes down on the mouse. It gave me the idea of something coming down from above, which tied in with Annie Shipton's wounds. When I saw the bridge I realised how it could be done.'

Andy and Jav applauded. 'Amazing, sir, you've done it again.'

'Hold on, sir,' called Steph from the lock. 'What happened next? How did they get the boat to go back down to the basin?'

'Easy, these boats are heavy but quite manoeuvrable when they're in the water. This lock is quite shallow, and that was essential to the whole plan. If it had been deep, the knife would not have reached the boat and the killer would not have been able to do what they did next.'

He went across the bridge and alongside the lock until he reached the front of the boat. Then he used the pole to give the boat a push and it drifted gently with the current out of the lock in the direction of Saltaire and the basin, with Steph still by the tiller playing the part of the dead Shipton.

'*Voilà!*' declared Oldroyd. 'And it was all done without me getting on to the boat.'

There was applause from Andy and Jav, and now too from Steph who came back to life and steered the boat back to the mooring. The boat was tied up and Steph joined the others.

'Wonderful stuff, sir, as usual!' said Andy.

'Thank you,' said Oldroyd, taking a mock bow. 'Although this all depends on a number of things: that the murderer knew about narrowboats and locks, and that they were sure no one would see what happened. It was very early and there were no other boats or people around. The killer would have abandoned things at any stage if anyone had appeared, but they thought they'd been lucky. It now appears that someone did see them, but they must have been concealed. And that person was Bert Marshall.'

'Anything else, sir?' asked Jav.

'The killer had to get very near to Shipton and her boat. I can't imagine they just appeared from nowhere and leaped on to the bridge with the bargepole. I think that confirms that they were not a stranger to the victim. Annie Shipton knew her killer – at least one of them; I haven't entirely discounted the possibility that there could have been two people involved. It would certainly have made things easier.'

'You mean someone she knew lured her into the old false sense of security and somebody else killed her, sir?' asked Steph.

Oldroyd shrugged his shoulders. 'Possibly. We may never know exactly what happened.'

They all gazed at the lock, the open gates and the footbridge.

'If we know the how, that still leaves us with the questions of who and why, doesn't it, sir?' said Jav.

'It does. As we suspected from the beginning, it's clearly someone with knowledge about boats and canals but that still leaves a lot of possibilities. We have the method, but we do not yet have a clear suspect.'

Five

Lucy Banks,
Mother of three,
Her husband John
Was lost at sea.

How will you live,
My Lucy dear?
How will your children grow?

Lucy Banks
Down our lane,
Left alone
In the pouring rain.

How will you live,
My Lucy dear?
How will your children grow?

From 'Lucy Banks' performed by Rowan © 1995 lyrics
by Bridget Foster, music by Bob Anderson

Ben Shipton rented a small terraced house in Oakworth near the
iconic Yorkshire village of Haworth, home of the Brontë sisters

in the early nineteenth century and site of the station used in the famous film *The Railway Children*. Since his split with Annie he had lived there rather frugally, working part-time giving guitar lessons. Like all the members of Rowan and unlike many of the popular rock bands of the time, he had not made much money out of his folk group career.

He and Brittany spent the weekend relaxing. They felt exhausted after their ordeal in Saltaire. On Monday they decided to go for a walk and followed a path that took them along old lanes, over stiles and by the dark millstone grit walls that criss-crossed the green fields. The lower fields contained cows contentedly grazing. As they got higher, the cows were replaced by sheep. It was a dry, breezy day, with white fleecy clouds moving across the blue sky.

Brittany was enjoying the fresh air and the views. 'I must say it's good to be back in Yorkshire and to see these wide landscapes,' she said, gesturing with her arms.

'Yes,' replied her father, who had been brought up in Leeds and still found it rejuvenating to escape into the country. 'I spent a lot of time touring when I was younger, but I always wanted to come back here to settle. So did your mum. She came from round here too.'

'I think Harry and I will move back over here eventually.'

Ben looked at her. 'There is something else I need to tell you. The police brought it up when they questioned me yesterday.' He paused and braced himself. 'Your mother had affairs with women including with Ros Collins from the Canal and River Trust. She must have told the police about it.'

Brittany turned, wide-eyed, to her father. 'Dad? Neither of you said anything about this before.'

'We decided not to.'

'Why? Did you think I would reject her or something? This is the twenty-first century, Dad, I don't judge people by their sexuality.'

'Neither do I. It was the fact that she was being unfaithful to me that was the problem, not her sexuality. We didn't want to tell you about her affairs. We thought it might upset you.'

'Well, I'm old enough to deal with that kind of thing now. It's really between you and Mum.' She shook her head. 'It's a bit of a shock to find this out when Mum's just been murdered.'

'I know. I'm sorry. I had to tell you now because the police might raise it at some point and I didn't want you to hear about it from them.'

'It's all right.' She put her hand on his arm. 'Let's not allow this to come between us, especially on this lovely walk.'

The path took them through a muddy farmyard and up a steep climb along the edge of a wall.

'Did our splitting up really upset you? I know we never much talked about it,' Ben asked.

'Well, yes. I mean, not so much as it would have done when I was younger, but I don't think it's pleasant at any age if your parents separate. I remember you and Mum having arguments, but you always made it up. I never thought you would go your own ways.'

'Nor did I. Mum changed when we went to live on the canal. You'd left home by then, so there could have been a bit of empty-nest syndrome. I don't know why, but she seemed to get harder and less tolerant. She got involved in campaigns and rows with people and made herself unpopular. Maybe she needed some kind of role. She never really had one after the group finished.'

'I can see that. And then she told you about her affairs?'

'Yes. They were mostly just flings, but one was with Ros Collins at the basin. Seeing her there all the time was a constant reminder. I couldn't deal with it in the end.'

'I can't say I blame you.'

'Apparently after I'd left, she got even more curmudgeonly and difficult. I suppose being by herself made it worse.'

172

They'd reached the top of the hill, where there were large sandstone boulders and a trig point. From here, they could witness panoramic views towards Airedale and Skipton in one direction, and across Haworth up to Oxenhope Moor in the other. It was a clear day, and in the far distance there were glimpses of the high fells of Upper Wharfedale.

'Wow! Look at that!' exclaimed Brittany as the wind rustled her hair.

'Fabulous, isn't it?'

They were quiet for a while as they enjoyed the view, and then they spent some time trying to recognise landmarks.

'Auntie Bridget and Uncle Bob seem OK, although they're obviously upset about Mum, but I'm worried about Auntie Liz. She's by herself, and she seemed . . . I don't know . . . very emotional, and needy somehow, when she saw me.'

'I think you're right. I wouldn't like to live alone. And you also have to remember she's lost a lot – her husband and their little girl, Meg, both from cancer. I don't know how she manages, to be honest. I don't think you can ever properly get over that.'

'I'd forgotten about Meg. I think I have some vague memories of her when we used to visit Bob and Bridget.'

'She was a few years older than you – a lovely girl.' He shook his head. 'Tragic. Losing her was one of the reasons they agreed to come and live on the canal, to try to make a fresh start. Then Roger got ill. I'm sure it was related to the stress of losing his daughter.' He took a deep breath and smiled, trying to change the mood. 'Anyway, enough gloom. Let's enjoy the rest of the walk. This afternoon we'll have to give some serious thought to your mum's funeral and go down to the funeral directors'.'

'Oh no! That just sounds awful!' The brutal reality of this made Brittany burst into tears. Her father put his arm round her shoulders.

'It's hard, I know. The sooner we get it done the better.'

'OK,' said Brittany with a wan smile. She dried her eyes, and they started the descent back to Oakworth.

~

Back in the room at The Navigation it was lunchtime, and the detectives were having a bite to eat. Jav was on his laptop, on which he had just received some interesting news by email.

'Listen to this,' he said. 'Someone has sent an anonymous message to the Bradford HQ, and they've passed it on to me. This person claims to have evidence that Nicholas Spenser bribed a councillor to get his project at the Mill Centre approved. They've included a photograph of Spenser with a Councillor Crompton, which they say was taken at the café in the Mill Centre on Saturday.'

They all gathered round the laptop.

'Well,' said Oldroyd. 'It looks like Annie Shipton's group opposed to the Mill Centre plans is still active. It's just an allegation, of course, and that photograph alone proves nothing. The interesting thing as far as the case goes is whether Annie Shipton herself suspected this shady deal, and threatened to use the information against Spenser? If so, it gives him a much more powerful reason to get rid of her.'

'I'll get a team investigating it straight away, sir,' said Jav. 'We should also be able to track the IP address where this message originated.'

'Good.'

'It seems highly likely that she did, sir,' said Steph. 'Even if that group didn't have the proof they now think they have.'

'In which case, as I say, Spenser moves up the list of suspects. His job could be on the line, as well as his precious project. We'll need to talk to him again, but we'll wait until you've done the analysis, Jav.'

'OK, sir.'

'Spenser still doesn't strike me as the kind of person who could carry out two brutal murders, sir,' said Steph. 'If he killed Shipton, we need to assume he also murdered Marshall.'

Oldroyd sighed. 'I agree. I don't like the man – he's an image-obsessed manager type, but he doesn't feel physically threatening. However, when people are under pressure, they can behave in unexpected ways. Anyway, I think we're making a bit of progress and—'

His phone rang. It was Tom Walker. Oldroyd went outside to take the call.

'Morning, Jim,' Walker said. 'It seems things have taken a turn for the worse over there – another victim, I hear?'

'That's right, Tom – found in the canal this morning, smashed over the head and dumped in the water.'

Walker whistled. 'Well, it's not what they expect in Saltaire, is it? Bradford, maybe, but I've always thought that out there they consider themselves a bit superior to the big city.'

Oldroyd laughed. 'You're probably right, Tom.'

'So, you are pretty sure the two are connected?'

'Yes, the victim talked to a witness about having seen something related to the first murder, so we're working on the assumption that they tried to blackmail someone and got silenced.'

'I see. They sound a ruthless person, whoever the murderer is.'

'Yes, and desperate too. We've got a few more leads and we're making slow progress. I'm fairly sure I know where the first murder was committed and I'm going to brief the press about that and see if anyone comes forward with any information.'

'That's good. The only thing is that we've got a few people taking leave soon and I'm going to need you back before long. Can you at least get things to the point where the others can carry on without you?'

'I'll do my best.'

'Good. By the way, I had you-know-who on the phone – said he'd seen you interviewed in Saltaire, and why was one of our Harrogate officers working for the Bradford people? I explained it to him – in simple terms, of course, like talking to a child – and he said it was fine. Can you imagine anyone so bloody pointless as that charlatan?! He's so out of touch with what's taking place on the ground that he finds out what's going on in his own force from the television. Then he shows what a complete fool he is by asking silly questions.'

Oldroyd said nothing.

'Anyway, you don't want to hear all this, you haven't time. You've got real work to do, not writing ridiculous fantasies about robot police.' Walker laughed. 'I'd like to see him replace you and your team with robots. The criminals wouldn't believe their luck. Bye for now.'

Much to Oldroyd's relief, Walker rang off and he went back inside.

'Is Superintendent Walker happy with things, sir?' asked Jav. 'I always thought he was a good person to work for – very fair, and he understood the job.'

'Yes, he is that. And he's OK with things for now, but we need to really get moving. He'll be calling me back to Harrogate before too long. I'm going to prepare a briefing for the press about how the first murder was done and see if that jogs anybody's memory.'

~

In the early evening, two experienced officers in plain clothes – DC Tanner and DC Haynes – conducted a careful search of the woods above the tramway. It had long been suspected that there was some drug-related activity going on there, but a lack of resources had prevented the police from investigating it. Now that there was a possible link to the recent murders, it had become a priority.

The officers proceeded carefully, examining every little clearing for evidence of drugs being used or exchanged. It was fungi season in the woods, and they were fruiting in abundance, including some with hallucinogenic properties such as fly agaric.

'Look at these,' said Tanner, smiling as he pointed to a large specimen of the distinctive red mushroom with its white spots. 'They don't need to buy drugs from some criminal supplier, they could use these.'

'Maybe,' replied Haynes. 'But I think they'd probably poison themselves in the process.'

They discovered places where groups had met and left cigarette ends, the remains of spliffs, tin foil, and stones slightly blackened by fire. They walked deeper into the wood and eventually heard voices. They signalled to each other, crouching in the undergrowth and moving very quietly towards the noise. Eventually they could see who it was: a group of young men in a naturally concealed dell, smoking and laughing.

The officers crept on slowly and then spread out until they were close enough to be able to spring out from opposite points around the clearing, much to the shock of the little group who hastily stubbed out and tried to hide what they'd been smoking and inhaling.

'Well, what have we here?' announced DC Tanner. 'A happy little gathering.'

One of the young men looked about to try to run off.

'I wouldn't bother,' said Haynes. 'We know the lot of you, and we'll come for you if necessary.' He pointed at each one in turn.

'Terry Dunway, Liam Shaw, Sam Wallace – and Ryan Nelson, the dealer.'

Nelson, who was slightly older than the others, stared at Haynes sullenly.

'We can see you've got drugs here. You are all detained for a drugs search, and you are under caution – you do not have to say anything, but anything you do say may be given in evidence. We'll also take all your details and arrange for you to come into the Shipley station to be interviewed, having been caught in possession of suspected class A drugs.'

'How do yer know they're class A?' asked Shaw.

'They might not be,' said Tanner. 'You might have been snorting flour and smoking dried dandelion leaves, Liam, but somehow I doubt that's what we'll find when we examine this stuff.' He pointed to all the detritus on the ground.

'What'll we get?' asked Sam, who was terrified of his mother finding out.

'That all depends on your police record. Some of you might just get a caution for a first offence, but you,' he pointed to Nelson, 'have form on this matter, don't you? So you might get sent down.'

Nelson said nothing, as if he knew that it was better not to say anything that might be incriminating.

'Who else knows about these little meetings in the woods?' asked Haynes.

'Nob'dy,' said Shaw. 'We don't snitch on people anyway.'

'Nobody outside your little group?'

'What d'yer mean?'

'OK, I'll spell it out. Did that woman who was murdered, Annie Shipton, know anything about this?'

'That old woman on a boat? Why the hell would she know owt about us?' Nelson looked at the others, who laughed at the very idea.

'OK. Just asking. She didn't join in with you? Nothing like that?'

'You're joking, aren't you?'

After the officers had searched the young men and confiscated their drugs, and arranged for them to attend the police station to be given a formal caution, the young men slouched off, with Sam hoping he could keep this from his mother.

Haynes contacted Jav on his phone. 'We've found the drug users in the woods, sir. It was a case of the usual suspects with Ryan Nelson as the dealer . . . Yes, I think there's enough on him for a custodial sentence . . . No, they categorically denied that anyone else was involved and they thought the idea of Annie Shipton being involved, or knowing anything about them, completely ridiculous . . . OK, sir, thank you.'

The call ended. Haynes and Tanner left the woods feeling the satisfaction of a job well done.

~

That evening Oldroyd picked up Louise from Harrogate station. He hadn't seen his daughter for months. When she stepped off the train, he gave her a big hug on the platform. She looked very well, and was dressed in smart jeans, trainers and a denim jacket.

'Dad!' she cried. 'Oh, it's so good to see you – and to be back in Yorkshire again.' She took in a deep breath of the air. 'I can't wait to see the fells and the sheep and everything. We must do some walking. And the house! I'm desperate to see that!'

Oldroyd laughed. 'I'm glad that you're so delighted to be home again . . . or is London home to you now?'

Louise frowned. 'Come on, Dad, I'm a Yorkshire lass. This will always be my home wherever I go in the world. Sean feels the same about Ireland.' She was taking about her current boyfriend.

'Does he? Well, you'll have to have a base in both.'

'I know, but we'll never be able to afford that, and I don't really approve of second homes, anyway. They destroy local communities.'

Oldroyd smiled. He was used to his daughter's strong moral attitudes on everything from feminism to inequality to vegetarianism. He was proud of her but felt that he wasn't strong enough to match her commitment. She reminded him of his sister.

Louise was quiet on the drive out to New Bridge. She was looking at the autumn fields, woods and hedgerows. Then she sighed. 'It's so beautiful here. There are some lovely parks in London but it's not the same. You can hear the traffic going past.' She stretched her arms behind her head. 'I can feel myself relaxing already. Actually, I never thought you'd move out into a village. I thought you were settled in Harrogate.'

'Deborah was the impetus behind the move. She wanted to have a garden and be further into the countryside. We looked at a lot of properties before we found this, and now we've moved, I really like it. I wasn't really sorry to leave that flat; I was lonely there for quite a lot of the time. The associations weren't good.' He stopped talking for a moment, and then nodded at the road ahead. 'We're nearly there now. It's not that far out of town.'

The car shortly drew up outside the house. It was at the end of an attractive early Victorian terrace with gardens at the side and back. There was a garage extension and an old wooden greenhouse in the garden. Velux windows on the roof indicated that the loft had been converted.

'Oh, Dad, it's lovely – so pretty!'

'I know. We're very happy with it.'

Deborah opened the door and called out a greeting. She hugged Louise, who had always got on well with her de-facto stepmother, and then they all went inside. Louise was given a quick tour and was then left to settle in briefly in the guest room.

A little later they all met in the sitting room for a pre-meal drink. Louise sat in a comfortable armchair, sighed and sipped her wine.

'Well, this is not just a visit . . . it's a holiday. I'm feeling less stressed already.'

'Good,' replied Deborah. 'That's what we want to hear. Has it been difficult recently at the women's refuge?'

'Oh, you wouldn't believe it. With the austerity cuts and all the social problems, relationships seem to be failing more and more . . . and there's more violence too, it seems. Women with children are turning up in a dreadful state.'

'That must be really hard,' observed Oldroyd.

'Yes, but it's what we're there for. I've got a wonderful team.'

'Me too,' said Oldroyd.

'Oh, are you still working with Andy and Steph?'

'Yes. And, in fact, on the present case, we're working with one of our former colleagues.' He explained about the involvement of Javed Iqbal, who'd previously been at the Harrogate station.

Deborah asked Louise a bit more about her work. 'The impact on the children must be terrible, especially if they've witnessed violence against their mother.'

'Yes. The mothers are struggling with their own problems and they find it hard to cope. A lot of the children end up being taken into care.' She shook her head. 'I don't know what's worse . . . never to have any children if you really want them, or to lose them later.'

'That's very bleak,' said Deborah. 'You must meet people in desperate circumstances. I admire you for doing it and still keeping positive.'

'Thanks.' Louise sipped her wine. 'It's not as if the old prejudices have all gone either. A young woman came in this week, only seventeen – she'd been physically abused at home and then thrown out because she was gay. Unbelievable.'

181

'That is awful,' said Deborah gently, 'but let's leave work behind for now. You're here to forget about it for a while. Let's go and eat.' She looked at Oldroyd suspiciously. 'Jim, you're very quiet.'

'I'm OK. Just thinking about what Louise has been saying.'

'Are you? Well, let's *all* stay off work, and have a nice evening.'

~

'I've got the report from Dr Coates about the body of Bert Marshall, sir,' said Jav.

It was the next morning, and the detectives were gathering in The Navigation as Jav consulted his laptop. 'She confirms that the cause of death was drowning, but that he would have been unconscious when he went into the water due to the head wound, which was inflicted by something metallic. And apparently it left a pattern on his head – two square shapes.' He shook his head. 'That's strange.'

'It was a windlass!' said Steph.

'You mean the thing we use to open and shut the sluice gates?' asked Andy.

'Yes! The square holes are for turning the metal cog, and the sluice gates come up or down depending on which way you turn it.'

'I think Steph's right,' said Oldroyd, nodding and smiling. 'But what we can conclude from that I'm not sure. It suggests again that the killer is someone in the boating community, especially if the two killings are connected. On the other hand, those windlasses are all over the place on the canal and especially in a basin and marina like this. Someone could have just picked one up that was lying around.'

'And probably chucked it into the water afterwards,' said Andy.

'Officers have conducted a search of Marshall's house,' continued Jav. 'He lived alone in a small estate of council houses just outside the town. The position of the house confirms what we were told at the Mill Centre – that he walked down the canal towpath to work, which is where he would have witnessed what happened on the day of Shipton's murder. He'd have been there early because it was his job to open up the Mill Centre.'

'If our theory is right, he must have seen somebody he knew acting strangely, and decided to stay out of view. He was the type of person who likes to find out what other people are doing and gossip about it later. He may not have been fully aware of what had happened, but later when he found out that Shipton had been murdered, he realised he could blackmail the person concerned,' said Oldroyd.

'Instead of telling us about it,' observed Steph.

'Yes, that was his undoing. I suppose there's a kind of rough justice in it,' reflected Oldroyd. 'It was a case of GHD.'

'What's that then, sir?' asked Jav with a smile. Oldroyd was famous for his acronyms for different types of murders.

'Greed Hides Danger,' he explained. 'People can be so dazzled by their desire to gain, that they don't see the danger they are putting themselves in. It's a common feature in blackmail cases where the blackmailer ends up dead.'

'They don't see that the person they're blackmailing can escape the situation by getting rid of their blackmailer,' said Steph.

'Exactly. It would have turned out much better for him if he'd done the right thing. Sadly, the temptation to make easy money was likely too great.'

'So, I expect the murderer arranged to meet him after dark and then took him by surprise, sir?' suggested Andy.

'Very likely,' said Oldroyd. 'Now, how are we getting on with Spenser and the councillor? By the way, if Marshall saw Spenser at that lock, he would have known that his boss would make an excellent blackmail victim, what with his being very concerned about his image and that of the centre. It could be that Spenser killed two people who were blackmailing him.'

'OK, sir,' said Jav. 'We've established that Councillor Crompton is on the Shipley Council planning committee and has spoken in favour of the Mill Centre development scheme.'

'Excellent, that puts him in prime position to being bribed. Anything else?'

'My team tracked down the drug users in the woods near the Glen.'

'Well done them.'

'It wasn't that difficult. It's not a very professional operation, just a few young men we've known about for a long time who tend to get into trouble over things. Interestingly, one of them was Sam Wallace, the cyclist who had the confrontation with Annie Shipton, so that appeared to be a promising link. However, they were all adamant that she knew nothing about it. My DC said they found the whole idea ridiculous, so I think we'll have to abandon that as a motive for Wallace or anyone else.'

'OK for now,' said Oldroyd. 'So, Andy and Jav, get on to this Councillor Crompton, and Steph and I will make another visit to Mr Nicholas Spenser. It's not looking good for him.'

'How are you doing?' Laura Ward popped into the bedroom on the narrowboat to see how Darren was feeling. He was still in bed, and if he didn't improve soon, she planned to call the doctor.

'Just the same,' he managed to say in a croaky voice.

She had a good look at him and took his temperature. It was slightly high. 'Drink some water. Do you fancy anything to eat?'

Darren sat up and drank from a glass of water, then slumped back down. 'No, thanks.'

She stayed in the room. She was anxious and wanted to talk despite him not feeling well.

'Darren, what do you think's going to happen next on this canal?'

He answered without moving. 'What do you mean?'

'Two people murdered. It makes me feel uneasy.'

There was a pause. It was an effort for him to reply. 'Everyone feels the same, don't they?'

'I don't know. I like it here in lots of ways, but I've never felt that we really belong. Too many stuck-up types. That bloke who was found in the water, Bert Marshall, he was working class too. Maybe someone's decided to get rid of people like us. They could have read that blog and heard that I had a go at Annie Shipton.'

Darren turned over. 'What're you talking about, you daft bat? You're paranoid. One minute you think the police suspect you of killing Shipton and then you think there's a killer on the loose who doesn't like people like us.'

'Shut up. I'm not paranoid. And I'm not just worried about us. What about Len? He doesn't fit in with that group, either. He could be next.'

Darren started to chuckle, and it then turned into a wracking cough. 'I wouldn't worry about Len. He might be getting on a bit, but I bet he can look after himself. He's got plenty of tools on that boat to whack any intruder over the head.'

'I suppose so. But what are we going to do?'

'Nothing. The police will get to the bottom of it before long. Just take care and don't go out alone at night. Anyway, I'll look after you.' He sneezed and blew his nose on a tissue.

She laughed. 'You're not much bloody use at the moment!' Then she sat down on the side of the bed.

'Don't bother getting in with me. I'm not up for that at the moment,' he said.

'Get lost! I wasn't trying.' She looked around restlessly. 'I wonder when Sam's coming round with some stuff? I could just do with a spliff. It would calm me down.'

'Don't know. It's been a while. Maybe he's been caught by the police.'

'God, I hope not. His mother would go mad. Anyway, try to get some sleep and I'll come back later to see how you are.'

'OK.' Darren turned over and pulled the duvet around him.

~

Councillor Alistair Crompton had the expression of a cornered animal as he faced Andy and Jav at the Shipley Council offices. The whole arrangement between him and Nicholas was blowing up in their faces. Crompton had had a long career as a councillor and had clung to his place on the planning committee. He'd never refused the odd sweetener from interested parties wishing to get their plans approved. He saw it as a perk of the job and almost his right, as he felt councillors were paid so little. It had always been done very discreetly.

Crompton had taken them into a small meeting room. It was an oak-panelled affair in the stylish 1930s building. He'd attended many meetings in the room but never felt as nervous as he did now. He had a feeling this was about the Mill Centre, and he felt sweat on his forehead. He wiped his brow with a handkerchief. He had to try to stay cool and keep his nerve.

'So how can I help you, officers?' he asked.

'OK, well, I'll come straight to the point,' began Jav. 'We've received an email alleging that you have accepted illegal payments in relation to a development proposal submitted to Shipley Council.'

'Which proposal would that be?'

'The extensions to the Mill Centre at Saltaire. The email included a photograph of you, taken on Saturday, talking to Nicholas Spenser at the café in the Mill Centre. Mr Spenser appears very keen for this scheme to go ahead. The person who submitted this photograph claims to have overheard you talking about the illegal payment at that meeting.'

Crompton attempted a derisive laugh, which didn't sound very convincing. 'Well, it's all rubbish, Inspector. Yes, I know Nicholas Spenser and, being on the planning committee, I naturally know about the Mill Centre scheme. But I can assure you that nothing illegal has happened. I was indeed at the Mill Centre on Saturday – Mr Spenser invited me to the opening of a display about the scheme. It's very impressive and, I can tell you in confidence, that I am inclined to vote for it, so Mr Spenser does not need to bribe me to get my support.'

'Does he know you're in favour of the scheme?'

'Not explicitly. We try to remain as objective as possible on issues like this, but I'm sure he's worked out my attitude from the favourable comments I've made about the proposals. Again, between you and me, I think the extension and the new facilities which come with it will be excellent for the Mill Centre and for the area.'

He was trying to put on a smooth performance, but Andy detected an underlying uncertainty. 'You're aware,' Andy said, 'that not everyone in the area takes the same view, and that there is a group opposed to these plans.'

'Yes, and I suspect that this so-called information came from one of them. Mr Spenser told me he thought they'd do anything to stop the plans becoming reality. That seems to extend to spying on people.'

'Did you know that the leader of that group was Annie Shipton, the woman who was murdered on the canal?'

'Mr Spenser has mentioned her a few times, but I'm not sure what that has to do with these allegations.'

Jav looked straight at Crompton. 'If Annie Shipton suspected there were illegal arrangements between parties like yourself and Spenser, she could have attempted to use this to blackmail you. And blackmail can lead to murder.'

Crompton shook his head. 'I see, so it's a lot more serious than bribery. I can only assure you again, Inspector, that no money has swapped hands. As for Nicholas and I being involved in murder, that really is preposterous.'

'Did you know Annie Shipton?'

'Not personally. I know she led the campaign against the Mill Centre plans. She was very vociferous about their opposition. In my view they're just a bunch of nimbies trying to stop any changes to their patch. The extension will benefit the area. If it brings in more tourists, that's good – we need that economic stimulus.'

Andy gave him a wry smile. Maybe other people like yourself will also benefit, he thought. The problem was they had no proof of anything.

'What did Mr Spenser say about Annie Shipton?' he asked.

Crompton shrugged. 'Not much. He obviously didn't approve of her, as she was the ringleader of the opposition, but he never said anything threatening about her.'

'Do you know a man called Bert Marshall?' asked Jav.

'Never heard of him.'

'He was a caretaker at the Mill Centre, and he was murdered over the weekend.'

'Good God! Another murder?'

'Yes. We believe he knew something about the murder of Annie Shipton and that's why he was silenced.'

'Well, I've never heard of this man.'

Andy and Jav looked at Crompton suspiciously, but could not take this much further at the moment. Much to Crompton's relief, they brought the interview to an end, informing him that he would be asked to make a statement and that if any further evidence of corruption emerged the police would take action.

'What did you think of that?' asked Jav when they were walking back to the basin.

'I think Crompton and Spenser are probably as guilty as hell in terms of the bribery, but we can't prove it, especially if no money has yet exchanged hands,' said Andy. 'From what we know, Spenser is so desperate to get his scheme through that he'd do anything.'

'They're closer than he was prepared to admit. Did you notice how he called Spenser by his first name at one point?' said Jav.

'Well spotted.'

'I think they had a too-cosy relationship. The question is, as the boss said, did Shipton know about it? We need to talk to somebody in that group opposed to the plans and find out how long they've suspected that Spenser might have been involved in bribery.'

Andy nodded. 'You're right. If she did know, that would have provided a serious motive for getting rid of her. If she didn't, then Spenser is probably in the clear – at least for the murders. Let's see how the boss and Steph got on with him.'

Staff at the Mill Centre were still reeling from the news of the murder of Bert Marshall, who had been a familiar, if not always well-liked, character around the place.

Despite his dressing down from Oldroyd, Nicholas was still concerned about how the public would react. Would they feel that, after two murders, Saltaire was a dangerous place to visit? Now that an employee at the centre had been killed, would they feel that the Mill Centre had something to do with all the death?

When Oldroyd and Steph arrived to see Nicholas for the second time, he assumed they had come to find out more information about Bert Marshall, but when Oldroyd explained about the tip-off they had received about himself and Crompton, he was shocked. This was what he'd dreaded. He struggled to maintain his composure while thinking frantically about the previous Saturday. Someone must have been lurking in that café and managed to take a photograph of him and Crompton while they were talking. It didn't seem as if they'd managed to record the conversation, which was just as well.

'I can assure you that these allegations are false, Chief Inspector. It's true that I know Councillor Crompton and I invited him to an event here on Saturday, but I've not given him any money in order to buy his favour. Can I ask who has supplied you with this information?'

'We can't divulge that,' replied Oldroyd.

'Probably a member of the opposition group. It's clearly still active after the leader's death.' Nicholas fiddled with a pen on his desk.

'Which brings me on to my next question,' Oldroyd continued in an abrupt manner. 'Did Annie Shipton ever mention that she had any suspicions about this to you?'

'No, I never had any dealings with her. She held me in too much contempt to ever speak to me. It's amazing for an alternative hippy type like her, isn't it? To become so conservative in her old age, and so opposed to change?'

'She never tried to blackmail you about these alleged pay-offs?'

Nicholas shook his head and smiled. 'Absolutely not, Inspector. This is starting to sound like a second-rate thriller.'

'In second-rate thrillers, people get killed, and it's not funny,' said Oldroyd, fixing Nicholas with his fierce grey eyes. He still didn't like the man.

Nicholas coughed and assumed a sober expression. 'Quite,' he said. 'But I can assure you again, Inspector, that I had nothing to do with Shipton's death.'

Oldroyd continued to glare at him. 'And Bert Marshall? We believe he saw whoever killed Annie Shipton at the scene of the crime. If that was you, he may have been the second person to blackmail you, and the second person you got rid of. Where were you on Sunday evening?'

Nicholas laughed. 'Now we are entering the realm of the absurd, Chief Inspector. Me, a double murderer? I'm just a mild-mannered man who runs an arts centre. I was at home on Sunday evening and my wife was there.'

'I've known many apparently mild-mannered people who had a vicious side to them,' replied Oldroyd with a sardonic smile. 'Anyway, we'll leave it there for now, but an officer will come to take a statement from you, and we'll be checking your alibis.'

'But . . .' Nicholas was speechless.

Oldroyd got up. 'Good afternoon, Mr Spenser.'

Outside, Steph chuckled. 'You were very hard on him again, sir. He doesn't seem a very likely culprit to me, at least not for the murders. I know you don't like him, but you're making him sweat a bit.'

'You're right, I am.'

'But be careful, sir. Remember what happened that time at Redmire Hall.'

Steph had worked with her boss for a long time and knew his personality well. He had a tendency to handle people he didn't like in a rough manner. In a murder case at Redmire Hall near Ripon there had been a number of rich, arrogant and entitled people involved, and Oldroyd had overstepped the mark a little, leading to a complaint being filed against him. Steph also knew that they were close enough for her boss to accept a comment like this from her, even though she was his junior.

Oldroyd shook his head as they walked through the old mill yard on the way back to the canal. 'Well, yes, I suppose you're right. I'm intolerant of arrogant people. You're also right that he's not a very likely suspect for the murders, though I don't think he was telling the full truth about his relationship with Councillor Crompton.' He looked at Steph with a wry smile. 'Let him sweat a bit. At the very least, it might make him think about treating his staff in a better way.'

~

Len Nicholson took a break from his work at dinner time and sat on a bank by the canal eating a corned beef sandwich and drinking from a large mug of tea. The early sun had gone and it was now overcast and cool. But it was pleasant to get out of his boat for a while and away from the smell of paint. The canal and the towpath were quiet.

When he'd finished his sandwich, he smoked a cigarette. Looking down the canal, he could see, in the distance, the incident tape surrounding the place where Marshall's body had been pulled out of the water.

He smiled to himself. He knew that everyone thought he was just an old bloke slightly off his rocker when he talked about the canal being cursed, but they were ignorant. Look at what had happened: two people were dead who hadn't respected the waterway. Annie Shipton: she had sown disharmony among the canal community with her rows and arguments. Bert Marshall: he was most likely a blackmailer from what Len had heard. The canal had rid itself of these bad spirits now and there would be calm, just like on the surface of the water on a dry, still day.

He looked at his boat and his mind went back over a whole lifetime spent on the waterways. There were very few people left who had lived a life like his – people whose earliest memories were of being on the river or canal, part of a family on a cramped boat. It entered into your soul and put you in touch with the spirits of the water. They protected you against the dangers – the deep locks, slippery stone surfaces at the side and the narrow, dark and dripping tunnels.

Len surfaced from his reverie when he noticed someone walking down the towpath towards him. It was Ros Collins. His brow furrowed. It wasn't that he disliked her personally, but he resented all the officials who were in charge of the waterways, introducing all kinds of regulations and rules. He believed in freedom for the people who really knew the waterways and had always lived on them.

'Afternoon, Len,' said Ros, who was having a brief walk in her lunch break. She liked Len. She respected his knowledge of the canal and found the story of his life fascinating, but she was aware that he was suspicious of her as a representative of officialdom.

'Afternoon,' replied Len, finishing his tea. He pointed to the police tape. 'What's goin' on dahn there? Are t' police still at it?'

'I expect so.'

'It wa' that bloke that worked at t' mill where all those pictures are, wa'n't it?'

'Yes.'

He looked at her closely. 'Two murders, eh? How are your bosses takin' it, then?'

'What do you mean?'

'Ah mean all them bigwigs that make up all these rules for t' canal and charge all the money for mooring and stuff. Not that you'll get any from me. Ah'm on t' move, so thi can't sting me.'

Ros smiled. 'I'm sure they're as shocked as we are, but there's not much they can do about it.'

Len grunted. 'Well, there'll be one less payin' those fees.'

Ros humoured his curmudgeonly attitude. There was no point arguing or remonstrating with him. 'That's true, but I'm sure that someone will soon replace Annie Shipton. We all hope that what's happened doesn't stop people from visiting the canal.'

Len grunted again. 'There's too many folk walkin' and runnin' round now and ridin' bikes up and dahn towpath. They get in t' way. One o' them runners nearly bashed into me t' other morning. It'll end up with sumdy getting knocked into t' watter.'

'But, Len, we couldn't survive without all these people. The canal's different now, you know that. It's not used much for industrial things any more but for leisure. Without that we wouldn't have any money to maintain it. It would go back to the nineteen-sixties when canals were being shut down and concreted over.'

Len grunted for the third time. 'Ah, well,' he muttered, but he knew that she was right.

Ros looked up into the cloudy sky. 'I don't suppose many people are going to miss Annie, apart from her daughter and her old friends – and they all seem to have fallen out with her at one time or another.'

'She wa' a bad spirit on the canal.'

'I know what you mean. But there was a nice side to her.'

'Did you know her well, then?'

Ros was lost in thought for a moment. 'Not as well as I thought I did.'

~

When Oldroyd got home that evening, Deborah was in Harrogate seeing her clients. He found Louise in the lounge with a rather dusty old photograph album.

'Have you had a relaxing day?' he called from the kitchen as he put the kettle on.

'Yes, thanks. I've mostly been chilling in the house, but went for a walk round the village earlier.'

Oldroyd came back with two mugs of tea.

'Dad, I found this in my room last night. I haven't seen these photographs for ages.'

'There's still a lot of stuff up there we haven't unpacked yet, and it's mostly in boxes in that room. Sorry. Your mum and I divided the family albums up between us.'

'Don't worry, I'm glad it was there. Look at this – there's me and Robert on the beach at Scarborough.'

Oldroyd sat next to her on the sofa and looked at the photograph of his son and daughter building a sandcastle. They looked about eight and six years old. His wife Julia was standing behind them and smiling. He must have taken the picture, but he didn't remember. They'd had many happy family holidays on the Yorkshire coast. He had a brief spasm of nostalgia for those times before he and Julia had parted.

'How is your mother? Have you heard from her recently?' Julia taught history in a sixth-form college in Leeds and lived in a terraced house in Chapel Allerton.

'She's OK, I think. A bit fed up with work, as usual. You know how she never says much about herself and her feelings. She's still alone, I think. Maybe she prefers it that way.'

'Yes.'

'I'm going to stay a night with her before I go back to London.'

'Good. She'll like that.'

'Look at this one.' Louise pointed to another picture. Here someone had taken a shot of all four of them in a restaurant somewhere. Louise and Robert were older.

'That was your birthday – were you thirteen? We're in Dolce Vita in Harrogate.'

'I know, I remember it. Look at Robert there. He's starting to look like you, but you can't see it in the earlier photo.'

Robert lived in Birmingham with his partner and their daughter. Oldroyd always regretted not seeing more of them. Robert seemed to have been more deeply affected by his parents splitting up than Louise.

He looked closely at the photo. 'Yes, but actually I thought Robert always looked a bit like me when he was a baby.'

'Did you? I can't really see it. Facial features are funny that way, aren't they? People see different things when it comes to likenesses. And sometimes resemblances to other people in the family only become apparent when the person gets older.'

'True,' said Oldroyd, sounding a little distracted. What Louise had just said had made him think about something. Something he'd noticed. Something that had seemed inconsequential at the time and yet had stuck in his mind. What was it?

'Anyway, Dad, let's get the tea on. I'm going to make some Mexican bean burritos with guacamole. You can come and do some chopping. There's going to be lots of delicious veg in them.'

Oldroyd smiled. 'It sounds great, but while we're talking about families, I sometimes wonder what my grandad would have thought about eating burritos and guacamole. The words would have been incomprehensible and the food far too spicy for him. It's a shame – they missed out, those older generations. I love having a choice of cuisines with all their different flavours.'

Louise laughed. 'Be honest, Dad – you'll eat any cuisine as long as there's plenty of it.'

≈

'I don't believe this. What a bloody mess! You absolute idiot!'

Samantha Spenser sat in the sitting room of their house, look-ing daggers at her husband while shouting at him.

Nicholas seemed completely cowed. He was desperate and had decided to tell his wife everything about his relationship with Councillor Crompton and how the police suspected them. He knew she would support him in finding a way through this crisis, however furious she was. There was too much at stake.

'And there's been another murder? Someone who worked at the centre?' she said.

Nicholas nodded.

'Well, I'm surprised you haven't been arrested. The police must now think you have a double motive for killing Shipton, and it would fit very nicely into the story, wouldn't it, if this man had been blackmailing you and you got rid of him too. So now I'll have to provide you with an alibi for that as well. Easy enough, though, as you actually were here all evening on Saturday and Sunday.'

'I didn't do it.'

'No, I'm sure you didn't. I don't think you've got the guts to kill someone. But it doesn't look good, does it? And you have been trying to bribe a councillor! What kind of a fool are you, putting all our futures at risk?!'

Nicholas put his head in his hands. 'I know it was stupid. I'm just desperate to get these plans through. It could make or break my career. If it's a success, it could set me up to move on to something bigger. Maybe a big arts organisation in London.'

'You won't be running a big arts organisation in London from prison, will you?'

Nicholas frowned. 'Look, although Crompton and I talked about it, nothing was ever actually done. No money changed hands. The police have no proof and we've both denied it. Everything should just die down when they've solved these murders.'

'That's assuming that none of this leaks. If Shipton's group Save Saltaire have got wind of this, they'll use it against you regardless of what the police do.'

Nicholas shook his head and tried to reassure her. He knew he didn't sound convincing. 'I don't think so. Getting rid of me wouldn't stop the scheme, would it? And they don't have any real evidence. As I said, it's just a photograph of me and Crompton in the café and what does that show? He was there to attend the opening of the display on my invitation and then we went for a drink. It was all above board.'

Samantha remained rigid, her arms folded. 'If it does all come out, I hope the trustees of the centre take the same view and support you. It's not exactly good publicity, is it? The centre director accused of bribery and under suspicion for a double murder?'

Nicholas shuddered at the stark description of his plight. 'I'm going to have a word with the chair, Malcolm Givens, before anything is made public. I'll explain everything. I know he'll support me – he's behind the scheme and he hates that protest group. I can present it positively as me taking a hit for the centre if it comes to it.'

She glared at him. 'Huh! Well, I hope you're right, because I'll never forgive you if we lose everything because of your stupidity. I never thought you would put your career before your family.'

'That's not fair, Sam.'

'Isn't it? What else am I supposed to think? You're so keen to get ahead that you're prepared to break the law and possibly ruin everything.' There were tears in her eyes. 'You're a selfish bastard.'

He couldn't think of a reply to this stinging accusation without making her more angry, so he gave her a weak smile and said nothing. It was, as she'd said, a mess.

∾

Andy and Steph had found a pleasant little family-run Nepalese restaurant in Shipley, recommended by Jav, and were tucking into plates of delicious curry along with papadums, naan bread and cucumber raita.

'I was ready for this,' said Andy. 'It's been a long day.' He and Steph had spent a lot of time in the afternoon with Jav going through the statements given by witnesses and suspects without discovering anything significant.

'Yes, it's lovely in here, isn't it? And they're all so friendly.'

Andy scooped up some of his lamb tikka with a piece of naan bread. 'So, Enola, what are your latest theories about who committed these murders?' Andy liked to refer jokingly to Steph as Enola after the films about the sister of Sherlock and Mycroft Holmes.

Steph took a drink of water and sat back for a moment. 'Well, it's a difficult one. My money was on Sam Wallace, the cyclist. He's strong, and you could imagine him bashing Marshall over the head and dumping him in the water. But after the boss demonstrated how the first murder was committed, I can't see Wallace planning it in such detail, and making a murder weapon like that, unless he had an accomplice. I think it has to be someone more directly concerned with the boats.'

'That doesn't narrow it down much,' said Andy. He raised his glass of water. 'I think it's all to do with sex.'

'You would say that.' Steph laughed. 'How?'

'We know Annie Shipton had affairs. That kind of stuff really stirs up strong feelings. There's nothing like sexual jealousy as a trigger for violence.'

'Ah, the *crime passionnel*,' said Steph, her bright blue eyes teasing. 'That used to get a lower sentence in France at one time, didn't it? I can understand why. I know how you would be driven to extremes if you thought I was involved with another man.'

'And what about the other way round?'

'Oh, yes. Hell hath no fury, as they say!'

'You're being very intellectual tonight.'

'What? Just a French phrase and an old saying from somewhere?'

'I think you went to better schools than me. Harrogate's a lot posher than Croydon.'

'Maybe, or perhaps I was just a better scholar. Anyway, you're thinking that the husband Ben or the spurned lover Ros Collins might be the killer?'

'Or another lover who hasn't emerged yet. It's possible.'

'Maybe she was having sex with everybody around that canal basin. There could have been an ex-lovers' alliance to get rid of her.'

'Are you taking the piss?'

Steph collapsed in giggles. 'Just a bit, but you could be right.'

They finished their main courses and had some pistachio kulfi for dessert, which was satisfyingly sweet and cold after the curry.

They walked back to their boat holding hands. The evening was cool, and the sky was now clear.

'I wonder when we'll be able to continue with our holiday,' said Steph, looking up at the stars. 'We were supposed to be spending time together away from work.'

Andy put his arms around her, and they kissed. 'I know. The problem with us is that we find our work fascinating and we can't tear ourselves away.'

She pushed him from her. 'So work is more fascinating to you than I am?'

'Not really, but it behaves itself and doesn't give feisty answers all the time.'

He ran off up the towpath and she pursued him, laughing.

～

Jav was in the sitting room with Nadia, half-watching a news broadcast. The girls were in bed.

'I've heard all this already. You can watch too much news – it gets depressing,' said Nadia. 'Tell me about your day. How are you getting on with the great Detective Chief Inspector Oldroyd?'

Jav smiled. 'You remember those days in Harrogate, don't you? How much I hero-worshipped him. We all did and, to be honest, we still do. Yesterday he demonstrated to us how the murder could have been committed by someone without them getting on to the boat. I think only his mind could have worked that out.' He explained what Oldroyd had done at the lock.

'That's amazing. And that was the same lock that Aleena visited on her trip?'

'Yes. He and Steph saw them. DCI Oldroyd said that seeing some of the kids standing on the little bridge and pretending to fire guns at the boat passing underneath gave him the idea that the victim could have been attacked from there.'

Nadia laughed. 'If those kids only knew they'd helped to solve a murder mystery, they'd remember it for the rest of their lives!'

'I know. Maybe if this works out for the best, we can tell them.'

'Anne Hopkins said Aleena was absolutely full of it. She told everyone they'd all seen a famous detective who worked with her father. Anne got them to do a diagram of how the lock worked and Aleena also drew a picture. Look.'

She got up and fetched the drawing from the table. It was a clear picture of the lock with a very colourful boat going through. Her classmates were standing in a line and waving to the people on the boat. In the background the detectives were watching. Steph was recognisable with her blonde hair, and Oldroyd was wearing a jacket that said *Chief Inspector* on it. At the bottom was written, *My class and two famouse detectives looking for edivence. They work with my Dad at SOLVING MURDERS!!!*

'That's brilliant,' said a proud Jav. 'She doesn't get all her spellings right, but she's having a go at difficult words.'

'I know. What's this though?' asked Nadia, pointing to another boat at the edge of the picture that was coloured black. A man with a beard was standing by the tiller and waving his arms. Black smoke was billowing out of the chimney.

'Oh, that must be Len Nicholson. He's a big guy with a massive beard. He makes a living painting boats, making signs and stuff like that. The boat's filthy and smoke comes out of the chimney on top just like she's drawn. It's very good, I can recognise everything in the picture. It's just the kind of thing that kids find fascinating and scary . . .'

'Ah, that's right. She mentioned an old man with a beard who shouted at them, and they ran off. It must have been him.'

'Yes,' replied Jav and considered this for a moment. They hadn't pursued Len Nicholson as a suspect because there didn't appear to be a motive, but he was well positioned to have followed Annie Shipton from his boat that morning. He would have seen her pass. And he was also very experienced in all aspects of boating. He could be worth investigating more thoroughly.

In the kitchen of her dad's terraced house in Oakworth, Brittany was speaking to her husband, Harry, at their home in Oldham and explaining what had happened in more detail.

'All Mum's friends are in a state – Auntie Liz, Auntie Bridget and Uncle Bob. But at least they all seemed really pleased to see me.'

'Well, you're the only child that group had who survived. It was very tragic about Liz's child. You're like the daughter to all of them. The daughter of Rowan.'

She laughed. 'It sounds like the title of an old ballad – like the ones they used to sing in the band – but I suppose you're right, they've always made a fuss of me. I feel terribly sad when I think that their retirement project on the canal has ended up like this.'

'I can understand it. Are the media making a nuisance of themselves?'

'Not really. There's a good team of detectives handling the case and the chief inspector in charge is very experienced in dealing with reporters. He told us all not to speak to them because they have a tendency to twist things and interfere with the investigation.'

'He's right about that. I think I saw him on one of the bulletins. How's your dad?'

'He's managing. It's a shock. I know they were separated, but I think he still had feelings for Mum. The problem was she just seemed to get more difficult the older she got.'

'She was never that easy, was she? Though I think she liked me.'

'She did. She took to you straight away. You were lucky!'

'I know. Anyway, any idea when you'll be back?'

'Hopefully sometime on Thursday. The school have been very good, but I would like to get back to work on Friday.'

'When's the funeral going to be?'

'It won't be for another two weeks. It'll be near Shipley at Nab Wood Crematorium.'

'Right. Let me know the date as soon as you can, and I'll arrange for the day off at work.' Harry worked for the civil service in Manchester. 'OK . . . go and be with your dad, and give me another ring tomorrow.'

'OK, love you. Bye.'

Brittany ended the call and went to see how her dad was doing in the living room. He was trying to watch a wildlife documentary, but finding it hard to concentrate.

He yawned and rubbed his eyes when she entered the room. 'How is he?' he asked.

'OK. I know he wants me back as soon as possible. He doesn't like being by himself.'

'I can understand that. I got very lonely when I first came here. I'd never lived by myself before, but you get used to it.'

'You missed Mum.'

'Yes, even though we couldn't live together any more without arguing all the time.' He took a deep breath. 'And now I'm thinking a lot about what went wrong and whether it was my fault. I don't like to think of her spending the last years of her life as alone and angry as she seemed to be.'

'It wasn't your fault, Dad. Everybody had problems with Mum. I wonder if she ever really dealt with the fact that Rowan was over and you weren't performing any more. Maybe she was depressed.'

Ben shook his head. 'I wonder if any of us really got over it. It was an exciting thing to do, you know, and it's such a different life being on tour most of the time. And when it all stopped, it was like a ride at the fairground coming to an end – the thrills are over, and you have to get off. I think it was especially hard for your mum because she was the lead vocal – the main face of the group, like Maddy Prior in Steeleye Span.' He laughed. 'But you won't remember them, they were well before your time.'

Brittany thought for a moment. 'Do you think that was why Mum was keen for you all to come and live together in the canal basin? That way you were all together again, and it was as if Rowan still existed?'

'Well, I'd never thought of it that way, but you could be right. I don't know. She's gone now and we can't talk about it with her.' He looked at Brittany, and there were tears in his eyes.

Brittany sat alongside him and gave him a hug. 'Oh, Dad! I knew you still cared about Mum.'

Ben wiped his eyes with a tissue. 'I did. I didn't want to leave. I just felt she was pushing me away somehow, but I don't know why.'

'Maybe she didn't know herself, but, as you say, we'll never know now.' She hugged him again. 'But we're still here and we can help each other to get through this.'

Six

The Standedge Tunnel on the Huddersfield Narrow Canal, linking Huddersfield with Ashton-under Lyne, opened in 1811 and is the longest, highest and deepest canal tunnel in Britain. There is no towpath in this long, dark passage under the moors, and boats had to be 'legged' through by men lying on their backs on a plank laid on the boat, and walking their feet on the underside of the tunnel to push the boat along. A professional legger was paid one shilling and sixpence for legging a boat for the three miles, which could take up to three hours. On the Yorkshire side, the tunnel starts near Marsden.

We legged the boats
By candlelight,
Under old Marsden Moor.
Cold and damp
Without a lamp,
Under old Marsden Moor.

Under old Marsden Moor, my lads,
Under old Marsden Moor.
Walk on the bricks
For your one and six,

Under old Marsden Moor.

You scrape your boots
Through the leather sole
Under old Marsden Moor.
Your legs and feet
Are weary reet,
Under old Marsden Moor.

Under old Marsden Moor, my lads,
Under old Marsden Moor.
Walk on the bricks
For your one and six,
Under old Marsden Moor.

From 'Legging Through' performed by Rowan © 1995
lyrics by Bob Anderson, music by Roger Aspinall

Next morning Jav arrived early at the canal basin and paid a visit to Gary Wilkinson at the shop. He thought Gary was probably the best person to ask about Len Nicholson.

It was quiet around the marina. Gary was just opening the shop and setting up his outdoor display of different-coloured ropes, gas canisters, water containers, pieces of ornamental ironwork and tools of all shapes and sizes.

'It seems you need a lot of stuff to run a narrowboat,' remarked Jav, looking around. 'It must be quite costly.'

'Nothing compared to the cost of running a house,' replied Gary and they went into the small office.

'What can you tell me about Len Nicholson?' began Jav.

'Len? Well, he's quite a character. I suppose he's one of the last remaining people on the canal who were brought up as narrowboaters, going back to when the canal was a working transport route. It's all tourism now apart from the few who make a home here.'

'How well do you know him?'

'He's been around all the time I've had this shop. He's not here permanently. He stays on the move to avoid paying mooring fees, so he'll go up towards Skipton or down to Bingley in his battered old boat. When he's here, he comes in fairly regularly to buy bits and pieces, and he usually goes right to The Navigation.'

'How does he get on with the other people around here?'

'I don't think he interacts very much. He sees them all as "comers-in" – you know? People who don't understand life on the water like he does. I've seen him chatting with Laura Ward. I think they get on well. There's a class thing going on too. They both see most of the people here as a bit posh – a lot of old hippies who've arrived here thinking they're living a version of the good life.'

'Did he ever have rows with anyone?'

'Not that I'm aware of.'

'And how did he get on with Annie Shipton?'

'I don't think he ever had much to do with her.'

'How did you get on with him?'

Gary smiled and shook his head. 'I found him amusing, Inspector. He's what you'd call a character. He has some strange ideas about spirits on the canal. He was in here the other day talking about places on the canal that are cursed and how the spirits on the canal never forget bad things that happen. He claimed to have seen and heard ghosts. It was all a bit batty but interesting. It's like listening to folklore from a different age, if you know what I mean.'

Jav was also interested in this for a different reason. 'Did he say what these bad things were?'

Gary shook his head. 'No, Inspector, it was all very vague and pretty harmless, I think.'

Jav was not so sure about that. 'Did he associate these bad things with any people?'

'Not to me. I never heard him threaten anybody.' He got up from the chair. 'Now, if you don't mind, I must get on. The shop is due to open soon.'

'Fine.' Jav got up and left. It was an outside chance that this stuff would turn out to be important, but he felt he had something interesting to take back to DCI Oldroyd and the others.

～

It was a fine morning, if a little misty again. Louise was travelling to Saltaire with her father, and she had offered to drive. Oldroyd had been telling her about the Mill Centre and she had decided to go with him, see the David Hockney paintings in the gallery and spend the day in the village.

'I'm sure you know Hockney was born in Bradford,' said Oldroyd as they waited in traffic. The journey to Saltaire from any direction was notorious for hold-ups. 'He spent a lot of time in California, but he's been back in England for a few years. He lived in East Yorkshire for a while, at the edge of the Yorkshire Wolds near Bridlington. There's a great display in the centre of his paintings of the Wolds in spring. There's also a painting of Saltaire in Hockney's style.'

'I'm really looking forward to it.'

'There's a lovely art shop and a nice café for lunch. Then maybe a walk in the park will complete a nice day out.'

Louise laughed. 'Thanks for the suggestions, Dad. They all sound lovely.'

When they arrived at Saltaire, Louise parked in the village, and they walked down to the Mill Centre and the canal basin.

'Is this where the murders took place?' Louise asked.

'Yes. Steph saw the narrowboat drifting along the canal over there and the other body was pulled out of the water a bit further down.'

'Steph! You never mentioned she was involved in this particular investigation.'

'No, well, her and Andy weren't really supposed to be, nor me for that matter. But they had just begun a boating holiday.' He pointed across the basin. 'That's their boat. And they ended up here just as the murder happened. We worked with Javed in Harrogate, and they roped me in too. It was a series of coincidences, but now we're all working together.'

'Oh, I must see her while I'm here. I haven't seen her for ages.'

Steph was a hero to Louise as she had once saved her life when Louise was in great danger.

'I'll tell her you're here and give her your number.'

'Thanks. Have a good day!'

They parted by the bridge over the canal and Oldroyd watched her go, thinking how nice it was to have her around again.

Bridget and Bob called on Liz to see how she was, and found her much improved. They persuaded her to go for a walk around Roberts Park.

'Just as far as you want, Liz,' said Bridget. 'Tell us when you've had enough.'

'I'll be fine. I feel much better today.'

They went over the iron bridge spanning the river and walked slowly across to the main promenade, then up to the bandstand and half-moon pavilion. The borders were still colourful with late-flowering dahlias, cannas and spiky cordylines, though the flowers were steadily fading as autumn progressed. On this week-day September morning, there were not many people around, just one or two dog walkers.

'Have you thought about what you might do now?' Bridget asked Liz.

'What do you mean?'

'Bob and I have been talking. We're not sure we're going to stay here on the canal after all the awful things that have happened. It won't be the same without Annie . . . and the whole place is, well, contaminated. I don't think I'll ever feel the same about it again.'

'Where will you go?'

Bob answered. 'We might look for a flat somewhere in this area. Maybe Skipton. We've always liked it as a town. We couldn't afford a house at today's prices and a ground-floor flat might be better for us as we get older, you know. And Bridget will be able to carry on with her flute lessons.'

Liz was walking slowly and still looked rather pale. 'I see. I haven't really thought about it, to be honest. Anyway, I'm not sure I could afford to buy or even rent anything, so I'll probably just stay. I've got a good set-up at the Mill Centre making my stuff, and I know all the markets round here.'

They reached the pavilion and went up the steps to the band-stand. 'You'd be by yourself if we left,' said Bridget.

Liz was walking between her friends, and she reached out and touched them both. 'Obviously I would miss you, but I know Bob and Brittany will visit me and I've made quite a few friends at the Mill Centre and on the markets, so I wouldn't be entirely on my own. And it's not far to Skipton. I could come up on *Meg*. You can't stay here just for my sake.'

Bridget smiled. 'Well, maybe at some point you could get a permanent mooring at Skipton. The basin there where the Springs Branch of the canal comes in is beautiful.'

Liz looked at Bridget. 'You're really keen for us to be near each other, aren't you?'

Bridget glanced at her partner who moved across and put his arm round her shoulders. 'Yes, she is. You don't want to see Rowan completely broken up again, do you, love?'

'No, I suppose I don't. As I said, we're all getting on a bit, and we've been friends for so long. It's been nice to be together even though we've had some difficulties with you losing Roger, and Ben and Annie splitting up. Now I don't think I can stay here, but there's only the three of us left unless Ben comes back. It just seems sad.'

'Well, if you choose a flat near here, that might solve the problem,' said Liz.

'Yes. Anyway, we haven't decided anything yet.'

They walked from the bandstand down to the river and along the path by the bank. It was near the spot from where there were boat trips in Victorian times, as illustrated in old postcards from that era.

'I must say it's very pleasant here,' said Bridget. 'Maybe we won't move away after all.'

Bob laughed. 'Let's forget about it for the time being. How about a coffee at the Mill Centre?'

'Good idea,' said Liz. 'I'm feeling a bit tired now. It will be good to sit down.'

~

'So, I'm not sure about Len Nicholson, sir. He has some strange ideas. Gary thinks he's harmless, but I believe we should investigate him more thoroughly.' Jav was finishing outlining his latest hunch to the others as they met at The Navigation for the first time that day.

'Well done, Jav,' said Oldroyd. 'He's clearly an eccentric who doesn't fit in well with the modern world. I imagine a lot of those ideas have been passed down to him from his parents and grandparents, whose lives were played out on the waterways. Tales about spirits on the water, ghosts and things like that; they'd be carried down the generations by people who respect the canals but also know the dangers.'

Steph took up the issue. 'The question is, sir, as Jav said, is it all harmless, or are we dealing with someone who's deranged? If it's the latter, he could have decided that Annie Shipton was one of these "bad spirits" or whatever and decided to do her in. Bert Marshall could have been another. Len might see himself as a servant of the canal or something, and think he's doing good work.'

'Hmm.' Oldroyd was not convinced. 'I think it's a bit outlandish, but it's worth pursuing, I suppose. We'll go back and talk to him, and maybe see what other people round here think. Let's find out if there's any record of him arguing with people or attacking anybody.'

'OK, sir,' said Jav.

'Actually,' continued Oldroyd, 'I think Phil Cunliffe might be worth asking first. Publicans usually know all about people in an area, especially the unusual ones. I'll talk to him at lunchtime – it's a good reason for going into the bar.'

'Any excuse, sir,' said Steph. 'Sizing it up for the end of the day?'

Oldroyd gave her a sly look. 'Well, as it happens, perhaps. I meant to tell you, Louise is staying with us for a few days, and she drove me in today. She's going to see the exhibitions at the Mill Centre and then go walking, but she said she would like to see you again.'

'Oh, that's lovely. How is she doing?'

'Very well. I'll send you her number and maybe you could go over to the Mill Centre at lunchtime.'

'I'd love to.'

'OK.' Oldroyd paused as they returned to business, and he gave one of his little pep talks. 'We're still waiting for the breakthrough in this case and, until we get it, you all know what we have to do: keep slogging on. No additional suspects have emerged since we identified the ones we have, so we need to go back to them again. I'm beginning to think that, as in many of these cases, the answer is going to lie in the past, in something quite deep or traumatic, and we haven't uncovered it yet. I'm wondering—'

'Sir,' said Jav, whose phone had vibrated with an incoming message. 'Sorry to interrupt, but there's information coming through from HQ. I've got a team doing background checks on all the suspects. It's taking them a long time but they're overworked at the moment. So, Ben Shipton attacked his wife three years ago. It was regarded as a minor assault and he was given a caution, but that shows he could be capable of violence towards her.'

Jav was reading the report. 'It says that Annie Shipton had a slight injury to her shoulder, following a row that had taken place on their narrowboat on the canal at Saltaire. Her partner, Benjamin Shipton, admitted what he'd done and that he was intoxicated at the time. There was no previous history of violence.'

'I imagine that was the point he left here,' said Andy.

Steph still looked disgusted.

'Well, whatever we think about the incident, we definitely need to call him back in urgently for further questioning,' said Oldroyd.

Darren Ward was feeling much better – not fit enough to go back to work, but he was able to get up in the morning after Laura left and get dressed. He drank some coffee but felt in need of something stronger . . . and not alcohol.

Sam Wallace, their usual supplier of coke and weed, had not been around for a while, but he was sure he'd seen Sam working on a house not far off in the old village. Darren decided to walk over and see if he could find him. When he got out of the boat, he felt a bit wobbly, but it was a very short walk along two streets to the house in Titus Salt's famous nineteenth-century model village.

Sam was working on the ground with an angle grinder, cutting some roof tiles for one of the larger end terraces which had been reserved for the mill managers and overseers in Victorian times. When he saw Darren, he switched off the cutter and pushed up his goggles.

'What's wrong wi' you?' he asked. 'You look peaky.'

'I've been rough for a few days. Bad cold.'

'What do you want?' Sam asked. 'I told you never to come to me at work.'

'I want some stuff. You haven't been to see us for ages. Where've you been?'

Sam glanced round. His workmates were all on the roof or the scaffolding.

'Keep your voice down or you'll get me sacked. T' boss won't like it if he finds out I'm into drugs. Look, we got busted by the police – they caught us in the woods. We've got to lie low for a while.' He picked up the grinder and pushed his goggles down. 'Anyway, I've got to get on wi' me work. I've got nowt for you at the moment. I'll let you know if things get any better. And keep your mouth shut or there won't be anything at all.'

He switched the grinder on, leaving Darren to walk back disconsolately to the basin. Sam hadn't said anything about the death of Annie Shipton and threat to their supply lines, never mind the fear that the police might try to pin the murder on them, thinking it was a deal that had gone wrong. They would have to find another supplier to replace Shipton. These were difficult times.

~

Lunchtime found Oldroyd in the main room of The Navigation looking longingly at the pumps on the bar. His favourite kind of beer: amber-coloured bitter, smooth with a deep flavour, was on offer but he would have to wait until he was off duty. He saw Phil Cunliffe who was drying glasses behind the bar and beckoned him over.

'I'm sure you know Len Nicholson, the painter who lives in that boat up towards the lock,' Oldroyd said.

Phil smiled. 'Yes, he comes in now and again. He's been here a while. Tends to move around a bit but he always comes back. He gets plenty of work here with the boats in the basin and the marina.'

'What do you make of him?'

'He keeps himself to himself. He's one of the old guard on the canal, not many left now, and he doesn't fit in with the modern crowd.'

'That's what Gary Wilkinson said. Has Nicholson ever talked about his views on spirits on the canal, things like that?'

'Well, now you mention it, he has. Some people are actually a bit scared of him. I have to admit, he looks a bit menacing, being a large bloke with a massive beard. There was a big row with someone in here about all that, stuff about spirits. It's a few years back now, but there was a bloke here then, Mat Holden, who used to enjoy winding Len up. He'd say that he thought canals were useless these days and they should all be filled in, stuff like that. Of course, Len got angry, couldn't see the funny side, and one evening he went for this chap and we had to pull him off. He was shouting some weird stuff about the canal always taking vengeance on those who disrespected it. We thought nothing of it, but a few weeks later

Mat Holden was found dead in the canal. Of course, it was fully investigated and there was no sign of foul play, as you coppers call it. Mat was a drinker and he often left here drunk and unsteady. The conclusion was that he'd fallen into the canal. It was winter, and the cold water caused him to have a cardiac arrest. He hadn't been hit or anything, there were no signs of struggle. But we all remembered what Len had said, and one or two people teased him about it. He wasn't sorry either about what he'd said nor about Mat dying. He just said something along the lines of people like him had it coming to them.'

'Do you think he had anything to do with it?'

'Naw, not really. He's all talk, and a bit strange. Spent most of his life on the bloody canal – enough to turn anybody odd – but it just made us think.' He smiled. 'It's interesting that none of the regulars ever teased him after that. They probably wanted to avoid ending up in the canal too.'

'But you think it's superstition rather than an actual threat?'

'Yes, coincidences like that freak people out, don't they? Len's come in here a bit less frequently since then and some of the regulars tend to avoid him. I don't think he's bothered. As I said, he's a bit of a loner.'

Oldroyd paused. 'I'm also interested in Annie Shipton and her husband, Ben. You've been landlord of this place the whole time the friends from the folk group have lived here?'

'And a long time before that, Chief Inspector. Over twenty-five years now.'

'OK, so you're aware that the Shiptons separated a while ago?'

'Yes, Ben went to live over in Oakworth, didn't he?'

'Yes. Did you know there was an altercation between them which resulted in the police getting involved and Ben Shipton being given a caution?'

Phil frowned. 'No, I didn't. Ben never struck me as violent. I know Annie could be difficult, but that's no excuse. You could hear rows coming from the boat occasionally, but nothing worse.'

'Can you remember when he moved out of the boat?'

Phil thought about this for a moment. 'Yes, actually. It would have been August just over three years ago, because it was my wife's birthday, and we usually have a bit of a do in here for the locals. I remember asking where Ben was and Annie saying he'd moved out.'

Oldroyd nodded. 'That correlates with the police report. It seems he left after the incident, as one of my sergeants suggested. Thanks, you've been very helpful.'

He looked again at the pumps on the bar, then left quickly before temptation proved too much.

∽

In the house at Oakworth, Ben Shipton received a call from Jav to arrange to speak to him again about Annie. He agreed to meet with the detectives in Saltaire.

Brittany came into the front room to find her father grim-faced.

'What's wrong, Dad? Are things getting to you today? It was hard yesterday at the funeral directors', wasn't it?'

'No, it's not that. Sit down.'

Brittany looked alarmed. 'Dad?'

Ben sat down too. 'There's something I haven't told you.' He found it hard to look at her. 'Because I daren't, and because I'm too ashamed.' He paused and was clearly making a big effort to stay composed. Then he blurted out, 'When your mum and I were arguing, I got hold of her arm and twisted it badly. She had to have it checked at the hospital, and she was so angry with me that she rang the police and reported me. I went to the police station and admitted what I'd done, although it was under provocation and in the heat of the moment.'

Brittany looked at him open-mouthed. There were tears in her eyes. 'Dad, that's no excuse.'

Ben put his hands to his face. 'I know, I know. I was absolutely in the wrong and I admit it. I was given a caution and I think I was lucky. It was after that I left and came here.' He looked at her. 'I didn't tell you because I was afraid you would reject me, and I couldn't bear it.' He started to cry.

Brittany got up and put her arm over his shoulders. 'Dad, I forgive you. I know you're not a violent man. I know you didn't mean to hurt her.'

Ben put his hand on hers. 'I didn't. I still feel bad about it.'

'What were you arguing about?'

'It was when she told me that she'd had affairs with women and wanted to continue. She insisted on having an open marriage. She didn't seem to think my feelings were important.'

'That was hard for you, and you lost it with her.'

'Yes, she was walking away from me, and I caught her arm to pull her back because I had things to say to her. I pulled her much harder than I intended. I never meant to hurt her.' He was crying again. 'Now the police have rung and want to talk to me again. I have to go back to Saltaire tomorrow. I'm sure it's about that, and I'm a suspect in the investigation into your mum's murder. Now there's evidence that I've used violence against her in the past and I failed to disclose the incident. But I swear to you, I had nothing to do with her death.'

'I believe you, Dad. Look, if they've no evidence to link you with Mum's murder it doesn't matter what's happened in the past. I'll come with you.'

Ben smiled and blew his nose. 'You don't hate me, then?'

'No. You shouldn't have done it, but I don't think you intended to hurt her.'

'Thanks,' said Ben. 'Thanks for believing in me.'

~

It was Wednesday evening, a full week after Annie Shipton's murder, and the weekly folk night went ahead as usual. Liz, Bridget and Bob decided to attend. They felt it was important to start enjoying themselves again. They sat in the pub at their usual table, not quite sure what to make of it all. The pub was full, such was the reputation of The Navigation's folk nights.

'I can't believe we were here last week at exactly this time, and Annie was with us.' Bridget was holding her wine glass with her arm resting on the table. Liz, who seemed very much recovered, reached over and patted Bridget's hand.

'I know, Bridget, it's a painful thought. When someone goes quickly like that it's a terrible shock. But I think Annie would have wanted us to continue being involved in music, even if it's only listening these days.'

'You're right,' said Bob. 'What saddens me is how few of us there are left. Ben is still around but not here with us, so only half of Rowan are together now.'

'It's inevitable,' said Liz. 'Nothing lasts forever, does it? At least we've still got each other. And Brittany and Ben will visit us.'

Bob laughed. 'You make it sound quite cosy.'

'I think it is cosy here on the canal. It's beautiful and relaxing being on the water. Oh, they're going to start!'

They all looked towards the small stage area where the folk group had arrived to applause, and were introducing themselves. The music was a kind of modern, electronic folk – very different from Rowan's style, which had been mainly acoustic guitar until they had started to perform in larger venues. The young group looked completely different too. The men had short hair and were clean-shaven, dressed in a sort of American preppy style of clothing. The female lead singer wore heels.

After listening for a while, Bridget turned away and frowned. 'Not my style. Too noisy for folk music. I always felt that we were better with acoustic guitar and not too much amplification. It's more intimate and closer to the old traditions, which is what folk should be, surely?'

'I agree,' said Liz. 'The vocals aren't clear, the drums are too loud. But maybe we're just showing our age again.'

'When I think of last week, at least one of the final things she did was to come to see a folk group and listen to music. What could be better?' said Bob, feeling quite emotional.

Liz played reflectively with her wine glass and nodded. 'Absolutely.'

Phil Cunliffe came over to their table when the singers had finished their first spot. 'Nice to see you all here tonight,' he said. 'I didn't know whether you'd come or not – thought maybe it was too soon. Annie was a great local character, and we'll miss her. She may have been difficult at times, but who isn't, eh? The world would be boring without people like her.'

Bob glanced at the other two and then spoke for them. 'Thanks, Phil. We appreciate that.'

'How nice was that?' said Bridget after Phil had returned to the bar.

'Lovely,' said Bridget.

All three were quiet for a while. Liz broke the silence.

'I'm worried about Brittany, you know. Do you think she'll be alright after the shock of losing her mother?'

'Yes,' replied Bridget. 'She's got her own life now with a job and a partner. Maybe her and Harry will start their own family soon. I don't think you need to worry about her.'

'No,' said Liz, looking glum. 'She'll be getting more and more established over in Lancashire and less likely to come over here.'

Bob looked at her. 'That's inevitable, isn't it?'

'I know. It's just that I miss her. She's a link with the younger generation. And I think of her as a substitute for Meg. I'm aware of that. I wish she was a bit nearer.'

'Yes,' said Bridget. 'It would be nice, but I don't think it's going to happen.'

'Have you heard anything about the funeral?' asked Liz, changing the subject.

'No. I expect Ben and Brittany are on with it at the moment,' replied Bob. 'There's a crematorium just up the road towards Bingley at Nab Wood. I expect it will be there.'

'Didn't Annie come from over in Lancashire originally? Burnley or somewhere?'

'Bolton, I think. She never talked about her childhood, did she? Or any family. I think she must have broken from them early on, maybe when she went to music college. She did once tell me that she was badly off when she was a child, and it was a teacher who got her interested in music. I don't expect anyone from over there will be coming to the funeral. Hold on, look who's here.'

Bob stopped talking as Laura Ward approached the table. She stood there a little uncertainly, avoiding eye contact and then said, 'I thought you all might be in here. I've come to apologise for last week. I shouldn't have said those things and then lose my temper like I did.'

Bob nodded. 'OK. We appreciate that,' he said, looking to the others for acknowledgement. 'Don't worry about it. Annie went over the top with what she wrote in that blog. It was right out of order.'

'It must be hard for you . . . losing a friend like that,' she continued.

'Yes.'

'The police have been round, but Darren and I had nothing to do with it. Nothing at all, nor with this other bloke found in the river.'

'We believe you,' said Bob. 'I don't know what was going on with Bert Marshall, though.'

'Right. Good. OK, then. Enjoy your evening.' Laura nodded, turned and walked out of the bar.

'Wow, I never expected that, did you?' asked Liz.

'No, but she's worried about the police being on to her so she's on her best behaviour now,' observed Bob.

'You don't think she did it, though?' asked Bridget.

'No. She might have wished Annie dead when she was angry, but I don't think she would stoop to murder.' He finished his beer with a grimace. The group had just launched into a particularly loud number that sounded more like heavy metal than folk.

'God, I've had enough of this. Let's go back to our boat and listen to some tracks there.'

'You mean some songs by that great group, Rowan,' said Liz, laughing.

'What could be better?' replied Bob with a big smile.

On the way home, Oldroyd, without being specific, told Louise that domestic violence had cropped up in the case.

'That doesn't surprise me,' she said. 'There's an epidemic of it in this country.'

'Is that partly because more cases are reported now?'

'Maybe, but poverty has a lot to do with it as well as some entrenched male attitudes. And it's pretty clear that there are still many incidents that go unreported.' She looked at him. 'One of the reasons is that women don't always trust you lot. There's a long history of violence against female partners being classified by the police as "just a domestic" and that being used as an excuse not to interfere.'

'Well, you're right. I don't blame women for being suspicious of the police, especially after what we've seen in recent years. But rest assured we get intensive training these days on these issues. What I particularly wanted to ask you about is men persisting in their abuse. How often do they come back and repeat what they've done – and go on to worse?'

'Very often . . . Oh, at last we're moving.'

After queuing for some distance, they'd reached the traffic lights at Apperley Bridge where they turned left to cross the River Aire and then up to Rawdon.

'And this can happen after the relationship is over and they're no longer living together?' Oldroyd asked.

'Yes. Some men blame the woman. Especially if there's been continuing conflict, like a custody battle over children.'

'I see.' Oldroyd was quiet for a while as he reflected on what his daughter had said.

They had reached Leeds Bradford Airport and were driving through the tunnel under the runway.

'It was great to see Steph, by the way,' said Louise. 'We met at the café, like you suggested. I haven't seen her since all that Whitby stuff. I'll never forget what she did for me. She's just the same – bubbly and friendly. She was asking me all about what I'm doing, and she was really interested in it. She told me she was involved in outing a detective inspector who was harassing women at the Harrogate station.'

Oldroyd smiled. 'That's right. Steph's been at the forefront of championing women in the force for a while. Things have certainly changed at Harrogate, mostly due to her. I don't think women are patronised any more or subject to sexual harassment.'

Louise gave him a sceptical glance. 'Well, that's good, Dad, but why did it take someone like Steph to force change? Couldn't you all see the problem yourselves? And how can you be sure it's gone away so completely?'

Oldroyd held up his hands. 'You're right. We're all culpable. Most people, and I'm one of them, just go along with things as they are because it seems like the norm, and everyone accepts it. It takes a strong person like Steph to come along and say, "Look, this is wrong". Then you start to see things differently, things that had never occurred to you before. Most people conform, don't they? They don't question things.'

'I suppose so. At least you admit that you accepted things you shouldn't have. The real problem today is the people who don't accept the need for change in areas like this. A lot of them are still in positions of authority.'

'Well, at least we're a model of progress in these areas now at Harrogate.'

'Oh, are you? I'm very glad to hear it.' There was a taunting tone in her voice. 'How many women are there in senior positions then? And how many people from minority groups?'

'Straight for the jugular! Not enough is the answer, but we're working on it.'

'Good,' said Louise as she drove down Pool Bank and into Lower Wharfedale.

～

After two days of dithering, during which he'd been to the police station after work to receive his caution, Sam Wallace decided to tell his mother about being caught by the police in the woods with drugs.

It was likely that she would find out anyway. She knew so many people in the area and everything seemed to leak out, however secret you thought it was. Then he would be in worse trouble, having said nothing.

He waited until they'd eaten tea. He cleared away the plates and washed up. He knew it wouldn't make this any easier, but might show he was feeling a little regretful.

'Mum, I've got something to tell you.'

She was sitting on the sofa reading a magazine. She looked up at him. 'Have you now? I thought there was something going on when you were so keen to clear away and wash up.'

'Yeah, well . . .'

She sniffed and nonchalantly continued reading her magazine.

'It wouldn't be anything to do with being caught by the police in the woods with your daft friends taking drugs and getting a caution.' She looked up at him. 'Would it?'

Sam's mouth dropped open. 'Eh? How do you know about it?'

His mother laughed scornfully. 'You never learn, do you? Beryl Dunway rang me. She got it out of their Terry. He was frightened of going to the police station to get his caution, so he blabbed the whole story to her. He was crying, she said.'

'Shit! The big, stupid baby!'

She put the magazine down. 'Yes, it is shit, isn't it, Sam? Now you've got a caution on your record for drug-taking as well as a reputation for fighting. I only hope Bill Ferguson doesn't find out. Or, if he does, he lets it pass without sacking you.'

'Why should he sack me? I do my work right.'

'Well, I'm pleased to hear that, because you haven't much else that's good on your record, have you? You haven't the bloody brains

225

you were born with. Somebody your age too – you're not a bloody teenager any more!'

Sam hung his head. He was completely outmanoeuvred and didn't know what to say.

'I hear the dealer's been arrested. Who was it?'

Sam looked alarmed. He hoped Terry Dunway hadn't said anything about Annie Shipton. They'd all agreed not to mention that to avoid suspicion about the murder.

'Ryan Nelson.'

'Oh, I've heard of him. He's been done for shoplifting. I know his uncle.'

'You know everybody.'

'Not everybody, but let's say enough people to find out what I need to know.' She yawned and got up. 'Anyway, Sam, I don't see why I should worry any more. It's up to you. Carry on like this if you want. But I've told you before, if you lose your job because of getting a criminal record, I'm not supporting you – you'll have to find somewhere else to live and I don't know how you'll pay for it.'

'I won't lose my job.'

'Good. Why the hell don't you keep your cycling up? They seem to be sensible people in that club.' She looked round the room. 'When you've finished washing up you can carry that basket of ironing upstairs.'

She walked out, leaving Sam to wonder about Ryan Nelson and whether he would keep Annie Shipton's name out of it, or would he do some deal with the police instead?

He frowned. There could be further trouble ahead. What would his mother say then? She was probably right – he should stick to cycling.

~

'You should have been upfront about this rather than waiting for us to check your record,' said Oldroyd to Ben Shipton. It was the next morning and a second interview of Annie Shipton's partner was taking place at The Navigation. Steph was also there. Brittany had been granted further time off by her school and had come over from Oakworth with him. She had gone to see Bridget and Bob.

Ben was sullen. 'I didn't think it was my place to raise it.'

Oldroyd was in a hawkish mood and his tone was implacable. 'Maybe not, but your caution for that assault on your wife is clearly relevant to the investigation, and you knew we would find out as soon as we searched the records, so why not just admit to it? We've seen the police report. You were handed a caution. Now it looks as if you're trying to conceal things, which raises our suspicions. So tell me what happened.'

Ben was weary. It was an effort to tell this story again after so long keeping it to himself. 'Our relationship was deteriorating. Annie had told me that she had had affairs with women. She wanted us to have an open marriage so that she could continue to see other people.' He winced at the unpleasant memory. 'I was shocked and angry. I . . . I felt betrayed. It was a ridiculous thing to ask – unfair. We argued about it on and off for days. One night I'd been in here feeling miserable and drinking. When I got back to the boat, she started again, saying it was up to me and she preferred it if I agreed, but she was going to have relationships with women anyway. She seemed to think it didn't matter if she was unfaithful with women instead of men, but I didn't see it like that. There was a bottle of whisky, and I drank some of it.

'Annie could be very nasty if she was in the wrong mood. She started goading me, saying it was my fault anyway – if I'd been a better lover, she might not have looked for other relationships.' Ben paused as he came to the central bit of his account. 'I was furious. As she said this, she turned to walk away, and I just grabbed her arm and pulled her back. I was drunk, and pulled her more roughly than I intended. She cried out and said I'd dislocated her shoulder. I said I hadn't, but she was angry, said I was a wife-beater and she was going to tell the police. The upshot was that we walked up to the hospital A&E department, and she got her shoulder looked at. It was strained but not dislocated. She wouldn't speak to me, and when we got back, she rang the police. I agreed to go in to be questioned – we didn't want the police to come here; we wanted to keep it all quiet. They gave me the caution. And that's it really. It was the only time I ever laid a finger on Annie and I'm still sorry about it.'

Ben stopped speaking and Oldroyd looked at him with his sharp grey eyes. 'You must have felt a great deal of resentment towards her after that,' he said.

'I did. It was the end of our marriage. I left the boat shortly after and moved to Oakworth. I didn't see much of her after I'd left.' He shrugged. 'It was a sad end to our relationship of many years, but that was it.'

'Did you move out because you were afraid you might attack her again?'

Ben thought about this. 'I didn't want to fight with her. I wanted to put some distance between us.'

'Did you still harbour anger towards her for her infidelity? And maybe jealousy about these relationships she was having?'

'No. I felt it was all over between us. I didn't care what she did.'

'Did you get your revenge by murdering her on the canal?'

Ben looked straight at Oldroyd. 'No. I didn't feel that strongly about it all. And I would never murder my daughter's mother. I love my daughter and I wouldn't cause her pain like that.'

Oldroyd looked at his notes. 'You have no alibi for the morning of the murder, do you? You claim you were at home, but nobody can confirm that. You know the canal and you know about boats and locks. You were still in contact with your wife. Maybe you were intending to visit for some reason, and she told you she was setting off early in the morning to go to Skipton. That could have been your opportunity.'

He looked at Ben who shook his head. 'I don't blame you for thinking this, Chief Inspector, I know I'm a suspect, but you have to believe me when I say I didn't do it.'

∾

Over in the basin, Brittany was on *Rowan* drinking coffee with Bridget and Bob. It was a wet day, and the drumming of raindrops on the boat roof was quite loud, but all of them except Brittany were used to such sounds, being seasoned narrowboaters. They were reminiscing about when Brittany was growing up.

'We lived in that little house in Grosvenor Street somewhere near Baildon, wasn't it? I can't really remember.'

'Yes, it was. We came to visit you a lot,' said Bridget.

'The house was full of guitars and music – there were always folk songs playing. Dad was teaching guitar in schools in Bradford, wasn't he?'

'That's right, a peripatetic instrument teacher.'

'What did Mum do? She always seemed to be at home.'

'Yes, she was. The problem with your mum was that she couldn't settle down. She really missed the life we had travelling round performing in different venues. She tried one or two things, but she hated any regular routine.'

'Then we moved to Shipley to a semi so they could get me into St Mary's. I'm glad they did because I liked it there, but we were always short of money. Dad told me they struggled to pay the rent on that place. Luckily, they only had me so I never wanted for anything. Mum always seemed to have a bit of money spare, if I really needed something for school. I don't know where she got it from – she must have saved it up. I remember my friends thought it was cool that my dad was a guitarist and they'd both been in a folk group.'

'Yes, those were happy years until your Auntie Liz and Uncle Roger lost Megan. That was terrible.'

Brittany drank some coffee and shook her head. 'I know, I can't imagine it . . . Oh, here she is.'

Liz Aspinall came down the steps, calling out a greeting as she did so. She was wearing skinny jeans and a white T-shirt with black and white images of long-haired guitarists emblazoned on the front. Her face was pale and scrawny. She looked surprised and then delighted to see Brittany and went straight over to give her a hug.

'Hello, love, I didn't know you were here.'

'Dad and I just arrived. The police wanted to speak to him again.'

'Oh. What for?'

'I don't know. It's probably just routine to check a few things.' Brittany and her father had decided not to tell anyone about the incident with Annie.

'Well, I'm just off to the shops and I wondered if anyone needed anything.'

'Not at the moment, Liz, thanks,' said Bridget.

'OK.' Liz looked at Brittany. 'Don't forget to come round to see me, will you?'

'Of course not, Auntie. I was planning to come over to see you next.'

'Good.' Liz glanced at Bridget and Bob. 'See you later, then.' She turned and her thin legs disappeared back up the steps.

'Oh dear, she doesn't seem very happy, does she? She's always so pleased to see me but I almost feel she relies on me somehow,' said Brittany.

'I know. She's been very needy since Roger died. Is it any wonder after losing Megan as well? I think she's always thought of you as some kind of substitute for her daughter. And then this trauma we're going through. It must make it all worse. I wouldn't like to be living alone on that boat at the moment.'

'She looks so thin.'

'She's been getting steadily thinner for a while. It's the running she does . . . and she doesn't eat much. I was wondering before all this happened if she was depressed. What do you think, Bob?'

Bob shook his head. 'Maybe. She probably looks to the future and just sees a life alone. It can't be much of a prospect. She's got us of course, one less now, but no family of her own left.'

'No,' said Brittany thoughtfully. 'I'll definitely go and see her when I leave here. I wonder how Dad's getting on.'

∽

Oldroyd frowned as he drank a cup of coffee. It was yet another case meeting, and he was feeling frustrated. There were leads and evidence, but there was no sign yet of a breakthrough. They had the method. They had the means. But they didn't yet have a motive – or at least one that pointed to a definitive suspect.

'What did you think of Shipton, sir?'

Oldroyd rubbed his eyes and shook his head. 'I'm not sure, is the honest answer. He's got the motive and opportunity, but his denials seem genuine.'

'Having separated from his wife, did he harbour so much hatred towards her that he would plan her murder?' said Steph.

'I agree it's doubtful, but we don't know if we've yet to discover more about Annie Shipton's past. There was certainly a lot going on in her life.'

231

'On that point, sir, I have more information,' said Jav. 'The drugs team at HQ have been examining the evidence submitted by the officers who found those drug users in the woods, and they were alerted by the mention of the name Annie Shipton. Apparently she's been a suspect as a dealer for many years in this area, but they've never been able to pin anything on her.'

Oldroyd looked up, suddenly more lively. 'Has she indeed? Well, that sheds more light on the whole business of Wallace and his involvement with her. Maybe that altercation on the canal was not about cycling, but something to do with drugs. They were all eager to deny that Annie Shipton had anything to do with them, weren't they? Maybe that group decided to bump her off for some reason. She may have cheated them.'

'It would also explain how Annie Shipton seemed to survive for years without any obvious income apart from some basic state benefits, sir,' said Steph. 'Dealing was how she got her money.'

'You're right. Good point.'

'I wonder if her old friends from the folk group knew about it?'

'We need to ask them. And we should get back to Wallace. We'll widen the investigation out to include his friends in the woods.' He seemed excited, like his old self again. 'Now, I've got some news concerning Len Nicholson. I spoke to Cunliffe. He's acted strangely about these "spirits on the water" before. Apparently, there was a bloke who used to wind him up about it and then he was found dead in the canal.'

Andy whistled.

'Yes. There was nothing to link him with the death of this character, who was a drinker and who everyone thought must have fallen in the water. But it's something of a coincidence, especially after Marshall's death. So, we need to talk to him, and also get hold of the police report from that incident. Is anything happening with Spenser?'

'We've taken a statement and checked his alibi. His wife confirmed that he was at home on Sunday evening,' said Jav.

'Hmm. Well, I'm still suspicious. Partners often supply false alibis for various reasons.'

'His wife also said he left the house on the morning of Shipton's murder at a time that would preclude him from committing the crime.'

Oldroyd grunted and then quickly finished his coffee, got up and rubbed his hands together. 'Well, things seem to be hotting up. We're getting more useful information about a number of the suspects. We don't yet know which line of enquiry will lead us to the killer, but let's get on to it.'

Steph smiled at Andy. They were used to their boss's various moods and knew that, when he became energised and upbeat like this, it was always very promising that a breakthrough was near.

~

Oldroyd and Steph donned their raincoats and walked down the wet and squelchy towpath towards Nicholson's boat. They could see smoke coming out of the blackened chimney as usual.

Oldroyd knocked on the grimy door but there was no response. They could hear the sound of Len singing in a loud but not very tuneful voice. Oldroyd smiled at Steph and then shouted, 'Len! Open the door, please. We need to speak to you!'

The singing stopped and they heard the clumping of Len's footsteps approaching. The rusty lock was turned, and the door opened a little. Len's big beard and dirty face peered through the crack. 'Oh, it's thi agean. What does thi want this time?'

'We just need to speak to you,' repeated Oldroyd in a firm tone.

Len frowned, but opened the door. 'Ah'm keeping it locked till thi find out who's bumpin' folk off. First that Shipton woman and then Bert from t' mill. What the bloody 'ell's goin' on?'

They followed him down into the boat where the smell of paint was strong. A number of small pieces of ornamental ironwork were drying. The room was hot and full of woodsmoke fumes. They sat on the ramshackle chairs and Oldroyd, in typical fashion, got straight down to business. 'I understand you knew a man called Mat Holden.'

Len's brow furrowed and he glared at Oldroyd. 'What abaht him?'

'You had a row with him and attacked him in the pub.'

'So that Cunliffe's been saying stuff?'

'Only because I asked him. You do know you've got quite a reputation for having some strange ideas about the canal and spirits and things like that, don't you?'

'They're only funny ideas to them 'at don't understand t' canal and its ways,' growled Len. His face seemed to be retreating beneath his huge beard and shaggy eyebrows.

'Apparently Mat Holden was found dead in the canal, and you said it was the canal getting revenge . . . or something like that, at least.'

Len pointed a fat finger at Oldroyd. 'That bloke said some bad stuff about canals, said they should be filled in. That's . . . what do thi call it?'

Oldroyd cleared his throat. The woodsmoke was getting to him. 'Sacrilege?' he suggested.

'Aye, that's it. What does thi expect's goin' to 'appen if thi talks that way? T' canal took him off an' he deserved it.'

Oldroyd returned Len's glare. 'So did you help the canal by pushing him in?'

'No, I didn't.' He raised his head in defiance and then his expression went thoughtful. 'You see, t' canal doesn't need my help. It can look after itself. T' spirits'll protect it.'

'What spirits are those?' asked Steph, trying to keep any derisive scepticism out of her tone.

Len looked at her with an expression of pity. 'It might sound daft to thi, but ah know they're here. Ah've felt 'em many times. And ah've said before to lots o' folk – if thi don't show respect to t' canal, things'll 'appen to thi. Whenever there's anybody found in t' watter, thi can be sure they did summat against it. And sometimes there's part of t' canal that seems cursed somehow. Ah was tellin' Gary Wilkinson at t' shop abaht it, but he didn't believe me. You've got to have lived yer life on t' watter to understand.'

'So because Mat Holden was scornful of the canal, you think it somehow lured him in to his death?' asked Oldroyd

'Aye, ah believe it did.'

'And how did it do that exactly?'

Len shrugged. 'That ah couldn't say.' He raised his finger again and wagged it while he spoke. 'And it's better to let those things be.'

'Yes,' said Oldroyd. 'Unfortunately, it's our job to do just the opposite. We have to find out how people died and why. So you've already told us that you were up early on Wednesday and heard a boat go past. Where were you on Sunday evening?'

'Yer mean when Bert Marshall wa' killed?'

'Yes.'

'Here. Ah don't go out much and ah didn't go to t' pub that night.'

'But there's nobody to vouch for you?'

'No, ah've lived alone for a long time now and ah'm used to it. Ah wouldn't want anybody else here. This is my place.'

It's unlikely that anyone would want to join you here, thought Steph, looking around at the grimy, dark interior littered with paint tins, brushes, rags and pieces of rusty ironwork. The smell of smoke mingled with paint fumes and thinners was quite a toxic brew.

'You told me last time,' continued Oldroyd, 'that Shipton and her friends were hippies and not really canal people. Was she someone you particularly disliked?'

'No, ah didn't really know her. She wa' a bit of a busybody, but ah wouldn't want to bump her off just for that, would ah?'

'No,' conceded Oldroyd.

Len stood up. 'Well, if thi's finished, ah'd like to get on wi' me work.'

~

The rain was still coming down as Steph and Oldroyd walked back along the towpath. It made the air cooler and fresher. The vegetation by the water smelled different.

'He doesn't seem to have a motive for killing Shipton, sir, even though he has no real alibi,' said Steph as they walked back to The Navigation.

'Nor for Marshall. If we're right about the blackmail theory, the second murder follows from the first. But I agree with you about Shipton, unless there's something we still don't know. No one's reported any conflict between them unless he took exception to her because the spirits on the canal told him she was a bad 'un.' He waved his arms in the air in a mocking gesture.

Steph laughed. 'All that stuff's ridiculous, isn't it, sir? The Curse of the Canal. It's the material of comic horror.'

Another beautifully painted narrowboat chugged past, and the water lapped gently on to the canal bank. The person at the tiller was wearing expensive-looking waterproofs from head to foot.

'It is. But, unfortunately, it's also very real for those who believe in it, especially someone like Nicholson who clearly sees himself as some kind of guardian of the old ways and one of the few people left who believes in "the spirits", as he puts it. Who knows how Shipton could have offended him? She clearly wasn't at all concerned about what she said to people even if it was offensive. I don't think we can eliminate him yet.'

~

Jav and Andy called at *Meg* to ask Liz Aspinall to join Bridget Foster and Bob Anderson on *Rowan* for further questioning. The rain was now very heavy. The large raindrops were plopping into the canal and mist clung around the massive shape of Salts Mill. Liz followed the detectives across the basin wearing only a thin jacket that was wet through by the time she got to *Rowan*.

The sitting area was quite cramped with five people crowded in. The detectives and Liz took off their coats, from which water streamed. The room smelled of damp clothes.

'Liz, you're soaked!' exclaimed Bridget. 'Haven't you got a waterproof?'

'No, my last one wore out and I haven't been able to afford another.'

'Oh, well, borrow one of mine to go back in.'

'OK, thanks.'

Jav began the interview. 'We thought it would save time if we got you all together to ask you a few more questions. We've received reliable information from our drugs squad that Annie Shipton was involved in illegal drug dealing over quite a lengthy period.'

Liz put her hand to her mouth.

'What!' cried Bob.

'Yes, I'm afraid there's no doubt. She was known to the squad, but had been very skilful in avoiding arrest. We found no evidence of drugs when we searched her boat. The question is whether any of you were aware of this?'

The three friends looked at each other and shook their heads. Bridget spoke. 'No, Inspector. We had no idea. What on earth was she thinking? What kind of drugs?'

'We think mainly cannabis and cocaine. Did any of you ever buy from her?'

'No, Inspector,' replied Bridget. 'I think I can speak for everyone. We've all smoked cannabis and done speed a long time ago when we were on the road, but not recently. Bloody hell, though . . . We now know how she supplemented her income without ever having a job. So had this been going on all the time she lived here on the canal?'

'Maybe,' replied Andy. 'Certainly for a number of years.'

Bob laughed sardonically. 'Well, we always knew Annie was a dark horse. It seems she was darker than we realised. I suppose she would never have told us in case something leaked out.'

'Were you ever aware of anyone visiting her boat? Strangers, or unlikely people, like young men?'

Again, the friends exchanged glances and shook their heads.

'Did she ever have odd telephone calls in your presence? Or any rows with anyone you didn't know?'

'No, Inspector,' replied Bob. 'She was clearly very careful to keep everything away from her life here in the basin.'

'Did any of you witness that confrontation she had with Sam Wallace?'

'I was there,' replied Bob.

'Sam Wallace was involved with a group of young men who we believe acquired their drugs from Annie Shipton. Was that argument with her just about Wallace riding his bicycle on the towpath or were other things mentioned?'

Bob frowned. 'They were definitely arguing about the bike, and it got very acrimonious. We had to pull him away from her. I do remember she said something like, "You want to be careful." I took that to mean she would report him to the police for threatening behaviour, but maybe she was implying that she would cut off the drug supply. I don't know.'

'OK, that's useful. Is there anything else you remember that might be relevant?'

The answer was no.

The detectives left, leaving Annie Shipton's friends stunned. Bob made some tea.

'Annie a drug dealer? I can't get my head round it,' said Liz.

'I know, but then, as I said to the police, there were depths to Annie. I'm not surprised that there were things she kept from us. It's amazing how you think you know someone, someone who you've been friends with for forty years, and then you find out there was another side to them,' said Bridget.

'I'm not sure it was a different side. It's consistent with the Annie we knew. She was utterly determined when she decided to do something. She never fancied a regular job when Rowan finished, so she looked for another way of surviving,' replied Bob.

'But to break the law like that and probably for years . . . ?'

Bob shrugged. 'I'm sure she had a way of justifying it to herself. Don't you remember, in the old days when we smoked weed a bit, she thought drugs should be legalised? And she often said she fancied something a bit stronger.'

'Yes, she did,' agreed Bridget.

'So she probably thought there was nothing really wrong with it,' said Bob. 'She was so careful and devious for all these years. If ever there was a dark horse, it was Annie.'

Liz put her head in her hands. She was shaking. 'How long is this nightmare going to go on? Two murders and now we find that our friend was a drug dealer! I don't think I can take much more.'

Bridget put an arm round her shoulders, looked at Bob and said, 'All this must be bringing back the bad stuff you went through with losing Roger and Megan.'

Liz nodded and burst into tears. 'It's never far from the surface. I suppose I can't bear to lose anything. Now Annie's gone, Ben's in Oakworth and Brittany's in Lancashire. There's only us left.'

Bridget hugged her and looked at Bob again. There was nothing else they could say. It was worrying to see how everything had really got to their friend who suddenly seemed very frail. It was hard for her by herself, and if things continued to be traumatic, she could very well have some kind of breakdown.

Seven

I think of you
In the misty rain,
With every leaf that falls.

I remember you
In the green of spring,
Listening to birds' calls.

I think of you,
I think of you,
Under the autumn trees.

I think of you
As the birds fly south,
And the light of autumn fades.

I remember you
In the winter cold,
Walking in frosty glades.

I think of you,
I think of you,
Under the autumn trees.

'Under the Autumn Trees' performed by Rowan © 1996
lyrics by Liz Aspinall, music by Ben Shipton

Oldroyd and Steph waited in The Navigation until the rain had eased and there was a chance that the Wallaces might be back home. Oldroyd rested with his feet up on a chair as he drank a mug of tea. He was feeling tired after the hectic pace of the last week and travelling from New Bridge every day. He yawned and turned to Steph.

'Well, you've lost a week of your holiday,' he observed. 'Just think, you and Andy could be above Skipton by now, through the Foulridge Tunnel and well into Lancashire.'

'Don't worry, sir, we wouldn't have missed this investigation for anything. Working with you and Jav again, it's amazing. Far too exciting to miss. We'll take up the holiday afterwards. I think you said we could still take our leave.'

'Of course, you've been working, so the last week doesn't count as leave.'

She smiled at him. 'Thanks, sir. Of course, we might have been put off by all the bodies found on narrowboats and in the water. Going to Mexico City might have been safer.'

Oldroyd laughed. 'I don't think so. There are few places as relaxing as on a canal. It's to do with the gently moving waters and the slow pace of everything. You'll soon slip back into it.'

'That's good to hear, sir. We'll need it after this!'

Oldroyd stretched his arms and got up. 'Right, let's get down there and see what Sam Wallace has to say for himself.'

Outside, the rain had stopped and there were a few patches of blue in the sky. The towpath squelched underfoot. Ducks and moorhens were making their way out of the dense reeds where they had sought refuge in the storm. A very smart narrowboat approached, its colourful paintwork wet and gleaming. Oldroyd wondered if it was the work of Len Nicholson. The proud owner waved to the detectives as the boat glided past. At that point the sun came out briefly and the temperature immediately started to rise.

As they walked down the still, gloomy passageway towards the house, they could see a light in the kitchen.

'Looks as if we've caught them at home again,' said Oldroyd, and he went up to the door and knocked.

A face appeared briefly at the window and there was a cry of 'Oh shit!' followed by the sound of someone running, and a shout of 'Sam! What the hell's going on?'

'Sounds like he's making a run for it,' said Oldroyd. 'Not very wise. Get down the back of the house and I'll stay here in case he comes round the other end of the terrace.'

'OK, sir.' Steph ran quickly down the rough, unmade road at the side of the house.

Soon there was a cry of surprise and, shortly after, Sam appeared with his arm up his back and Steph behind him. His jeans were dirty at the knees.

'He was attempting a getaway, sir. I told him to stop but he ignored me, so I had to trip him and use an arm lock. I've put him under arrest on suspicion of conspiracy to supply class A drugs. I've said if he calms down and cooperates we can de-arrest him.'

Janice appeared at the door looking furious. 'Sam! What are you playing at, you stupid fool? Bring him in,' she said to Oldroyd.

In the kitchen, Oldroyd faced a very sheepish Sam across the table. Janice and Steph stood behind him. Sam looked down at the table, avoiding eye contact.

'OK, first of all,' began Oldroyd, 'it's never a good idea to run away from the police like that. Why did you do it?'

Sam shook his head but remained looking down and didn't say anything.

'Sam!' yelled Janice and he looked up at her quickly.

'Cos you lot never believe blokes like me. You allus think we're guilty.'

'Well, are you guilty? And what of?' replied Oldroyd with typical directness.

Sam squirmed, turning uneasily in his chair.

'T' police caught us in t' woods wi' some drugs. They did us for it. That's all, but you allus come back to get us for more. You never leave us alone.'

'OK, well, I'm not interested in busting you for more drug offences. What I'm concerned about is who supplied them to you, and it wasn't Ryan Nelson, was it?'

This caught Sam's attention for the first time. He looked at Oldroyd. 'What's he been saying? He was supposed to . . .'

'What? What was he supposed to do, Sam?'

Sam fidgeted, frowned and swore under his breath. He felt cornered. 'All right. We got the drugs from that woman Annie Shipton.'

'Bloody hell!' said Janice in disgust.

'Mum, shut up, will yer!' Sam shouted at her and then turned back to Oldroyd. 'I don't know where she got 'em from. She never told us owt. She never said much. Just delivered stuff to us – well, usually Ryan – and then we'd meet in t' woods and share it out. Did Ryan snitch?'

'No, we've found that Annie Shipton has been a suspected drug dealer for a long time. It seems she was a very clever operator, however. Our drugs team were never able to pin anything on her.'

'We thought you would think that we killed her because we fell out over money or summat and you'd pin the murder on us. We didn't do it.'

'Look, we don't generally go round trying to frame people, though I know it has happened, and I know you don't trust us

244

because of that. But what I'm going to have to push you on is your relationship with Annie Shipton.'

'What about it?'

'We know you were in a dispute with her about cycling on the canal towpath and you had that row with her where you nearly came to blows. That in itself made you a suspect. But was there more to it than that? Wasn't it awkward having a row with your supplier? Did she threaten to stop supplying you unless you stopped cycling on the towpath? Now tell me the truth and I'll overlook the fact that you tried to run away.'

'No, she didn't. When we had that row, she said something to me like "be careful", but she wouldn't stop supplying us, would she? It wa' brass for her, wa'n't it?'

Oldroyd nodded. 'I suspect you're right. She needed the money.' Then he fixed Sam with his penetrating gaze. 'So you and your friends could have killed Shipton over a dispute about money or you could have lost your temper with her about the cycling or both. You're telling me that none of that is true?'

Sam looked at Oldroyd. 'No, it's not true. We didn't kill her.'

'OK. We'll leave it there for now but you're still a suspect.'

Janice spoke to Oldroyd as she saw the detectives out. She looked worried. 'I'm absolutely sure he would never plan to kill anyone,' she said.

Oldroyd empathised with her as a single parent trying to do her best. 'I shouldn't tell you anything, but I'd say although we haven't eliminated him, he's not our top suspect.' He saw that she was relieved. 'I reckon him and his mates might pass some drugs on to other people, but I'm not looking into that. I will say, however, that he needs to get away from that group.'

'I just don't know what to do with him. He's in his twenties now and he behaves like a teenager. I got him interested in cycling, but it seems he just used his bike to meet up with his cronies in the woods.'

Oldroyd shook his head. 'It takes some people longer to grow up than others, especially young men like him. Is he working?'

She nodded.

'That's a good sign. He needs to be in a place of his own. You probably look after him too well. If he had to fend for himself, he might start to see things differently.'

'You're right, but rents are so high it's hard to find anywhere he could afford.'

'I know. He's not the only person in their twenties still living at home.' He smiled at her. 'Best of luck. Don't give up on him.'

She shrugged her shoulders 'Have you got kids?'

'Yes.'

'Then you know that we never give up on them, do we?'

He smiled at her. 'No, we don't.'

~

'So we didn't get anywhere with any of that. Damn!' Oldroyd hit the table with his fist, and shook his head.

It was late in the day and the detectives were back at The Navigation facing the fact that nothing new had emerged from their questioning of Sam Wallace or of Foster, Aspinall and Anderson. 'I sense we're not far off. The killer is one of the people on our list of suspects, but we haven't got that crucial link yet.' He was still struggling to make sense of things that had been sparked off in his mind.

'We've got all the information in now,' reported Jav. 'Spenser's alibis for the time of each murder have been corroborated by his wife. Foster and Anderson give each other alibis and nobody else has a supported alibi for both murders. It's very inconclusive. We've got lots of people with motive and opportunity, but no forensic evidence to link any of them to the murder scenes.'

'OK, look, we might as well call it a day. We're all tired. But I'm going back to Annie Shipton's boat. There was something in there that rang a bell with me, but I can't remember what it was. I think it might be important.'

'OK, sir,' said Steph, who sensed that her boss was getting a little desperate.

~

It was raining again when Oldroyd arrived at *Moorhen* and the late afternoon light was poor. For the first time the canal looked grey and uninviting as the rain chopped up the surface of the water. Mallards were sheltering under clumps of tall reeds with their heads laid on their plumage.

There was a sinister feeling about the still and deserted boat. As he unlocked the door and went down the steps, there was a slight rumble of thunder in the distance. It was dark inside and he switched on the light to reveal the forlorn interior. He frowned and tried to remember what it was that he'd seen on his last visit shortly after the murder that might give them a clue. The rain was now slanting across the windows and pattering on the roof as he walked around examining everything in the room.

He looked at some magazines on a table, some paintings, and examined Annie Shipton's papers again. But it wasn't until he looked at a framed photograph that he remembered what he had seen.

It was the photograph of Annie, Ben and Brittany that Steph had found by Shipton's bed. Brittany looked about eleven, with long hair and a lovely smile. Yes, the clue was in the picture.

As Oldroyd nodded to himself, there was the sound of the door banging. Startled, Oldroyd looked back to the steps. There was no one there. He'd forgotten to shut the door behind him, and the wind had slammed it closed. Quickly, he removed the photograph from the frame and placed it in his jacket pocket. Then, with some relief, he went back up the wet steps, locked the door and left the boat.

He hurried through the rain to the pub. Jav had already left, so Oldroyd called him.

'Jav, yes, I've found what I was looking for. Can you contact Ben Shipton and get him to come in again tomorrow? It's only a hunch, but I think he may be our killer after all. I think we should be ready to make an arrest.'

~

It was late afternoon the next day when Brittany and her father finally arrived in Saltaire, due to some problems with the car.

Brittany decided to pay Liz a visit while her dad spoke to the police. She knocked at the door of *Meg*. 'Hi, Auntie Liz! It's me.'

She heard Aspinall's voice. 'Brittany? Come in, love.'

Brittany went into the sitting area to find Liz in a chair staring into space. Her thin face was pale, and the lines seemed to have deepened since the last time Brittany had seen her. Her hair had lost its frizziness, and looked grubby. For the first time she looked old to Brittany, although her eyes brightened when she saw the young woman.

'This is a nice surprise,' Liz said. 'I didn't know you were coming over today.'

'I've come with Dad. The police want to talk to him again about something.' She sat down in a chair next to Liz and looked at her. 'Are you OK, Auntie? You don't look very well.'

'Oh, I've been off colour recently. It's because of all that's happened. I was just meditating on things.'

'What kind of things?'

Liz smiled at her. 'Life – you know, when stuff like this happens it makes you think about all sorts.' She reached across and took hold of Brittany's hand. Her arm was shaking but her grip was surprisingly firm. 'I've lost a lot in my life, but at least I know I've still got you.' She gave Brittany a very intense, searching stare. Her face was twitching, and her eyes looked as if they were about to fill with tears.

'Of course you do,' said Brittany, feeling uneasy.

'You see, if I didn't, I'd have nothing else left.' Her tone was desperate. With her other hand she clung on to Brittany's shoulder.

Brittany got up, carefully extricating herself from Aspinall's clutches. 'I can see you're feeling very bad today, Auntie. I'm going to make us some tea, OK?'

Liz looked as if she might grab Brittany again. But then she suddenly slumped back into the chair, looking exhausted.

∼

Oldroyd faced Ben Shipton in their room at The Navigation. Andy sat behind Ben, and Steph and Jav stood at either side of their boss. It was meant to be intimidating and it was. Ben looked around, feeling uneasy.

'What's all this about, Chief Inspector? I've told you everything I know about Annie. I had nothing to do with the murder of that other chap – never met him in my life.'

'I hope that's true,' replied Oldroyd. 'But I want to ask you again your relationship with your wife.'

Ben sighed. 'Fire away. I've nothing to hide.'

'In the period before Brittany was born, you were still on the road with Rowan, weren't you?'

'Yes.' Ben looked puzzled as he wondered where this was leading.

'So you and Annie were together most of the time?'

'Yes, we were the leaders of the group after the other founder members had left. I occasionally travelled to perform with other groups. It was a useful way of making a bit of extra money.'

Oldroyd looked up sharply. 'Were you still doing that when Annie got pregnant?'

'Yes, I think so. It was then that we decided to disband the group and we came to settle near here.'

Oldroyd paused again. 'You told us about your wife's infidelity with women. To your knowledge, was she ever unfaithful to you with other men?'

Ben looked shocked. 'No . . . I mean . . . what on earth are you getting at?'

Oldroyd produced the photograph and showed it to Ben. 'You see, I'm interested in this picture of you with Annie and Brittany.'

'That was taken at a friend's house. I remember it well. It was a birthday party. What about it?'

'Your daughter has beautiful hair in that picture, but it's distinctly red, unlike yours or her mother's. She must have dyed it recently because it's not red now. When I first met her, something seemed different, but I couldn't think what. I'd forgotten that I'd already seen this photograph in *Moorhen* on the wall. Red is the natural colour of her hair, isn't it?'

'Yes, that's true, but Annie's father had red hair so it must have come from him. That's how we always explained it.'

'What about you? You don't appear to have red hair.'

'Well, no, but it could have been in my family, I suppose.'

'You suppose. Does that mean that as far as you are aware there is no red hair in your family? You don't remember anyone with red hair or being told about anyone with red hair.'

Ben was puzzled and confused. 'No, I . . . I don't know. Maybe? What are you driving at, Chief Inspector?'

Oldroyd leaned forward to face Ben very directly. 'At this. Red hair colour is quite rare because it's a recessive gene – that means that a person with it has to have the gene for it from both parents, not just one. If there is no red hair colour in your family, you cannot be Brittany's father.'

The force of this statement struck Ben like a physical blow. His eyes widened. 'What? That's ridiculous!'

'I'm afraid not. And what I'm wondering is, to put it bluntly, that at some point not too long ago, your wife told you that you were not Brittany's father. That's when you left Saltaire. You were so enraged that you planned her murder.' Ben was unable to answer. 'You'd already attacked her once and now you had a much stronger motive to be violent again than the business of having an open marriage and her affairs with women, didn't you? To not be the father of the girl you always thought was your daughter meant a very deep betrayal which would've hurt you enormously.'

Ben had gone pale. He tried to shake his head, but slumped forward in his chair as if he might pass out.

Oldroyd looked towards Andy. 'Andy, get him a glass of water. Jav, can you hold him up?'

Jav grasped Ben's arm and gently pulled him upright in the chair.

Ben put his hands over his face and moaned. 'Oh, God, no!'

Oldroyd gave Steph a worried glance. This reaction wasn't quite what he'd expected. 'I see that this is a shock to you,' he said.

'You don't understand. It's . . . Annie didn't tell me . . . but some things have just slotted together in my mind. I told you that when Annie got pregnant, I was spending some time away. It was also when we had guest performers in the group, some by former members. Annie was always fond of Roger Aspinall, and he came by regularly to cover for me. Roger had red hair.'

It was Oldroyd's turn to be shocked. His mind worked frantically, trying to make sense of this new information. And then he remembered seeing the picture of Roger with Liz and their daughter Megan. Roger had red hair, too, like Brittany's had been. 'Are you saying that your wife had an affair with Roger Aspinall but never told you about it?'

'She didn't tell me. I swear. But she must have done. Oh, Annie!' He burst into tears. 'Brittany!'

'Where is Brittany?' asked Oldroyd, suddenly on the alert.

'She's gone to see Liz on her boat.'

Oldroyd leaped to his feet, knocking his chair over. 'Oh, bloody hell!' he shouted. 'I've got it completely wrong! Quick, we must get over there. Brittany could be in danger. Andy, stay here with him until I give you the signal.'

As Brittany was making tea in the small kitchen area of *Meg*, Liz came in quietly behind her. Brittany turned with the mugs and was startled to see her.

'Sit down, Auntie,' she said. 'I'm bringing the tea.'

Liz ignored her. She was blocking the doorway and there was a knife in her hand. There were tears in her eyes and her expression was tortured. She put her other hand on the side of Brittany's face and then stroked her hair.

'My little girl,' she said in a strange voice. 'Your auburn hair was beautiful.' She stroked her own hair. 'Look, mine's reddish, too, now. I think I dyed it because of you.'

Brittany was frightened by this sudden intensity. She moved away and put the mugs down.

'Auntie, what's the matter? What are you doing with that knife?'

Again, Liz didn't seem to have heard her. 'I'm your mother now,' she said, looking at the knife. 'I'm sorry about Annie.' A spasm of hatred crossed her face. 'But she was horrible to me. She told me about her and Roger – and she laughed. She laughed at me! I'll be a better mother to you. My husband was your father, so really you belong with me. We'll be happy together. I can change the name of the boat if you want, to *Brittany*. That'll be nice, won't it? Just don't ever leave me. I can't live by myself any more.' She seemed to see the knife again, as if she'd forgotten she was carrying it. 'I've got a cake and I'm going to cut us a slice each,' she said with a smile.

Wide-eyed with fear, Brittany backed away from Liz. 'Auntie, what are you talking about? Uncle Roger's not my father he's—'

Liz now looked angry. 'Don't say that! He was. Annie told me!' Then she saw that Brittany was terrified. Liz put her arms around her. 'There, there. Don't be frightened, my sweet girl. Mummy will look after you. You won't ever leave me, will you?' The knife brushed against the young woman's back.

Brittany was about to scream when the door burst open, and the detectives piled down the steps into the boat. Steph and Jav quickly overpowered Liz, who dropped the knife, howled and then collapsed sobbing in a heap on the floor.

'Thank God!' exclaimed Oldroyd, who was horrified to see the knife. The young woman could have been in real danger.

～

The sudden arrival of a police car with blaring siren and flashing lights brought people out around the basin, and there was a small crowd watching when the pathetic figure of Liz Aspinall was brought out of her boat and taken off in the vehicle. Steph was comforting Brittany in the boat. Andy was watching from *Moorhen* with the agonised Ben, whom Andy had had to restrain.

Bob and Bridget came to *Meg* looking devastated.

'What's going on, Chief Inspector?' asked Bridget, going straight over to Oldroyd, whose expression was supremely solemn. 'That was Liz taken into the police car, wasn't it?'

'Yes, I'm afraid it was. She killed Annie Shipton and Bert Marshall and she's been arrested.'

Bridget put her hands to her face and burst into tears. 'No!'

'What?' said Bob, open-mouthed with the horror of the revelation.

'I'm afraid so,' continued Oldroyd. 'I can't tell you any more at the moment, but I'll send an officer around to you in a day or so and they will explain what happened. I'm sorry.'

'Where's Brittany?'

'She's with my detective sergeant in the boat. She's had a bad shock, but she'll be OK. She's not physically hurt.'

'And Ben?'

'I'm here.' Ben appeared with Andy. 'Is Brittany all right?' he asked. 'I must go in to see her.'

'She's fine,' repeated Oldroyd. 'You can go down into the boat to see her. Ask my sergeant to tell you briefly what happened.' Ben hurried down the steps of *Meg*, where Bob and Bridget stood, looking completely shattered.

'What's going to happen to Liz?' asked Bridget, struggling to control her weeping.

'I really can't tell you any more,' said Oldroyd. 'The best thing for you is to just go back to your boat and we'll be in touch. I'm very sorry about what's happened.'

Oldroyd watched them supporting each other as they shuffled back to their boat looking old and bowed over. It was another huge blow to the legacy of Rowan after so many years of friendship and creativity. He felt it added a terrible poignancy now to their often melancholy songs.

Ben and Brittany came out of *Meg*.

'How are you?' asked Oldroyd, looking at Brittany very carefully.

'We just want to go home,' said Ben. 'We have a lot to take in and a lot to talk about.'

'OK, if you're fit to drive,' said Oldroyd, and then spoke gently to Brittany. 'An officer will be round very soon to take your statement.'

Brittany sighed. 'OK.'

'We'll just pop in to see Bob and Bridget. They must be feeling awful,' said Ben.

'Yes, I think they will. It's a terrible shock for you all.'

When they'd gone, Oldroyd took a deep breath. 'Well, I got that one wrong. I'm just glad that no one was harmed. We might as well go over to The Navigation and pack up. What a quick and dramatic ending to it all!'

Oldroyd walked over to the pub with Jav, Steph and Andy in silence, then he said, with a twinkle in his eye, 'Well, you won't hero worship me any more, now that you know I'm fallible. I was so pleased at finding the clue about the red hair in one photograph that I missed a similar clue in the other.'

'You still got closer than any of us, sir,' said Steph. 'And we got there in the end without further loss of life.'

'I don't think we even considered Aspinall as a suspect, sir,' said Jav. 'She didn't appear to have a motive. Don't feel bad about it.'

'No,' replied Oldroyd, who nevertheless was very subdued as they cleared things away from their room at The Navigation. It was his usual feeling of tiredness and anti-climax at the end of an investigation, combined with some disappointment. Not just at his failure to identify the perpetrator, but that he had potentially placed someone at risk in his rush to find the suspect. Despite everything he'd achieved over the years, it made him feel something of a failure. How could he have misread the evidence?

He called Superintendent Walker to inform him that the case was over.

'Well done, Jim. I trust Bradford will be grateful for your work. They don't know how lucky they are. I'll be glad to have you back here. You're a voice of sanity in this daft world of managerialism and endless number crunching. You won't believe the latest from so and so. He's . . .'

Oldroyd shut his eyes and gritted his teeth. The last thing he wanted to hear at this point was one of Walker's rants against Watkins. He managed to contain it by replying to Walker's questions in monosyllables.

'Anyway, remember me to young Iqbal and I'll see you tomorrow,' Walker said at last. Oldroyd knew that Walker wouldn't be interested in any mistakes that might have been made. He was just satisfied that the case had been solved. Steph was right: he should be happy with that too.

Jav was waiting to go. 'I'll finish everything off at this end, sir. I expect you'll be coming over to our HQ to interview Aspinall.'

'Yes, I'll be there soon. I want to get it all finished off today, so it doesn't run on into next week, as far as I'm concerned, anyway. I think Superintendent Walker wants me back. You can take it all forward from here.'

Jav smiled at him. 'Of course, sir, and I want to say that it's been a privilege working with you again. I'm really glad that you were able to join us, and I hope we all meet up before too long.'

'I hope so too,' said Oldroyd, smiling. 'You've done a great job organising this investigation. And tell that little daughter of yours that I couldn't have solved the case without her and her class. They gave me an important clue.'

Jav laughed. 'She'll be absolutely delighted, sir!'

Andy and Steph came to say goodbye to Jav. 'Where are you going now?' he asked.

'We're going to continue with our holiday on the canal,' said Steph. 'Our leave's been approved. We weren't far into it, so we're going to pretend that we're starting all over again. We're going up to Skipton and then on to Gargrave. Apparently the canal goes through some very peaceful countryside further up and we need to relax after all this. We were going to stay here a bit longer and explore the galleries and the village, but I think we'll leave Saltaire behind for a while until all this trauma has slipped into the past.'

'I don't blame you,' said Oldroyd.

Back out at the basin, a number of people had been watching the arrest, and now that it was over, they gathered to talk to each other.

Darren Ward, who was now feeling much better, had been watching events from his boat. He saw the police car and the detectives leave, and ventured into the basin where he was joined by Ros Collins and Gary Wilkinson.

'What the hell was all that about?' asked Darren.

'It looks as if they've arrested Liz Aspinall,' replied Gary.

'The thin woman with the frizzy hair who lives by herself?'

'Yes.'

Darren looked incredulous. 'Bloody hell! Does that mean she committed those murders?'

'It looks like it,' said Ros. 'Her hair wasn't frizzy when they took her away, though. She looked awful.'

Darren shook his head. 'Wait till I tell Laura. At least the police won't be on our backs any more. She killed one of her friends in that old folk band?' He shook his head. 'Always thought they were a bit weird, that lot.'

257

Ros was also feeling relieved but didn't say why. 'They're OK. It's just music from a different era, isn't it? You've got to feel sorry for Bob and Bridget, the two left. It's going to be very lonely for them now. I wouldn't be surprised if they sold up and left the canal.'

'Yeah,' said Darren. He puffed out his breath. It felt like the tension that had been growing around the canal area for over a week had suddenly relaxed, and it was a great relief.

'Anyway, see you later.' He went off back to his boat.

'I wonder what was going on,' said Gary. 'I suppose it will all come out at the trial.'

Ros looked over the basin towards *Moorhen* and *Meg*. The two boats were silent and empty. It was sad. 'Annie was a complex woman,' she said. 'She was attractive and charismatic, but there was also a very hard side to her. And she didn't seem to mind hurting people. I suspect that the answer to your question lies in things that happened a while ago.'

'Hi, how are you?' said a voice behind them. It was Phil Cunliffe from The Navigation. 'It's all kicked off this afternoon, hasn't it? Did you see what happened?'

'I heard voices raised. I came out of the office and the police were running around. A little while later a police car arrived and Liz Aspinall was taken out of her boat and into the car,' said Ros.

'So I gathered,' said Phil. 'It's definitely all over. The detectives are packing up and leaving – they've had an incident room in the pub. It's a relief, isn't it? I began to wonder who was going to be the next victim. I can't believe Liz Aspinall was the killer, though.'

'That's what we were saying,' said Gary. 'You never really know people, do you? She was such an insignificant-looking woman. The basin is going to be a bit quieter now – we've both lost a couple of our regulars.'

'Yes, but you know what the public are like. They enjoy seeing the places where grisly crimes have taken place. I wouldn't be surprised if we get an extra influx of visitors in the next few weeks once the story breaks in the press.'

'So, it will be good for business?' asked Ros with an eyebrow teasingly raised.

Phil shrugged. 'Well, you know what I mean. People can be ghoulish.'

'At least they won't be too frightened to come here,' said Gary. 'Things should get back to normal.' He gave a grim laugh. 'But it doesn't look as if I'm ever going to get the two hundred pounds that Annie Shipton owed me.'

'Nor me the rent she owed,' said Ros. 'But never mind. At least we're all here, it's a lovely day, and there's no longer a threat hanging over the place.'

The three of them looked across the basin. A narrowboat chugged past and a woman sitting on the top waved to them. It had an elaborately painted name – *Sandpiper* – and an ornate flower container on the top full of pelargoniums and petunias. Two large and elegant swans glided past in the other direction. People were walking along the towpath and over the footbridge to the Mill Centre. It was a beautiful scene, and it was surprising how quickly things were returning to normal.

At the Mill Centre, news came through that the murderer had been arrested. As usual, it was Julie Wilton who heard about it first. She rang Gary at the shop to confirm what she'd been told before passing Nicholas Spenser the news.

Nicholas, who'd had a nerve-wracking time since the police had visited and his wife had torn a strip off him, was very relieved to hear the news until he learned who the murderer was.

'Liz Aspinall? Doesn't she rent one of our creative workspaces? I hope nothing will reflect badly on us. We can't seem to escape from these damned murders.'

Even Julie, who admired her boss, was rather disgusted by this self-centred and insensitive response, and didn't stay to hear any more of his comments.

Nicholas immediately rang his wife to give her the good news.

'So, darling, this means that I'm no longer a suspect.'

His wife, however, sounded unimpressed. 'In the murder inquiry, yes, but there's still that business of intending to bribe a councillor. We don't know what repercussions that's going to have, so don't start crowing to me that you're in the clear. I told you before, you behaved like an idiot and put me and the boys at risk. And you're not out of trouble yet.'

When the call ended, Nicholas frowned. Unfortunately, she was right. He would have to sweat it out for a bit longer. There were some powerful forces against him. Who had tipped off Shipton's group about his relationship with Crompton? It implied that there were people in the council against his scheme. He was out of his depth with the politics of it all. But at least he felt he'd learned his lesson: he'd been losing sight of what was really important. His career was not worth the risk of flirting with breaking the law, alienating large numbers of local people or risking his marriage and the well-being of his family. No, he would break completely with Crompton and there would be no sweetener for him.

～

After the trauma of the police questioning, and Liz's behaviour and arrest, Ben and Brittany barely spoke as Ben drove slowly back to Oakworth. On the boat, Steph had outlined what had happened

260

and confirmed that Aspinall was the killer. It was almost too much to take in.

When they got back, Ben made a drink, and they sat together in the lounge, sipping in silence.

Brittany was the first to speak. She put her hand on Ben's arm. 'Dad . . . Don't think this makes any difference to me. You're still my dad even if you're not my biological father. It's a shock for both of us, but we can get through it.'

He held her other hand and said, 'Thank you.' There were tears in his eyes.

Brittany continued, 'It's so ironic that it was my hair that gave the police the clue. I never really liked my red hair. I never thought about where it came from. I've always dyed it different colours since I grew up.'

'I know.'

Brittany looked at him. 'You were not at fault. It was Mum and Uncle Roger. Fancy doing that and keeping it a secret all these years. I don't know how anyone could do it. What was wrong with Mum? Why did she have that awful side to her?'

Ben shook his head. 'I don't know. When we first met, I was attracted to the fact that she was a strong personality who stood up for the things she believed in. She had a lot of charisma when she performed with the group. She seemed to get more cantankerous as she got older. I used to think it was because she couldn't build any kind of life for herself when she was no longer performing. Now I'm sure it was also because of the guilty secret she was keeping from us. It turned her sour.'

She sighed. 'I can't help feeling sorry for Auntie Liz. I think what Mum said to her and how she said it was the last straw. I'm not trying to justify what she did.'

'Me too. She's going to prison with nothing left. It's a horrible prospect.' He shuddered at the thought.

'Well, I'm going to go to see her in prison. I just have to. She's been part of my family for all these years.'

'Even though she killed your mother?'

Brittany frowned. 'Yes. I know some people would think that was terrible, but I can't just leave her there. She's had so much pain in her life, she's lost so much, and people close to her have betrayed her. I think she's been tipped over the edge; I don't think she's in her right mind. If I abandon her now, that would feel like another betrayal and another loss. I can't do it.'

Ben squeezed her hand. 'I think that's wonderful. And I feel the same as you about us. You are my daughter and always will be. I love you.'

They were both weeping as they gave each other a big hug.

Late in the afternoon, Oldroyd faced Liz Aspinall in an interview room at Bradford Police HQ. She was now composed, but looked an exhausted wreck – a husk of the lively woman who had once composed songs and performed in Rowan.

Oldroyd was tired himself and, as he often did at this point in an investigation, felt no triumph but more a sense of tragic loss. The thrill was in solving a puzzle, but confronting the culprit often reminded him of the darker side of his job – facing the terrible things of which human beings were capable.

'I take it that you decided to kill Annie Shipton when she told you that Roger was Brittany's father?'

'Yes.' Her voice was weak. It was clearly an effort to speak, but she seemed to want to tell her story and there was no attempt to deny what she'd done. 'I never really liked her. She was self-centred, domineering. And worse than that, she had a nasty streak in her. We all had rows with her over the years about different things. We tolerated her because she had a good voice, and a good business sense. She organised the tours and wrote some of our best songs.'

'When did things go seriously wrong?' asked Oldroyd, and an agonised look crossed her face.

'I was struggling badly after Roger's death. I'd never really come to terms with losing Megan. One day I was over in her boat, and I was asking her about Ben and why they'd split up. She took it completely the wrong way, thought I was prying. She said my husband hadn't been as faithful to me as he pretended. She had a horrible smirk on her face. I asked her what she was talking about, and she said that Roger was Brittany's father, that they'd had an affair when Roger was making a guest appearance with the group. She said that was where Brittany got her red hair from.

'It was like being kicked in the stomach. I'd never thought about her hair before, why would I? We all thought the red hair came from Annie's family. She couldn't prove what she was saying but she put the doubt in my mind. I'd always known they liked each other. She used to flirt with Roger all the time. Then I researched about the genes for red hair, found out it wasn't in Ben's family, and I believed her.' She paused and looked down at the table.

'Did you see any other physical resemblances between Brittany and your husband?'

'No.'

Oldroyd nodded. When Louise had been looking at the photograph album he'd started to wonder about Brittany. He'd looked at so many mugshots over the years that he'd become an expert in faces. Brittany didn't look like her supposed father in the photograph of her as a child, but when he saw her now, he could see some faint resemblances to the photograph of Roger Aspinall. In itself this meant very little. It was the red hair that was the clincher.

Liz continued. 'I felt a deep hatred for Annie. It felt like she was taking Roger from me all over again, and I'd already lost so much.

And she was enjoying it. She was taunting me. She was laughing.'
Liz shook her head. 'Something snapped inside me. I began to have
strange thoughts and feelings and I couldn't stop them.' She put her
hands to the side of her head. 'I thought I could kill her and then I
could be Brittany's mother. If Roger was her father, I could be her
mother.' She began to weep. A police officer gave her a tissue. 'At
last, I could replace Megan and then, with Brittany's partner Harry,
the three of us could be a family again.'

Oldroyd paused at the almost unbearable sadness of what she was
saying before continuing. 'I think I know how you did it, using a knife
and a bargepole,' said Oldroyd. 'But I want you to take me through it.'

She paused and wiped her eyes again. 'I planned a way of killing her that would leave no trace of me at the scene. She deserved
it. I wasn't going to go to prison if I could avoid it. I wanted to be
with Brittany. My chance came when Annie said she was leaving
early in the morning to go up to Skipton. I already had everything
prepared, and I'd practised what I was going to do. I got up very
early – it was still dark. I put on my running gloves to prevent
fingerprints and took the bargepole with the knife strapped to the
end and hid it near to the lock. I came back, changed into the rest
of my running gear. When I saw that she was up and getting ready
to go, I ran back up to the lock. When she arrived there, it appeared
that I was running back to the basin. We said hello, and I offered
to help her get through the lock.'

'Didn't she suspect anything?'

Liz shook her head. 'No, not Annie. She never understood
how she could hurt people. She just carried on. I don't think it ever
entered her head that I might attack her. I think she believed that
she was invulnerable.'

'Go on.'

'Everything worked perfectly. I opened the bottom gates,
retrieved the bargepole when she wasn't looking, stood on the little

bridge over the gates and stabbed her when the boat came into the lock. I couldn't believe how easy it turned out to be. The knife went straight through her neck. I felt nothing but satisfaction as she bled to death by the tiller. Then I used the bargepole to push the boat out of the lock and send it back downstream. As I expected, she'd put the throttle into neutral once she was coming into the lock. It was all stuff I'd done many times before. I could do it all without getting on board. I thought that if the boat appeared back at the basin, it would be unclear what had happened, and it would make any investigation more difficult.'

'Yes, it took me a while to work it out. Curiously, I got the idea from thinking about mousetraps – how the metal bar comes down and kills the mouse. One small detail – what happened to the windlass? We couldn't find one on the boat.'

'She knocked it into the water when she fell back on to the tiller.'

Oldroyd nodded.

'Then I hid the bargepole again, very carefully this time as I knew there would be a search near the lock. I went back and disposed of it completely later so it would never be found. I ran back to the basin by a different route while the boat drifted down. I was pleased with the way it had gone. I was sure that I'd left no trace on anything.'

'What about the knife?'

'I threw it in the canal further down and well away from the lock.'

'You were lucky that there was nobody on the towpath or any other boats nearby.'

She shrugged. 'It could have gone wrong if anyone had appeared. I took my chance, and the coast was clear when I stabbed her. Once she was dead, I was ready to abandon everything if I had to and run off, but it was very early and there was nobody about.'

'Except there was: Bert Marshall.'

She shook her head. 'I'm sorry about him, in a way, but he was a blackmailer. He came to the boat after dark and told me what he'd seen. He must have been hiding in the woods by the lock. I knew from the things he described that he really had seen what happened. I agreed to get some money for him by Sunday. He came to the basin again late on Sunday night. He didn't seem to suspect anything. I expect he was blinded by greed. I hid, came up behind him, and smashed him over the head with an old windlass. Then I pushed him into the water and threw the windlass in. Again, I didn't think there was any way I could be linked with the attack.' She thought for a moment and frowned. 'I know it sounds callous, but it was much easier once I'd killed Annie.' She shook her head. 'I must have gone through some kind of barrier.'

'You covered your tracks very well. We didn't really suspect you at all until the very end.' He looked at her closely. 'You wouldn't actually have harmed Brittany, would you?'

She looked at him, her face etched with the deep despair of loss and defeat. Her eyes had taken on a vacant and distant expression.

'I would never want to,' she said, 'though, listening to myself, I think perhaps I've gone a bit mad . . . I don't know what I might do. Anyway, I've lost her now as well.' She stared ahead for a moment, and her face was gaunt. Then suddenly she began to sing slowly and mournfully, her voice cracking at times.

> *I think of you*
> *In the misty rain,*
> *With every leaf that falls.*

> *I remember you*
> *In the green of spring,*
> *Listening to birds' calls.*

> *I think of you,*
> *I think of you,*
> *Under the autumn trees.'*

She seemed to lose herself in the song, and in memories of the past.

Oldroyd gestured to the police officer and left the room quietly as the eerie sound continued. He found it hard to get it out of his mind for quite a while afterwards.

~

It was later than normal when Jav arrived home from work. He had phoned Nadia to say that the investigation was over, and he just had to stay in Saltaire for a while to finish a few things off.

Aleena rushed to meet him in the hall. 'Did you catch who did it, Dad?'

Jav laughed. 'Yes, we did, but it was mainly due to Chief Inspector Oldroyd. He's a very clever man.'

Aleena's eyes sparkled. 'Oh! I'm going to be a detective when I grow up. And I'll arrest people.' She pointed an imaginary gun at her father. 'You are not oblarged to say anything, but it could be used as incidence against you.'

Nadia came into the hall and smiled. 'Are you arresting Dad? Won't you let him have his tea first?'

Jav put his hands up. 'Is that a gun you've got? Most officers don't carry guns in the British police force, you know. And I think you mean "obliged" to say anything and "evidence" against you, though we don't caution people like that any more.'

Aleena ignored the last thing he said. She loved the words 'obliged' and 'evidence' and kept saying them to herself. 'Right, I'm going to arrest Fatima and put her in jail in my bedroom.'

Her parents laughed. 'I don't think she'll be very pleased about that! And there isn't time anyway,' said Nadia. 'Tea's ready.'

Aleena, however, ran upstairs, still repeating 'obliged' and 'evidence'.

'You can't stop her,' said Jav. 'It looks like she's got to wind up her case too.'

They both laughed again, hugged each other and went into the kitchen.

～

On the next day, Saturday, there was a family gathering at New Bridge before Louise left to stay with her mother in Leeds for a few days and then returned to London.

Oldroyd, Deborah, Alison and Louise went on a circular walk to Almscliff Crag, a prominent rocky outcrop overlooking Lower Wharfedale. At the end they were going for a meal in the local pub.

It was a mild September day, with an almost cloud-free sky and a pleasant breeze. Ideal for walking. Although it was autumn, it was not misty, and the leaves were not yet falling like in the Rowan song. The path went across a number of cow-filled fields and over stiles as it headed gradually on to a high ridge, from which the crag was visible in the distance.

Oldroyd and his daughter kept up the pace in front.

'I must say I'm glad to be out here today,' observed Oldroyd, who never felt more relaxed than when he was wearing his walking boots and trousers. He breathed in the bracing Yorkshire air. 'I'm fond of Saltaire and the canal, but it was all getting a bit oppressive and sinister. There was this old guy.' He explained to Louise about Len Nicholson. 'He made the canal sound positively spooky with his talk of water spirits.'

Louise looked around and took a deep breath. It still felt good to be back in Yorkshire's sweeping countryside. 'I suppose he learned all that from his family and a community that has now disappeared.'

'Yes, generations of people who lived on the waterways and developed their own folklore.'

They were walking along the ridge. The ruins of the medieval Harewood Castle were visible in the trees near Harewood village in the direction of Leeds. Alison and Deborah were deep in conversation behind them.

Oldroyd put his arm around Louise's shoulders. 'I feel so lucky to have you. I'm never going to take you for granted.'

Louise laughed. 'I'm glad to hear that, but what's brought this on?'

Oldroyd explained about Liz Aspinall. 'You started me thinking about her on the day you arrived, and you said something about how awful it was to lose a child, maybe worse than never having one. She lost her daughter and never really recovered. And it was worse after her husband died when she was left on her own. She became fixated on making herself the mother of her friend's daughter. I thought she was the kind of traumatised person who could snap and do something drastic, and that was what happened. It was all very tragic, and it's made me feel grateful for what I've got. Despite the fact that your mum and I split up, everything's turned out well.'

'Oh, Dad!' Louise put her hand on his arm. 'And I'm glad to be of help.'

'They're funny things, families, aren't they?' continued Oldroyd.

'Tell me about it,' replied Louise. 'I'm working with the consequences of family breakdown every day.'

'This case we've just completed rested in the end on who was a girl's father.' He turned to Louise. 'What if you found out that I was not your biological father? How do you think it would affect you?'

'Wow! That's a big one! I don't think you can ever really know how you would react unless it happens to you, but I can't believe it would change the way I think about you as my dad.'

'Good!' said Oldroyd with a smile. 'I've always believed that your parents are the people who brought you up, regardless of whether they're your biological parents or not. Parenting is a relationship, isn't it? Not just a scientific fact.'

'I think that's right. When you think how many people are happily brought up by adopted or foster parents, the key thing is that the child bonds with someone.'

'Yes. In this case the girl did bond with the man who brought her up as her father and she would have never known any different if the mother hadn't chosen to tell someone else about it. And that, I'm afraid, produced an explosive cocktail of betrayal and envy and bereavement.'

'Resulting in murder?'

'I'm afraid so.' He lowered his voice after a quick glance back. 'Look, those two are talking away and just following us. They've no idea about where the path goes. When we go over this stile here, we'll hide behind a wall. They'll walk on for a while oblivious until they suddenly realise that we're not ahead. Then we'll come up behind and startle them.'

'Let's do it.' Louise laughed, and they quickened their pace towards the stile.

Folk Songs Written and Performed by Rowan

Under the Autumn Trees

I think of you
In the misty rain,
With every leaf that falls.

I remember you
In the green of spring,
Listening to birds' calls.

I think of you,
I think of you,
Under the autumn trees.

I think of you
As the birds fly south,
And the light of autumn fades.

I remember you
In the winter cold,

Walking in frosty glades.

I think of you,
I think of you,
Under the autumn trees.

© 1996 lyrics by Liz Aspinall, music by Ben Shipton

The Shepherd

Old Adam was a shepherd
On the moorlands of the north,
He walked o'er twenty mile a day
Was never paid his worth.

Upon the moors,
Upon the moors,
The moorlands of the north.
Upon the moors,
Upon the moors,
Was never paid his worth.

He dug his sheep out of the snow,
As ewes gave birth in frost,
He walked in ice and sun and rain,
And counted not the cost.

Upon the moors,
Upon the moors,
As ewes gave birth in frost.
Upon the moors,

Upon the moors,
And counted not the cost.

He lived and died in a shepherd's hut
Or so the legend tells.
He was buried deep amongst his sheep
High on the misty fells.

Upon the moors,
Upon the moors,
Or so the legend tells.
Upon the moors,
Upon the moors,
High on the misty fells.

© 1993 lyrics by Bob Anderson, music by Bridget Foster

The Ballad of Mary Flint

I'll tell the tale of Mary Flint,
She worked at Shuttle Eye –
A weaving mill
In a Yorkshire town,
But she was doomed to die.

She was doomed to die, O Lord!
She was doomed to die.
Cast from the fold
To bitter cold
Where she was doomed to die.

Mary had a pretty face,
The master's son thought so.
They met at night,
By a silvery light
And Mary couldn't say no.

By the dark of winter-time
She was great with child.
Her father thrust her
Out of doors.
The snowstorms they were wild.

She was doomed to die, O Lord!
She was doomed to die.
Cast from the fold
To bitter cold
Where she was doomed to die.

She wandered o'er
The whitened moor.
The master's son was gone.
She gave birth to their little child
And laid across his door.

Next day they found them
Stiff in death
And piteous to behold
The child and mother lying there,
Between them not a breath.

She was doomed to die, O Lord!
She was doomed to die.

Cast from the fold
To bitter cold
Where she was doomed to die.

Her flinty father
Now knew pain,
He hugged his child and hers.
The master's son in full disgrace
Ne'er showed his face again.

This tale's a sad one
You'll agree
The young girl's fate was cruel.
And her little child ne'er lived till morn
They were lost in tragedy.

They were doomed to die, O Lord!
They were doomed to die.
Cast from the fold
To bitter cold
Where they were doomed to die.

© 1994 lyrics by Liz Aspinall, music by Roger Aspinall

Lucy Banks

Lucy Banks,
Mother of three,
Her husband John
Was lost at sea.

How will you live,
My Lucy dear?
How will your children grow?

Lucy Banks
Down our lane,
Left alone
In the pouring rain.

How will you live,
My Lucy dear?
How will your children grow?

Lucy Banks,
Listen to me,
I'll take you,
And your children three.

And you will live,
My Lucy dear,
Your children they will grow.

Lucy Wright,
And your children four,
Remember John,
But grieve no more.

You live with me,
My Lucy dear,
And all our children grow.

© 1995 lyrics by Bridget Foster, music by Bob Anderson

Legging Through

We legged the boats
By candlelight,
Under old Marsden Moor.
Cold and damp
Without a lamp,
Under old Marsden Moor.

You scrape your boots
Through the leather sole
Under old Marsden Moor.
Your legs and feet
Are weary reet,
Under old Marsden Moor.

Under old Marsden Moor, my lads,
Under old Marsden Moor.
Walk on the bricks
For your one and six,
Under old Marsden Moor.

When through at last
The daylight comes,
Away from old Marsden Moor,
You screw your eyes
At the bright blue skies,
Away from old Marsden Moor.

But we've hardly time
To stretch our legs,

Near to old Marsden Moor.
To look around cos
We're back underground,
Under old Marsden Moor.

Under old Marsden Moor, my lads,
Under old Marsden Moor.
Walk on the bricks
For your one and six,
Under old Marsden Moor.

© 1995 lyrics by Bob Anderson, music by Roger Aspinall

ACKNOWLEDGEMENTS

As ever, I would like to thank my family, friends and members of the Otley Writers' Group for their help and support, and the many people around the world who buy my books.

Salts Mill art gallery and the model village of Saltaire are well worth a visit. The Leeds and Liverpool Canal does go between the two massive mill buildings as Steph and Andy discovered, but I invented the canal basin, the marina, the chandlery/shop, the office of the Canal and River Trust and The Navigation pub. I had in mind Hirst Wood Lock on the canal west of Saltaire as the basis of the murder scene.

The West Riding Police is a fictional force based on the old West Riding boundary. In this story, Harrogate and Bradford are different districts within the West Riding Police. Harrogate was part of the old West Riding, although it is in today's North Yorkshire.

ABOUT THE AUTHOR

John R. Ellis has lived in Yorkshire for most of his life and has spent many years exploring Yorkshire's diverse landscapes, history, language and communities. He recently retired after a career in teaching, mostly in further education in the Leeds area. In addition to the Yorkshire Murder Mystery series, he writes poetry, ghost stories and biography. He has completed a screenplay about the last years of the poet Edward Thomas and a work of faction about the extraordinary life of his Irish mother-in-law. He is currently working (slowly!) on his memoirs of growing up in a working-class area of Huddersfield in the 1950s and 1960s.

Follow the Author on Amazon

If you enjoyed this book, follow J. R. Ellis on Amazon to be notified when the author releases a new book!

To do this, please follow these instructions:

Desktop:

1) Search for the author's name on Amazon or in the Amazon App.
2) Click on the author's name to arrive on their Amazon page.
3) Click the 'Follow' button.

Mobile and Tablet:

1) Search for the author's name on Amazon or in the Amazon App.
2) Click on one of the author's books.
3) Click on the author's name to arrive on their Amazon page.
4) Click the 'Follow' button.

Kindle eReader and Kindle App:

If you enjoyed this book on a Kindle eReader or in the Kindle App, you will find the author 'Follow' button after the last page.